## "Your job is to protect me, not comfort me."

Acting purely on instinct, Jack shoved the bedroom door fully open and then brushed the back of his hand against Peggy Jo's flushed cheek. "My job is to take care of you. And that includes giving you a shoulder to cry on, if you need it."

"I don't need—"

He placed his index finger over her lips, adeptly silencing her rejection. "If you're feeling a little shaky right now, that's to be expected. And if you don't want any of your friends to see you weak, then turn to me, Miss Peggy Jo. I'm your man."

She stared at him, and for a couple of seconds he thought she was going to succumb. But suddenly the barriers came back up. "You're mistaken, Mr. Parker. You're my bodyguard. Nothing more. Now, if you'll excuse me, I'd like to go to bed."

Dear Reader,

The year is almost over, but the excitement continues here at Intimate Moments. Reader favorite Ruth Langan launches a new miniseries, THE LASSITER LAW, with *By Honor Bound.* Law enforcement is the Lassiter family legacy—and love is their future. Be there to see it all happen.

Our FIRSTBORN SONS continuity is almost at an end. This month's installment is *Born in Secret,* by Kylie Brant. Next month Alexandra Sellers finishes up this six-book series, which leads right into ROMANCING THE CROWN, our new twelve-book Intimate Moments continuity continuing the saga of the Montebellan royal family. THE PROTECTORS, by Beverly Barton, is one of our most popular ongoing miniseries, so don't miss this seasonal offering, *Jack's Christmas Mission.* Judith Duncan takes you back to the WIDE OPEN SPACES of Alberta, Canada, for *The Renegade and the Heiress,* a romantic wilderness adventure you won't soon forget. Finish up the month with *Once Forbidden...* by Carla Cassidy, the latest in her miniseries THE DELANEY HEIRS, and *That Kind of Girl,* the second novel by exciting new talent Kim McKade.

And in case you'd like a sneak preview of next month, our Christmas gifts to you include the above-mentioned conclusion to FIRSTBORN SONS, *Born Royal,* as well as *Brand-New Heartache,* award-winning Maggie Shayne's latest of THE OKLAHOMA ALL-GIRL BRANDS. See you then!

Yours,

Leslie J. Wainger
Executive Senior Editor

Please address questions and book requests to:
Silhouette Reader Service
U.S.: 3010 Walden Ave., P.O. Box 1325, Buffalo, NY 14269
Canadian: P.O. Box 609, Fort Erie, Ont. L2A 5X3

# BEVERLY BARTON
## Jack's Christmas Mission

*Home Sweet Home*
*Bakery & Cafe*
*11109 E. Winner Rd.*
*Independence, MO 64052*

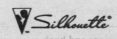

INTIMATE MOMENTS™

Published by Silhouette Books

**America's Publisher of Contemporary Romance**

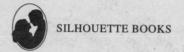 SILHOUETTE BOOKS

ISBN 0-373-27183-2

JACK'S CHRISTMAS MISSION

Copyright © 2001 by Beverly Beaver

## BEVERLY BARTON

has been in love with romance since her grandfather gave her an illustrated book of *Beauty and the Beast*. An avid reader since childhood, Beverly wrote her first book at the age of nine. After marriage to her own "hero" and the births of her daughter and son, Beverly chose to be a full-time homemaker, aka wife, mother, friend and volunteer. The author of over thirty-five books, Beverly is a member of Romance Writers of America and helped found the Heart of Dixie chapter in Alabama. She has won numerous awards and has made the Waldenbooks and *USA Today* bestseller lists.

In loving memory
of my sister-in-law Winnie Sue Bradford,
whose beautiful smile and boisterous laughter
brightened the world around her. We love you, Sis.

# Prologue

"I love you to death!"

Peggy Jo Riley stared in disbelief at the message scrawled in red paint on the mirror. Half a second later her mind registered that not only was her dressing room at WLOK totally ransacked but that her secret admirer had somehow gotten inside the television studio and into her private quarters, adjacent to her office. An adrenaline rush surged through her body, jangling her nerves. Her mouth opened to scream, but the sound froze in her throat, becoming a silent cry. What if *he* were still in here somewhere? Hiding in a closet? Behind the paneled screen where she often changed clothes? Beneath the daybed? Her accelerated heartbeat roared inside her head, temporarily deafening her to all other sounds.

The sudden touch of a hand on her shoulder jarred Peggy Jo into action. She yelled as she whirled around to face her attacker, ready to retaliate with the self-defense tactics she had learned from the experts who had appeared on her television show last year.

"Don't!" the woman cried. "It's me. Jill."

With fear still pumping through her system like an insidious poison, Peggy Jo took several deep, calming breaths as she looked directly at her agent, Jill Lennard. Suddenly she remembered that Jill had driven in from Atlanta today because they had made plans to go out for dinner, after she taped two episodes of *Self-Made Woman*.

"Oh, God, Jill, I'm sorry," Peggy Jo said. "I almost attacked you. I thought—"

Jill shoved past Peggy Jo to take a closer look at the dressing room. Shaking her head, she voiced a strong curse word. "No wonder you went berserk when I touched you. I was afraid this would happen. This is absolutely the last straw." Jill backed out of the room. "Come on, we're getting the station's security to check for an intruder, and then we're calling the police."

"How could he have gotten in here?" Peggy Jo didn't resist when Jill grabbed her arm and pulled her out of the dressing room and into her office.

"I don't know how it could have happened, but after this, maybe Chet Compton will listen to me. As the station's manager, it's his job to make sure there's enough security to see to it that no unauthorized people can just wander around in the building. This incident goes to show you what I've been trying to tell you for months now— this guy, whoever the hell he is, isn't going to stop with just writing you dozens of sick fan letters and making threatening phone calls." Jill gave Peggy Jo a gentle shove. "Sit."

Peggy Jo plopped down in the chair behind her desk. "I'll call security first, just in case he's still in the studio." Her hand shook as she picked up the telephone receiver.

Jill nodded and said, "Right. Call studio security, then call the local police. And if that detective dares to suggest that these threats aren't real, that I'm probably behind them as some sort of publicity stunt, I'll strangle him."

As Peggy Jo dialed an inside line, she clutched the receiver tightly and curled her other hand into a fist to stop the trembling. "I thought...no, I hoped it wouldn't come to this. I just don't understand why this is happening. It's not as if I'm some national celebrity."

"Look, honey," Jill said, rummaging in her purse for her cell phone, "I'm going to contact the Dundee Security Agency right now. You need around-the-clock protection."

"No, don't. I've told you I don't want a bodyguard."

"You can't refuse," Jill said, as she continued scrambling around in her oversize black shoulder bag until she came up with her address book. "You promised me that if things went beyond harassing letters and phone calls, you'd let me contact the Dundee Agency. I'm holding you to your promise."

Peggy Jo sighed, then nodded agreement just as the studio security officer answered his phone. She explained hurriedly what had happened. He assured her that he'd give the studio a thorough check for an intruder and notify Mr. Compton about what had happened.

She simply couldn't believe things had reached this point. And why now? Just when she had the world by the tail, when everything was almost perfect in her life. After all the years of struggling to overcome the past and be the best person she could be, at long last everything had fallen into place. Professionally and personally, she'd never had it so good. Her local Chattanooga television program *Self-Made Woman* was going into national syndication after the first of the year, and she'd be making more money than she'd ever dreamed possible. And her second self-help book had made the *New York Times* extended list and gone into a third printing. Her private life was filled with peace and contentment. She had a beautiful, healthy six-year-old daughter, who was the joy of her life. And even if she didn't have a significant other, she didn't lack for male companionship whenever she wanted it. And best of all, those relationships were always on her terms. She had come a long way from the days when she had allowed a man to run her life.

The minute she finished talking to Ted Wilkes, head of security, she dialed the police and was immediately put through to Detective Gifford. Despite the hint of distrust in his voice, the burly fifty-year-old police veteran told Peggy Jo that he would come to the studio posthaste. As she hung up the receiver, she heard the last few words of her agent's conversation.

"Then we can expect him first thing tomorrow morning?" Jill said. "Good. Thanks, Ellen. I appreciate your sending one of your top agents for this job. Peggy Jo is more than a client. She's a good friend."

"Him?" Peggy Jo snarled. "They're sending a man?"

"Yes, they're sending one of their top agents. A guy named Jack Parker. Ellen assures me that he's the best."

"I don't want a male bodyguard," Peggy Jo said. "When we discussed this and I promised to agree to a bodyguard, you said you'd get a female agent."

"I tried. Honest I did." Jill widened her big brown eyes, a you-must-believe-me expression on her face. "The Dundee Agency has only a handful of female agents, and right now they're all on assignments or they've already taken off for the Thanksgiving holiday this weekend."

Peggy Jo groaned. Great! That's all she needed, some big, sweaty, bossy man in her face twenty-four hours a day. It wasn't that she hated men. There were a few she genuinely liked. But she'd had her fill—personally—of swaggering, chest-beating, womanizing hell-raisers. She'd been married to one long time ago, and that experience had left a bitter taste in her mouth. And her own father had taught her how disloyal and unreliable men can be. No, Peggy Jo Riley depended on no one except Peggy Jo Riley, and the thought of a bodyguard, especially a male bodyguard, didn't sit well with her.

She intended to lay down some ground rules with Mr. Jack Parker the moment they met. He had to know, up front, that she wasn't a helpless female who loved the idea of being protected by some big, strong man. She intended to make it perfectly clear to him that he was her employee and she was the boss. She would be issuing the orders and making the decisions. And if he didn't like it, he could just go straight back to Atlanta. Or straight to hell, for all she cared. Nobody—absolutely nobody—told Peggy Jo Riley what she could and couldn't do. Least of all some man!

# Chapter 1

Jack Parker checked into the Reed House hotel in downtown Chattanooga, paid the bellhop an extra twenty bucks to bring him a bottle of Crown Royal, then turned on the sports channel and tossed his black Stetson on the bed. He had approximately twelve hours to acquaint himself with the details of this new case, one he'd been reluctant to take. He had heard about the Dundee Agency's new client, Peggy Jo Riley, and knew her type well. The type who preached that men where the bane of every woman's existence, and all the ills of society could be laid at the feet of the male sex. Hell, who hadn't heard of the latest guru to American womankind, the up-and-coming Chattanooga talk-show hostess whose program was going into national syndication the first of the year?

Jack shoved his Stetson aside on the bed, then lifted his duffel bag, laid it on the spread and unzipped it. He removed a video tape of Peggy Jo's show, *Self-Made Woman*, a paperback copy of her latest book, *Putting Yourself First*, and a file folder of information about the woman herself.

Good thing he'd eaten on the drive over from Atlanta. He'd picked up a couple of barbecue sandwiches and a bag of chips. That would tide him over until breakfast. He'd be up past midnight going over the information, skimming the book and studying the video. The more he knew about Peggy Jo, her lifestyle and her daily routine, the better able he'd be to protect her and to hopefully figure out who was harassing her. With her attitude, she had probably pissed off half the men in the state, but only a real nut case would become a stalker and pose a threat to her.

After taking off his denim jacket, Jack sat on the edge of the bed to remove his black boots. As he massaged his feet, he thought about why he'd asked Ellen, Dundee's CEO, to give this case to another agent. Could he be totally honest with himself? He sure hadn't been up front with Ellen. What he should have said was, "I don't want to have to guard some man-hating feminist twenty-four/seven because her attitude sticks in my craw." Because Jack knew better than anyone that a woman could be just as guilty of mistreating a man as a man could of mistreating a woman. As a boy he had watched his mother slowly but surely drive his father to suicide. It wasn't that he didn't like the ladies; on the contrary, he loved the ladies and they loved him. But because he understood the dangers of commitment, nobody owned Jack Parker. No woman would ever rope and tie him and put her personal brand on his backside. Love 'em and leave 'em had been his philosophy since he'd been a teenager. And so far, that motto had served him well.

Jack realized that he and Peggy Jo Riley would mix like oil and water. When he had pointed out to Ellen that a female agent would probably be more to Ms. Riley's liking, Ellen had laughed.

"She requested a female agent, but unfortunately Lucie, J.J. and Kate are all on assignments," Ellen had said. "And you're my only experienced agent who's free, so you're taking this assignment. Get your gear together and head for Chattanooga pronto.''

Jack padded barefoot across the carpeted floor, switched channels and inserted the tape into the video machine. By the time he had unbuttoned his shirt and unbuckled his belt, the theme music for *Self-Made Woman* reverberated throughout the hotel room. A jazzy instrumental rendition of a once-popular song by Helen Reddy that he recognized immediately. "I Am Woman." The announcer introduced the hostess of the show to resounding applause from her audience. Jack plopped down in a chair in front of the TV and studied his new client as she marched front and center.

Peggy Jo Riley was no ordinary woman. One look told him that she was tough, self-confident and aggressive. He was a pretty good judge of women. He'd known more than his share and could usually size up a filly immediately and never be proven wrong. Ms. Riley spoke with a soft, country Southern accent that could easily melt the polar ice cap. As he listened to her rhetoric, he surmised several things— that she was intelligent, charming and had a fairy godmother complex. She wanted to help all the women of the world to fix their problems, be it problems with men, with work, with feelings of inadequacy or incompetence. No wonder the media was comparing her to Oprah.

As he watched and listened, Jack automatically began sizing her up, checking out her physical attributes or lack thereof. He'd never preferred a specific type. He liked 'em all. Blondes, brunettes and redheads. Short, tall, thin, plump. The bimbo type as well as the brainy type. So why was it that he knew instantly that Miss Peggy Jo wasn't his type?

Hell, what difference did it make? He wasn't going to be wooing her into his bed. She was a client, an assignment, just like any other. But he couldn't remember when he'd dreaded taking on a case as much as he did this one.

As he watched Peggy Jo speaking, laughing and commiserating with her female guests, he did an immediate reevaluation. On this particular show she didn't come across as a man hater, despite the fact that one of her guests was a male therapist who specialized in treating men who abused their wives and children.

Jack noticed the way her eyes glazed with tears when she spoke with a victim and the firmness of her handshake when she thanked the therapist for his valuable input. This was a woman who cared—genuinely cared.

When a knock sounded at the door, Jack paused the video, then stood and traipsed across the room. He opened the door, took the bottle of whisky from the bellhop and thanked him. After pouring himself half a glass of liquor, he picked up the file folder and carried it with him to the chair before restarting the video. Alternately he glanced at the TV screen and read a few pages of data on his client. He just couldn't connect the high school drop-out and abused teenage wife he was reading about with the self-confident television hostess he saw on screen.

Peggy Jo was no raving beauty, but with her green eyes and freckles she possessed a healthy, clean-cut vibrance. She wore her long, dark-red hair pulled away from her full cheeks and square jaw, but allowed it to hang freely halfway down her back. A neat yet feminine style. She was plump, by today's standards, not that he heeded today's standards. Probably five-five, with an ample bosom, small waist and broad hips. Not a large woman, but Rubenesque. She dressed conservatively, in a classic camel tan jacket and black slacks and wore gold jewelry that glistened in the harsh studio lighting.

"Well, Jacky-boy," he said aloud, "you're going to have your hands full with this one. She sure is a contradiction. She looks like the type of woman made for loving, but her bio reads like a woman who'd sooner jump into a box of rattlesnakes than into bed with a man."

He had a sinking feeling that his good-ole-boy charm

wouldn't work on this woman. He knew before even meeting her that this was going to be the most difficult bodyguard case he'd ever handled for Dundee.

Hetty met Peggy Jo at the front door, a concerned look on her wrinkled face and a sad gleam in her brown eyes. Peggy Jo had found a prize in Wendy's nanny, who also served as her housekeeper. Hetty Ballard was a childless widow who had worked with children all her life, first as a grade school teacher and after retirement, as a baby-sitter. Hetty loved children and in the six years she had been with Peggy Jo and Wendy, the woman had become family; a substitute mother to Peggy Jo and a grandmother to Wendy.

After taking Peggy Jo's coat the moment she removed it, Hetty hung the black wool garment in the hall closet. "That man called here a few minutes ago. He said to tell you that he's at the Reed House and he'll meet you at the station first thing in the morning."

"Jack Parker is already in Chattanooga?" Peggy Jo headed down the hallway toward her daughter's room.

"He sounded like a real nice man," Hetty said. "Got a good Texas accent and was real charming."

Peggy Jo stopped abruptly, glanced over her shoulder and frowned at Hetty. "We've hired the man to be my bodyguard. Our relationship will be completely professional. So, if you have any ideas of trying to put any kind of romantic spin on his living here at the house, you can forget it right now."

"You're accusing me unjustly." Hetty followed Peggy Jo down the hall. "I promised you, after my last attempt at matchmaking, that I would stay out of your love life." Hetty lowered her voice to a whisper. "Or lack thereof."

Although she had heard it quite clearly, Peggy Jo ignored the last comment as she opened the door to Wendy's room.

"She's supposed to be asleep, but my guess is that she's been trying to stay awake until you got home," Hetty said.

Only a soft pink night-light illuminated the darkness in Wendy's bedroom, an area of pastel colors that created a perfect vision of a little girl's haven. Peggy Jo had decorated the room from memories of the room she had always wanted as a child but never had. White French Provincial furniture. A canopy bed. Frilly pink curtains and bedspread. A Victorian dollhouse. One wall filled with shelves containing a doll collector's dream come true. And stuffed animals of every size and variety. And inside the walk-in closet were enough clothes to dress half a dozen six-year-olds.

"Mommy?" Lifting her head from the lace-adorned pillow, the raven-haired child smiled the moment she saw her mother.

Peggy Jo rushed over and sat on the side of the bed. "You're supposed to be asleep. It's after nine."

Wendy scooted out from beneath the covers and threw her arms around Peggy Jo's neck. "I couldn't go to sleep until you got home. I wanted to tell you that Missy's got the flu and Mrs. Carson's going to let me be an angel in the play. You've got to call Missy's mother and see if we can use her costume."

Peggy Jo hugged her daughter to her, savoring the bliss of being loved and needed by this special child. She had decided years ago to never remarry, so for an old-fashioned woman like she was, that meant never having children. But when her friend Ginny had died in a car accident, along with her husband, Wendy had been left an orphan at six months old. Adopting Wendy had been an easy decision. Peggy Jo's maternal yearnings could be fulfilled without compromising her moral standards and without risking a second marriage. She had given Wendy all the love in her heart and everything that money could buy, including a private school. But recently Wendy had begun asking why Peggy Jo couldn't get her a daddy.

"I'll call Missy's mother first thing tomorrow," Peggy Jo said. "Right now, I have something to tell you."

On the drive home from the station, she had thought about how she would explain to Wendy that a man would be moving into their home tomorrow. The last thing she wanted Wendy to do was become attached to a hired bodyguard. But for the past several months Wendy had become as obsessed as Hetty with finding her mother a mate. Every man Peggy Jo dated became a potential daddy candidate.

"Sweetie, we're going to have a houseguest." Peggy Jo eased Wendy onto her lap. Wendy's big blue eyes rounded in surprise. "His name is Jack Parker, and he's a bodyguard. Since Mommy's TV show is going to be seen all over the United States and Mommy is going to be famous, Aunt Jill thinks I need someone to look after me."

God, she hoped that explanation made sense to a six-year-old. She had gone over several different versions, and this one seemed simple and honest, without being frightening.

"Oh, Mommy, we're going to have a man around the house," Wendy mimicked Hetty's repetitive declaration that what they needed was a man around the house. "He's going to take care of you and me, and I can tell Missy and Jennifer and Martha Jane that I do so have a daddy."

"No, Wendy." Peggy Jo clasped her daughter's chin gently. "Mr. Parker isn't going to be your daddy and he isn't going to take care of us. What have I told you about us girls?"

Wendy's smile quickly turned into a frown. Her rosebud mouth became a pout. "That we don't need a man to take care of us. That we can take care of ourselves."

"That's right."

"But you said he was going to look after you," Wendy whined. "Daddies look after mommies and little girls, don't they?"

She wished she could tell Wendy that, yes, all daddies

look after their wives and little girls, but she had never lied to her child and she wasn't going to now. "Some daddies do, sweetie, but some daddies don't. That's why it's very important for us girls to always know how to take care of ourselves and never depend on any man."

Peggy Jo knew that some women had fathers and husbands who had never let them down, who had always taken care of them and looked after them, but she hadn't been that lucky. She had been forced, at an early age, to face the harsh reality that some men were uncaring.

"I know. There is no Prince Charming," Wendy said as she cuddled close to her mother. "Fairy tales aren't real. They're just made-up stories."

"That's right," Peggy Jo said. "Life can be wonderful and beautiful, but it can never be like it is in fairy tales. Life is what we make it. It's up to us to make it good for ourselves." She loved her daughter far too much to fill her head with hopeless dreams of happily-ever-after when that dream so seldom came true in real life. Others might think her hard-hearted for giving Wendy a realistic view of love and life and relationships, but she knew better. As a mother, it was her job to protect her child and that's what she was doing.

"Okay, Mommy. I won't pretend that Mr. Parker is my daddy. I promise."

Peggy Jo sighed. "Mr. Parker is going to work for me. I'm going pay him a salary to be around all the time and make sure nobody bothers me."

"Will he keep me from bothering you?" Wendy asked, with wide-eyed innocence.

Peggy Jo hugged Wendy close, then chuckling softly, she lifted her child and put her back into bed. After pulling the covers up to Wendy's chin, Peggy Jo kissed her.

"You never bother me, sweetpea. And Mr. Parker will never keep you away from me. I'll tell him that Ms. Wendy Riley can see me and talk to me any time she pleases."

After yawning, Wendy smiled. "I love you, Mommy."

"I love you, too."

When Peggy Jo exited the room and closed the door behind her, she made her way down the hall to the kitchen. Hetty sat at the table, a mug of hot chocolate in her hand and another waiting for Peggy Jo, who immediately pulled out an oak Windsor chair and sat across from Hetty.

"I knew that after the day you've had, you'd need something chocolate." Hetty nodded toward the Santa mug. As soon as Peggy Jo tasted the delicious drink, Hetty asked, "So, how did you explain to Wendy that we've got a man moving in with us tomorrow?"

"It wasn't easy." Peggy Jo sipped the cocoa. "At first she thought Mr. Parker might be her new daddy, but I cleared that up right away." Peggy Jo glowered at her housekeeper. "If you hadn't talked so much about our needing a man around here, she wouldn't have—"

"Don't blame me because that child wants a daddy. All of her friends have daddies, even the ones whose parents are divorced."

"I can give Wendy everything else she needs and wants, but I cannot give her a daddy."

"Can't or won't?" Hetty glanced at the ceiling, her expression making a statement.

"Both. Can't and won't. Marriage is just fine for a lot of women, but not for me. After my own father deserted me, and Buck treated me like dirt, I swore that I'd never let another man have any control over my life. And that's a promise I intend to keep."

"All men aren't like your father and Buck Forbes," Hetty said. "My Jim was a wonderful man. I wish you had known him. He would have changed your mind about men."

"We've had this discussion before, and there's no point in beating a dead horse." With the mug in hand, Peggy Jo scooted back her chair and stood. "Just make sure the guest bedroom is ready for Mr. Parker. He'll be coming home with me tomorrow evening.''

"I'm fixing a pot roast and my blackberry jam cake. I've never known a man who didn't like my country cooking. And we sure do want to make Mr. Parker feel right at home, don't we?''

Peggy Jo rolled her eyes, shook her head and left a chuckling Hetty alone in the kitchen. If she wasn't genuinely frightened by this unknown person who was terrorizing her, Peggy Jo wouldn't even consider allowing a man to become her twenty-four-hour-a-day companion. But despite her determination to never rely on another man as long as she lived, she realized that under these circumstances, she would be a fool not to hire a bodyguard. And if there was one thing Peggy Jo Riley never intended to be—ever again—it was a fool.

The next morning, as she was going over her notes for the taping, WLOK's station manager, Chet Compton, came into her office. He handed Peggy Jo a cup of coffee, then placed his hand on her shoulder.

"You're here bright and early this morning,'' he said, his voice low as he leaned over to speak to her. "Something wrong?''

Peggy Jo tensed, but didn't move away from the man she had dated on and off for the past several years. When Chet had gotten serious and started acting territorial, she had ended their personal relationship, which she had considered to be nothing more than two good friends dating. Chet had not taken the rejection kindly, and for months afterward, tension had suffused the station whenever Chet came into Studio B, where they broadcast the show live daily and taped other shows for holidays and vacations.

"I'm expecting someone to meet me here around eight,'' she said. "Jill has hired a bodyguard for me, and he'll start work today.''

"A bodyguard? Do you think that's necessary?" Chet squeezed her shoulder. "I think there's enough manpower around the station to keep an eye on you. You must know that not only am I your willing slave, but so are most of the guys who work here, especially Ross Brewster. That guy would walk over hot coals for you."

"None of you, including Ross, is a professional. And after what happened in my dressing room yesterday, Jill and I agree that I need a trained bodyguard with me until this stalker is caught."

Peggy Jo eased away from Chet and moved across the set to inspect the job the production manager had done in arranging the Christmas decorations. The three programs they'd tape today would be shown the week after Christmas and she wanted everything to be perfect. She had a reputation for being detail oriented and often hard to please, but only those with sloppy work habits ever complained.

Chet followed her. "So, does the set meet with your approval?"

"Mmm-hmm." She nodded. "When Leda and Burt come in this morning, I want to see them first thing and explain why I've hired a bodyguard. So, please don't put your own spin on it before I've spoken to them."

"Hey, you hired both of them. They're your people, not mine."

Peggy Jo forced a smile. Chet hadn't been thrilled with her when, after her former director left WLOK, she had hired Leda Seager to replace him, without consulting with Chet first. And Chet had been adamantly opposed to her demanding that the show's original production manager be fired for incompetence. He had also rejected Peggy Jo's choice of a replacement—Burt Morgan, a brilliant young African-American man who had a knack for dealing with the crew. When he hadn't come up with any compelling argument against Burt, Peggy Jo had hired him. She was glad she did.

Peggy Jo picked up the loosely structured script for today's first show off the seat of her chair, then sat, the script in one hand and the coffee mug in the other. She spoke to Chet, but didn't look at him. "I need to go over this script. Is there anything you want to talk to me about this morning? Some other reason you're here on my set?"

"Apparently not." He turned and stormed off the set.

She wasn't usually so rude, but she'd learned that with Chet she had to be. The guy took even normal friendliness as a come-on. Peggy Jo laid the script in her lap, then glanced up in time to see Chet's back as he retreated out the door, almost running into Ross Brewster, the station's twenty-year-old gofer. Chet grumbled. Ross apologized, then hurried toward Peggy Jo, a small white paper bag in his gloved hands.

She liked Ross, though she was careful not to encourage his boyish crush on her. Why was it that when she'd been a teenager, she'd had a problem getting guys to notice her, and now, when she didn't give a damn, she seemed to attract men like honey attracted bears?

Ross rushed forward and offered her the white paper bag. "Cream cheese Danish," he said. "I know it's your favorite. I came by the bakery on my way here. You're early this morning, aren't you? I thought I'd get here first."

Peggy Jo accepted the gift graciously, even opened the bag to smell the mouth-watering confection, before she handed it back to Ross. "Thanks. I appreciate your thinking of me, but—"

"Look, I know Chet has already told me to back off." His shoulders slumped as he took the bag. "And I know what he must be thinking. But, honest to goodness, Peggy Jo, I'm not stalking you. I think you're the absolute greatest, but I'd never harass you."

"When did Chet tell you to back off?" she asked.

"Last week," Ross said. "He told me that he thought I

was the one stalking you and said if I didn't stop immediately, he'd fire me.''

"Damn," Peggy Jo cursed under her breath. "Ross, I apologize for Chet. I don't think you're my stalker. All I was going to say is that I appreciated your thinking of me, but I'm deliberately cutting back on sweets from today until Christmas. Otherwise, I'd wind up with five or ten extra pounds come New Year's day.''

Ross's pale cheeks flushed scarlet. "I'll get rid of these right away. Would you like me to run out and get you some fruit. A banana or an apple or—''

She lifted the coffee mug. "How about pouring out this slop and making some fresh coffee in the pot in my office?''

"I'll get to it right away. And, thanks, Peggy Jo, for believing me about not being your stalker.''

While he glanced over his shoulder, smiling like an idiot, Ross headed for the door and ran smack-dab into a big man wearing a black Stetson. Peggy Jo's stomach did a nervous flip-flop. Was this...? It had to be him. A stranger in a Stetson, jeans, denim jacket and black boots. Heaven help her, the Dundee Agency had sent her a cowboy. A big, rugged John Wayne wanna-be.

The man grabbed Ross by the shoulders to steady him, then laughed good-naturedly. "Gotta watch where you're going, son, or you'll wind up in a heap of trouble.''

"Yes, sir. Sorry, sir." Ross all but ran out the door and down the hall.

Peggy Jo swallowed hard. The tall, broad-shouldered cowboy entered Studio B, and when he saw her, he removed his hat and smiled. The bottom dropped out of Peggy Jo's stomach. Jack Parker was drop-dead gorgeous in a rough, rowdy, hard-edged way that she bet few women could resist. And he had a killer smile that implied he knew just how damn appealing he was.

She would have to send this guy packing as fast as possible. No way in hell was she going to let herself fall victim to this good ole boy's devastating charm.

# Chapter 2

"Howdy, ma'am," Jack said. "I'm the Dundee agent you hired. Jack Parker." He held out his hand.

The woman stared at his proffered hand, hesitated, then clasped it in hers. He liked the feel of her small, soft hand and the strength of her firm handshake. But he was a bit uncertain about the way she looked him square in the eye. He was accustomed to ladies being a little more subtle and not quite so straightforward. But, being the man he was, he couldn't help noticing how green her eyes were and how long her thick, dark lashes were. Under different circumstances and with a different woman, he would have commented on her eyes. But knowing what he did about this particular lady, he figured she wouldn't take kindly to a compliment that she was sure to see as flirting.

When he held on to her hand a minute too long, she jerked free and stepped backward just enough to show him that she needed a perimeter of personal space around her in order to feel comfortable. Jack prided himself on being a good judge of body language, so he heeded her message.

"I suppose, to be polite, I should say it's nice to meet you and I'm glad you're here." Peggy Jo maintained direct eye contact with him. "But in all honesty, Mr. Parker, I really don't want a bodyguard and I greatly resent the fact that I need one."

"Call me Jack," he said, and smiled. But when she didn't return the friendly gesture, he realized he'd been right about this woman. His gut instincts had warned him that she wasn't going to be easily charmed, that she was going to make this assignment the job from hell. And his gut instincts were seldom wrong. "By all means, Ms. Riley, be honest with me."

"I'm sorry if I'm being impolite, but—"

"Why don't we clear the air immediately?" he suggested. "You hired me because you need protection, and you want the Dundee Agency to put its manpower and brainpower to work on finding out who your stalker is. But you hate the idea of having a strange man being with you twenty-four/seven."

Her eyes widened, apparently surprised by his frankness.

"It's not necessary that you like me," he told her. "But it is necessary that you trust me. Can you do that?"

She took a deep breath. "I'm not sure. It's difficult for me to trust others, especially men."

"Don't think of me as a man." Jack noted the startled look on her face and barely restrained a chuckle. "Think of me as your protector, someone whose sole purpose is to keep you safe from harm."

"I'm used to taking care of myself. I hate the idea of having to rely on anyone else to protect me."

"I admire your self-reliance, but with an unknown stalker determined to keep you off balance, the only smart thing to do is rely on me and the Dundee Agency until we apprehend this guy and take you out of harm's way."

"Yes, of course. I understand." Peggy Jo nervously rubbed her hands together. "I promise that I'll do my best to cooperate with you, as long as you remember that I'm your employer.''

''Meaning?'' Jack knew damn well what she meant. She wanted him to agree that she was the boss. Heck, she could call herself whatever she wanted—employer, boss, the one in charge—as long as she realized that he was the expert and if he issued her an order, she'd damn well better obey it.

''Meaning just that. I'm the employer and you're the employee. Our relationship is strictly business. No first names. No unnecessary familiarity.'' Peggy Jo finally broke eye contact as she surveyed Jack from head to toe, leisurely, as if she were studying him under a microscope. ''And as soon as the Dundee Agency has a female body-guard available, I want you replaced.''

Jack laid his hand over his heart and sighed dramatically. ''Oh, Miss Peggy Jo, you wound me, you do. You haven't even given me a chance to prove my worth and already you're talking about replacing me.''

''Cut the crap, Parker,'' she said, her expression somber. ''Your 'aw shucks, ma'am' attitude is wasted on me.''

''You're one tough cookie, aren't you, Miss Peggy Jo? Tell me, is ball-busting a second job for you or just a hobby?''

She gasped. The nerve of the man! How dare he speak to her that way. Just who did he think he was? Obviously, he didn't know a damn thing about her or he would have realized that she didn't take back talk from anyone—and never from a man!

''Let's get one thing straight—'' Peggy Jo punched the tip of her index finger into Jack's chest ''—if you make another remark like that, I'll fire you and get Dundee to send me another agent. One with a more agreeable attitude.''

The man laughed. He actually laughed. Right in her face! She felt her skin burning, felt a heated flush creeping up her neck. He glanced down at where her finger hovered over his chest. When she jerked it away, he reached out and grabbed her wrist. A wild rush of adrenaline pumped through her body at his touch. Their gazes collided. She tugged to free herself, but he held tight.

"I apologize, Miss Peggy Jo," he said, a warm, winning smile on his face. "I'm not usually such a jackass. As a matter of fact, I'm known for my Southern charm, but I figured charm wouldn't work with you, so I tried a different tactic. Obviously, I made a mistake. So how about forgiving me and letting us start all over again?"

The pressure of his grip on her wrist lessened until she could have easily broken loose. But she didn't. She stood there for an endless moment, their gazes locked, her breathing ragged, and allowed his statement to sink into her befuddled brain. She didn't like the way this man made her feel—all soft and hot and feminine. And vulnerable.

"I think you switched tactics on me again, didn't you?" When she pulled on her wrist, he released her. "If I have to choose between the jerk and the charmer, then I'll take the charmer. But you're right—all the charm in the world won't work on me, Mr. Parker. I'm immune."

"Does this mean you aren't going to fire me?"

He was still grinning, damn him, as if he knew perfectly well that if she fired him after his sincere apology, then she'd have to admit to herself that she couldn't stand her ground against him.

"No, I'm not firing you. But keep in mind that I can dismiss you at any time."

"Yes, ma'am." He saluted her and clicked his heels.

"So, now what?" she asked.

"We start by going over some ground rules," he replied, a mischievous twinkle in his golden-brown eyes. "My ground rules."

Before Peggy Jo could comment, she looked past Jack to where Ross Brewster stood just inside the doorway, a couple of mugs in his hands. She motioned for Ross to come to her.

Jack glanced over his shoulder. "Who's this guy?" Jack asked, and when Peggy Jo glared at Jack questioningly, he explained, "I need to know the identities of all the people who work here at WLOK and what their positions are and their relationships to you."

Peggy Jo nodded, understanding his need for this information. "This is Ross Brewster," she said as Ross approached her.

"I've brought you some fresh coffee," Ross said, handing a mug to Peggy Jo. "And I brought some for you, too."

Jack accepted the bright purple mug emblazoned with the WLOK emblem. "Thanks."

"Ross is a student at UTC," Peggy Jo said. "He works here at the studio every morning before classes and various hours between classes."

"Nice to meet you," Jack said, and shook hands with the young man. "I'm Jack Parker, Miss Peggy Jo's bodyguard. We'll probably be seeing a great deal of each other for a while."

Ross visibly flinched. "A bodyguard?"

"Yes," Peggy Jo said. "With the stalker getting more bold—bold enough to ransack my dressing room here at the studio without being caught—I decided that it was in my best interest to hire someone to watch my back."

"I think that's a really good idea," Ross said, his gaze scanning Jack from head to toe. "Do you carry a gun?"

Jack grinned. "Sure do." But he made no move to reveal the whereabouts of his weapon.

Ross swallowed, then cleared his throat. "Oh, yeah. Mr. Compton said to tell you that Leda and Burt are here."

"Thanks."

Ross smiled, then walked backward, exiting slowly, melting away like snow in the sunshine.

Peggy Jo turned her attention back to Jack and before he

could ask her, she said, "Leda Seager is the director of
*Self-Made Woman* and Burt Morgan is our production manager. I wanted to speak to them and explain about your
presence on the set…well, actually, your presence in my
life. I asked Chet to let me speak to them first. I was afraid
that if he told them about you, he would…well, he
might—"

"Chet? Chet Compton, the station manager. Right?"

"Yes, but how did you know?"

"His name stuck in my mind after I read your file that
Dundee put together quickly and gave me before I left Atlanta yesterday. If I recall correctly, Chet's also a former
boyfriend of yours."

"Chet was never my boyfriend," she corrected. "He and
I dated occasionally, but we've never been anything except
friends. And not even that anymore. We're business asso-
ciates and that's all."

"Who broke whose heart?"

"What?"

"If you two were friends before you started dating and
now that you don't date any longer, you aren't friends, then
that tells me somebody took the relationship seriously and
got hurt when it ended."

"You're quite astute, aren't you?" Peggy Jo sipped her
coffee. "Chet wanted more than friendship. I didn't."

"Any chance Chet is your stalker?"

Peggy Jo wanted to reply in the negative, but she
couldn't. Chet had a temperamental nature and tended to
be possessive. She didn't like the idea of suspecting him,
but she knew she couldn't rule out the possibility.

"Probably not," she said. "But it's possible."

"And what about Ross? It's obvious the boy's got a
crush on you."

Peggy Jo shrugged. "I doubt it's Ross. He's such a sweet
boy. But then again, I suppose he could be considered a
suspect."

Jack harrumphed. "Just how many lovesick fools do you have in your life?"

Peggy Jo narrowed her gaze and glowered at him. "What happened to that good-ole-boy charm of yours?"

"Sorry, ma'am." The corners of his mouth lifted, but didn't quite form a smile. "Let me rephrase that. How many men do you suspect might be your stalker?"

Before Peggy Jo could answer his question, Leda and Burt entered the studio. She glanced at her watch and realized that she had only a couple of minutes to introduce Jack Parker and explain his presence before it was time for a quick rehearsal. They would begin taping the first of the Christmas week episodes in less than an hour. And the audience would be allowed into the studio in about thirty minutes.

"I'll go over all the possible suspects with you on my lunch break later today," Peggy Jo said. "But for now, come meet two very important people who have helped advance my television career."

Jack stood on the sidelines, off to himself just enough to keep a close watch on his client without being seen by either the camera or the small local audience that fitted snugly into the studio. As he watched and listened to Peggy Jo Riley doing her thing, he marveled at how adept she was at putting her guests at ease, even those with whom she disagreed. Why hadn't she used a little of that charisma with him? he wondered. She'd been downright hostile. Of course, *he* hadn't put his best foot forward with her, either. The score was pretty much even in the ornery and unpleasant department. *Face it, Jacky-boy, you aren't used to women taking an instant dislike to you. Miss Peggy Jo kinda bruised your ego, didn't she?*

When she had threatened to fire him, why had he all but pleaded with her for a second chance? Ego! Male ego! It would be one thing if he quit, but another thing altogether if she fired him. He intended to contact Ellen tonight and tell her that he wanted a female agent to replace him on this job as soon as one became available. That way both he and the client would be happier.

The well-rounded young woman Peggy Jo had introduced to him as Kayla Greene, her assistant, came up beside him and said softly, "Isn't she wonderful?"

"Huh?" Jack glanced at the friendly Ms. Greene, whose gaze was glued to the set where her boss lady was discussing with a dietician how to eat well during Christmas without putting on extra pounds.

"I'm talking about our Peggy Jo," Kayla said, keeping her voice low. "Isn't she wonderful? Everybody in the whole state of Tennessee just loves her. That's why I can't figure out why anyone would want to hurt her. Do you think it's possible that her stalker is just some misguided guy who's in love with her?"

"Sure, the guy stalking her could think he's in love with her, but that doesn't mean he isn't dangerous."

"I'm really glad that Ms. Lennard talked Peggy Jo into hiring you. If anything happened to her, we'd all be just devastated."

Jack laid his hand on Kayla's plump shoulder. She gazed up at him and smiled. He indicated with a nod that he wanted her to move back farther away from the set. She followed him into the nearby corner.

"What is it?" she asked, her blue-gray eyes sparkling and her round cheeks flushing a rosy pink.

"I was wondering if you've got any idea about who Miss Peggy Jo's stalker might be," Jack said. "You probably know everyone she works with and the guys she dates and—"

"I've got my suspicions, that's for sure. If it's somebody who cares about her, then it might be Mr. Compton. He's been peeved at her ever since she stopped dating him."

"Yeah, I already know about him, and he's at the top of

my list. But what about someone else? What about Ross Brewster or Burt Morgan?''

When Kayla shook her head, her halo of chestnut-brown curls bounced about her moon-pie face. "It's not either of them. Ross is such a sweet guy and Mr. Morgan is super-nice. They both adore Peggy Jo."

"Mmm-hmm." Jack patted his Stetson on his leg. "So, Chet Compton is your only suspect?"

"I didn't say that. I just said it might be him. But if I were a betting person, I'd put my money on either Buck Forbes or Tia Tuesday."

"According to my files, Buck Forbes is Miss Peggy Jo's ex-husband, so I can see why you'd consider him a suspect, but who is Tia Tuesday?"

"Tia? She's the airhead bimbo on a local rival station who has an exercise-and-fitness show on at the same time *Self-Made Woman* airs. Our show has been beating hers in the ratings ever since her show debuted last year, and the woman has made no secret that she despises Peggy Jo. She's been saying some pretty mean things ever since Peggy Jo's show got picked up for national syndication."

"Is that it?" Jack asked. "Anybody else?"

"Those are the only people I know about, but couldn't the stalker be somebody Peggy Jo doesn't know?"

Jack nodded. "Yeah, that's always a possibility." He patted Kayla on the shoulder. "Thanks for you help."

"Anytime. I'd do anything for Peggy Jo."

Jack glanced back at the set where his client was finishing up the last shot of the segment with the dietician. As soon as the spot concluded, Peggy Jo shook hands with her guest and thanked her profusely, then turned and walked off the set. She came straight toward Jack, walking with a confident strut, as if she owned the world. There was some-thing downright appealing about a woman who was that self-assured. He couldn't help wondering if her cocksure attitude was for real or just for show.

"You weren't interrogating Kayla, were you?" Peggy Jo asked, her voice slightly on edge.

"I asked her a few questions," Jack said, his tone defensive. "After all, she is your assistant and I thought she might have some insight into who your stalker might be."

"Let me guess—her number-one suspect is Tia Tuesday." Laughing softly, Peggy Jo shook her head. "Tia might dislike me, but she isn't my stalker. For one thing the woman can't go anywhere in Chattanooga without being recognized. Believe me she has the most recognizable boobs in town."

"Ah, one of those." Jack couldn't stop the wide grin that spread across his face. "But even the most recognizable boobs in Chattanooga could hire somebody to do her dirty work for her."

"Okay, you're right." Peggy Jo reached out to touch his arm, but paused, her hand in midair. "Look, we'll talk on my lunch break. Right now, I need to freshen my makeup and glance over the information on my next guest, a counselor who's going to discuss dealing with depression during the holidays."

Jack nodded, then when she headed toward the door that opened into the corridor that led to her office, he followed her. The minute she realized he was marching along behind her, she stopped and turned to face him.

"I'm just going to the powder room," she said.

"Where you go, I go."

"You are not going into the bathroom with me!"

"No, but I'll be standing guard right outside. So just holler if you need me."

"Wipe that smirk off your face, Mr. Parker. I hardly think I'll be accosted in the bathroom. And I'm perfectly capable of doing anything I need to do in there without your assistance."

With that said, she turned and stomped down the hallway, shoved open the door to her office and made a beeline straight to her private bathroom. Jack leaned against the doorjamb, crossed one ankle over the other and waited.

Usually an optimist, Jack didn't understand why he couldn't shake this pessimistic feeling he had that things with Miss Peggy Jo were bound to get worse. It was clear as the nose on his face that the woman was determined to dislike him. And even though she was well-known as a feminist, he didn't think she hated all men. No, her feelings of animosity toward him were personal. But what could it be about him that rubbed her the wrong way? He wasn't bad looking. He was fairly smart. And he had a likable personality. Most ladies found him downright irresistible.

Heck, maybe he reminded her of her ex-husband in some way. If that were the case, he'd just have to show Miss Peggy Jo that he wasn't anything like Buck Forbes. He'd never struck a woman in his entire life, not even with provocation. Why, he'd rather cut off his right hand than to ever hit a member of the fair sex.

Jack noticed a shadow outside the office door. Just as he took a step forward, a perky young lady carrying a bouquet of red roses came prancing into the room.

"A delivery for Ms. Riley," she said.

"Do you work here or are you delivering for the florist?" Jack asked, wondering if the station's security people had allowed a delivery person to simply walk into Peggy Jo's private office.

"I work for Humphrey's Florist," she replied.

Jack growled under his breath.

"Sir, is something wrong?"

"No. At least nothing that's your fault."

"Where shall I put these?"

"Set them on the desk." He inclined his head toward the ornate cherry desk.

She hurriedly placed the arrangement on the desk, and when Jack reached for his wallet, she shook her head. "It's already been taken care of by the person who sent them."

The minute the woman left, Jack walked across the room, snatched the attached card from the flowers and opened the small envelope. But before he could look at the card, Peggy Jo emerged from the bathroom, took one look at the roses and cursed.

"Damn! Get those things out of here. Right now!" She glared at the gorgeous floral arrangement as if it were a grotesque two-headed snake.

"You want these roses tossed out?" he asked. "You don't even know who they're from."

"I don't care who sent them," she said. "Anyone who knows me well enough to be sending me flowers would know better than to send me red roses."

An alarm went off in Jack's head. He glanced at the card he held in his hand. Hellfire! Peggy Jo's sicko stalker had no doubt sent the flowers.

"What does it say?" she asked.

He hesitated, then lifted his gaze and looked her square in the eye. "'Red roses for a dead lady.'"

Her mouth rounded in a soundless gasp. "They're from *him*."

"It would appear so." Jack stuck the note in his pocket, then lifted the clear glass vase and dumped vase, flowers, water and all into the nearby wastebasket. "I'll contact the florist and see if they have any idea who the sender was."

"Do you think they'll know?" Peggy Jo stood ramrod stiff as she gazed at the wastebasket.

"Probably not. Our stalker will be smart enough not to give himself away by letting himself be identified by the florist."

Why the hell did she keep staring at the discarded flowers? It was as if they held her under some sort of demonic spell. What was the significance of red roses? And why did she hate the one flower that most women adored?

"Miss Peggy Jo?"

"What?" Still she continued to stare, as if hypnotized by the floral arrangement that she had told him to deep six.

"How about filling me in on the fascination you have for those dumped flowers?"

She snapped her head around and all but growled at him. "I'm not fascinated, I'm repulsed."

"Why?"

"Why? How can you ask such a question. The person who is tormenting me sent those flowers, and you ask me why they repulse me."

"You told me to get rid of the roses before you knew who they were from. Come on, level with me. Remember I'm the one guy you're supposed to be able to trust."

With her gaze boring a hole into him, she said, "My ex-husband used to send me red roses to apologize. Every time Buck beat the hell out of me, he sent me red roses the next day and a note saying 'I'm sorry.'"

# Chapter 3

Jack sat beside Peggy Jo as she drove along the busy downtown street in the late-afternoon rush-hour traffic. He hadn't been surprised when she had rejected his offer to drive. Just another example of her I-gotta-be-in-charge-at-all-times attitude. He had turned in his rental car and explained to his client the necessity of him being with her at all times, and that most definitely included when she was en route to and from work. Her stalker knew where she worked and probably knew where she lived. It would be a simple matter for him—or her—to follow Peggy Jo, perhaps even to cause a minor accident in order to force Peggy Jo out of her car. There were so many clever ways for a stalker to make personal contact with his or her victim. Although everyone, including the client herself, believed her harasser to be male, Jack wasn't ready to rule out the possibility that the culprit might be female. It would be easy enough for a woman to hire a man to make the phone calls for her.

Despite Peggy Jo's adamant assurance that it was highly

unlikely that her ex-husband was her stalker, Jack put Buck Forbes at the top of the list. When he'd suggested that Forbes should be considered as their number-one suspect, Peggy Jo had reminded him that she hadn't seen or heard from her ex in thirteen years, so why would he suddenly begin harassing her? Put like that, it didn't make much sense. But stranger things had been known to happen, so getting the police and the Dundee Agency to check out Buck Forbes was a top priority. Of course, the upcoming Thanksgiving holidays might slow things down a bit. That and the fact that the local police department had been less than cooperative.

The drive across the Market Street Bridge from the downtown business district to North Chattanooga took them across the Tennessee River. Sunset came early in late November, so the streetlights were already shining brightly, eliminating the darkness as Peggy Jo and Jack made their way toward home.

"So, how long have you lived here?" Jack asked.

"Here in Chattanooga or here at my present address?"

"Both."

"I was born and raised here," she replied. "But you must already know that. Surely your file of information on me states those mundane facts."

"I'm trying to make conversation," Jack said. "You know, just being friendly. Trying to break the ice."

"This isn't a date, Mr. Parker." She cut her eyes in his direction for a brief glower, then returned her gaze to the road ahead. "There's no need for idle chitchat."

"Look, hon—Miss Peggy Jo, we're going to be spending a lot of time together during the next few weeks or longer, so it might be nice for both of us if we tried to get along, if we made an effort to like each other."

He felt rather than saw her tense. What was it with this gal? Had an abusive husband turned her off so completely that she couldn't even be civil to a man? She was like a spooked filly who didn't want any human hands on her.

"So, tell me about him," Jack said.

"About who?"

"Your ex-husband. All I've got in my files is his name, the dates of your marriage and divorce. Stuff like that."

"What do you want to know?" Her fingers tightened on the steering wheel. "Do you want to know how many times he beat me, how many times he told me what a stupid, ugly, fat, worthless piece of trash I was? Or would you like to hear the gory details of how he nearly killed me? How he did kill our unborn child?" Her voice cracked at this last admission.

Jack's guts knotted painfully. The very thought that a man would raise a hand to a woman, let alone beat her, enraged Jack. God help him, if he could get his hands on Buck Forbes right this minute, he might kill him. He knew he'd sure like to give the sorry bastard a taste of what he'd given Peggy Jo. The man had actually hit his pregnant wife!

"You lost a child because of—"

"I was four months pregnant. I came home fifteen minutes late from my job as a receptionist, and he accused me of cheating on him with my boss. The accusation was ridiculous, of course, but that didn't matter. He beat me until I was unconscious. I woke up several hours later in the hospital. I'd suffered a miscarriage."

"God, honey, I'm sorry." Jack's hand reached for her in the semidarkness inside her car, but the moment he touched her, she cringed. He removed his hand instantly. He'd read in his file on her about the miscarriage, but hadn't known it was a result of her husband's brutality.

"I had put up with his cruelty for over three years. But after that night, I went to a shelter for abused women and I filed for a divorce."

"All men aren't like Buck Forbes." Jack felt the need

to defend his sex, to convince her that most men weren't savage animals.

"I'm well aware of the fact that there are a lot of good, kind, loyal and loving men in the world. I just didn't happen to have one of them for a father or a husband."

Before Jack could respond, she pulled the Chrysler Sebring into the driveway of a large Craftsman-style house. The old house had a real sense of hominess to it, as if it had been built to accommodate a large family. He had noticed that the neighborhood, which was in the Riverview area, was comprised of both large and small houses, some neatly remodeled and others still in need of repair. His information on her residence stated that she lived in an older section of the city that was part of a mass renovation project.

Peggy Jo turned to face Jack. "Before we go inside, we need to go over a few ground rules."

"Shoot." Jack studied her face by the soft light of the nearby streetlight. An odd little spasm tightened inside him and he wondered at the cause.

"You're a guest in my home, a temporary visitor." She paused as if uncertain how to explain. "You'll be treated with hospitality, of course, but...don't try to ingratiate yourself to my housekeeper, Hetty, or to my daughter."

Jack stared at her, puzzled by her statement. "I'm afraid you've lost me. In what way do you want me not to ingratiate myself to your housekeeper or your daughter? Are you saying don't be charming, don't make friends?"

"Exactly—don't make friends. You're a transitory fixture in our lives, and I don't want Hetty trying to make something personal out of a relationship that is strictly business. And I certainly don't want Wendy becoming attached to you in any way."

Realization dawned. "Ah. I understand. You don't want me playing daddy to your daughter. And you don't want the housekeeper trying to play matchmaker for us." Jack chuckled. Lordy. Lordy. He'd known some uptight women in his life, but Miss Peggy Jo sure did take the cake. Not only was she cautious and afraid for herself, but for her child, too. Poor little girl. And to be honest, he wasn't sure whether he was referring to Wendy Riley or her mother.

"Just do the job you've been hired to do and keep your Southern charm to yourself." With that said, Peggy Jo opened her car door, got out and rounded the hood.

Jack followed quickly, up the steps and onto the large wraparound porch. Before they reached the front door, it opened to reveal a stout, gray-haired woman standing just inside the foyer.

"Come on in, you two," the housekeeper said, smiling broadly. "It's getting cold out there." She ushered them inside hurriedly, then held out her hand. "Let me take your jacket and hat, Mr. Parker."

So, this was Hetty, Jack thought. A motherly type. Round and cheerful and fussing over them like a mother hen.

He handed her his denim jacket and black Stetson. "Thank you, ma'am."

Her smile widened until it reached from ear to ear, deepening the faint lines around her brown eyes and in her rosy cheeks. "You can call me Hetty. I'm the housekeeper and nanny around here, but Peggy Jo will tell you that we're all family in this house."

"Nice to meet you, Hetty." Jack offered her his hand. "You can call me Jack."

Hetty hung his coat and hat on the ornate oak hall tree, then took his hand and gave it a firm shake. "I'm sure glad to meet you, young fella. We're glad to have you with us. I've been telling Peggy Jo for months now that her crazy admirer wasn't going away and what we needed—what she needed—was a man around here."

"Well, Hetty, I'm your man." Jack winked at her.

Hetty giggled. "My, my, I like you already."

"If you two are finished with your mutual admiration

society meeting...'' Peggy Jo said with a look of exasperation.

"Oh, just ignore her," Hetty said. "Come on in and meet the real boss around here."

Peggy Jo sighed, then asked, "Where is Wendy?"

"She's eating supper in the kitchen," Hetty replied.

"Why is she eating now? She knew I'd be home in time for us to eat together."

Hetty smiled, then glanced over at Jack. "Wendy had me set up things in the dining room for you and our guest, so the two of you could have supper together."

"What!" Peggy Jo's eyes narrowed to slits as she frowned.

"Don't go fussing at her," Hetty said. "She can't help being excited. It's the first time her mama has brought a man home with her."

"This is ridiculous. I told her plainly that Mr. Parker is an employee, hired by me to...to watch over me." Peggy Jo marched through the living room and into the dining room.

As Jack and Hetty followed, Hetty said, "You should know, for future reference, that her bark is much worse than her bite."

"Yeah, I figured as much," Jack replied. "But she sure does have a mighty fierce bark, doesn't she?"

"Candles!" Peggy Jo shrieked. "Soft lighting, our best china, crystal and silver. Hetty Ballard, what sort of nonsense have you been putting in Wendy's head about Mr. Parker and me?"

Nonplussed by the accusation against her, Hetty plopped a wide, meaty hand on her hip. "You're accusing me unjustly. I've kept my mouth shut the whole livelong day. Wendy came up with this idea all on her own. And don't you dare scold her, and I mean it. She thinks we've done something really special for you, and she can keep on thinking that if you don't spoil this for her."

"But I can't let her think that there's anything romantic going on between Mr. Parker and me," Peggy Jo said. "I thought she understood last night when I explained the situation to her."

"She's a six-year-old who doesn't have a daddy, and no matter what you tell her about Mr. Parker—" Hetty grinned "—about Jack, she's going to hope…"

"I'll have to speak with her again." Peggy Jo headed for the kitchen. "We can't have her dreaming up some romance—"

Hetty grabbed Peggy Jo's arm, halting her. "Don't spoil this for her. Not tonight. Save your talk for tomorrow. One day can't hurt."

Jack could tell that Peggy Jo was mulling the matter over in her mind, going through a battle trying to decide. Maybe he should step in and handle this situation.

"How about letting me talk to Wendy?" Jack suggested. "After you and I enjoy dinner by candlelight."

Peggy Jo sighed; her shoulders drooped in defeat. "All right. I'll wait until after dinner. But, Mr. Parker, I will explain your presence in our lives, in our home, to Wendy. Not you."

If Hetty hadn't become like a member of the family these past six years, Peggy Jo would fire her. Ever since Wendy started asking why she didn't have a daddy, Hetty had spurred the child on in her requests for a father. And Hetty knew good and well that she never intended to remarry.

"Come on out to the kitchen and meet my daughter," Peggy Jo said to Jack Parker, then glanced at Hetty. "Go ahead and serve dinner for us here in the dining room. But only tonight. If in the future Wendy comes up with any more nonsense like this, you're not to encourage her."

Peggy Jo couldn't be truly angry with her daughter. She understood how much a father meant to a little girl—and to a big girl, too. Sometimes she felt guilty that she wasn't able to give Wendy something as important as a father. To this day she missed her own father almost as much as she missed her mother. One of the most difficult things she had coped with in the therapy sessions she'd had during her time at the shelter and for years afterward, had been accepting the fact that although her father had still been alive during her difficult marriage, he hadn't been able to be a real part of her life.

The moment she entered the kitchen, Wendy jumped up and came barreling toward Peggy Jo, then lifted her arms and cried out, "Mommy, you're home!"

Peggy Jo picked up the fifty pounds of adorable mischief, who immediately straddled her legs around Peggy Jo's waist. The two exchanged a big bear hug, then Wendy giggled as she stared at the man who came through the doorway directly behind Hetty.

"Are you the man who's going to look after my mommy?" Wendy asked, squirming to be put down.

Peggy Jo obliged her by setting her back in the chair at the table. "This is Mr. Parker, the gentleman I told you I'd hired. He's going to be our guest for a while." Peggy Jo pointed to the plate of food in front of Wendy. "Now that you've met him, you can finish your supper and then one hour of TV before your bath."

"Hey, there, Mr. Parker." Wendy lifted her fork, but she didn't take her eyes off Jack.

"Howdy, there, Miss Wendy." He came forward, crouched to his haunches and shook hands with Wendy. "It's mighty nice to meet you."

"You know what—you talk like a cowboy." Wendy hunched her shoulders and covered her mouth to smother a giggle.

Jack petted her under the chin, which made her giggle more. "Well, little darling, that's because I am a cowboy. Born and raised in Texas on my daddy's ranch."

"You've got a daddy? Does he still live on his ranch?"

Peggy Jo noticed a flicker of something in Jack's eyes, a momentary sadness mixed with something else. But the emotion lingered for no more than a flash. If she hadn't been staring right at him, she would have missed the instant reaction to the mention of his father.

"Wendy, you're being much too personal," Peggy Jo said. "Mind your manners."

Jack smiled at Wendy. "It's okay, darling, you didn't say anything wrong. The answer is yes, I had a daddy, but he died when I was thirteen."

"Oh. I'm sorry."

"Enough talk, missy," Hetty said. "You finish off your pot roast, and as soon as I serve your mama and Mr. Park— Jack their supper in the dining room, I'll cut you a piece of my jam cake."

"Jam cake?" Jack rose to his feet and drew in a deep breath as if smelling the aroma of the special dessert.

"Made from scratch. My own dear mama's recipe," Hetty said.

"I think I've died and gone to heaven." Jack sighed dramatically. "Living in the house with three beautiful ladies and having jam cake on my first night here."

Wendy and Hetty both cooed, like captivated fools. Jack Parker was a charmer all right. A snake charmer! He might have the other two "beautiful ladies" eating out of his hand before nightfall, but he didn't impress her one bit. However, Peggy Jo reluctantly admitted that she'd have to be on guard. She had a sneaky feeling that Jack's Texas sweet-talk had a way of wearing down a woman's resistance, judging by the heat she felt inside her body. Heat that had nothing to do with her temper, she realized.

After dinner alone together in the candlelit dining room, Peggy Jo showed Jack upstairs. The food was the best he'd eaten in years. Hetty sure was a good cook. But the company had left a great deal to be desired. No matter how hard he tried to be captivating and witty, his efforts failed with Miss Peggy Jo. She was determined to remain unaffected by the charisma that had lured many a good ole gal straight into his arms. Of course, he didn't want this particular gal in his arms. All he wanted was to make his job a little easier by putting her at ease around him. Undoubtedly, that wasn't going to happen anytime soon. Peggy Jo Riley had constructed a ten-foot barbed-wire fence around herself, and only a fool would try trespassing. And Jack was nobody's fool.

As he followed her upstairs, he heard the sound of childish laughter and splashing water. Hetty was probably giving Wendy her bath. Peggy Jo led him down the hall and into a large, neatly decorated room that had been painted an odd shade of brown. Sort of a reddish brown. The heavy wooden furniture appeared to be antique. Either that or really good reproduction pieces. He strolled in and took a good look around. He liked it just fine.

"This room has its own bath through there." She pointed to the closed door on the right. "There's a small TV in the armoire and a phone on the nightstand. And once you bring in your suitcase, feel free to use the closet and the empty top drawer in the dresser for your things."

"Thank you, ma'am. I didn't bring much. Just some underwear, socks, pajamas bottoms, a couple of shirts and jeans. I travel light and I'm not much for dressing up. But if you'd prefer that I wear a sport coat, I can—"

"How you dress is of no concern to me." Peggy Jo stood tensely just inside the room. "Please, if you need anything, just let Hetty know."

When she turned to leave, Jack caught up with her before she crossed the threshold. "Wait up."

She glanced over her shoulder. "Yes?"

"Where's your bedroom?"

"I beg your pardon?"

"Don't go getting yourself in a tizzy." He hated that

defensive expression on her face, the tense way she stood
there, as if she were halfway afraid of him. Hell! He had
put the fear of God into quite a few men, but never a
woman. "I'm your bodyguard, remember. I'm here to protect you. If I'm to do my job the right way, I need to know
certain things about this house and about your routine at
home."

As she sighed quietly, her shoulders relaxed. "Yes, of
course. My bedroom is directly across the hall. Wendy's
bedroom is to your left, and Hetty's room is next to
Wendy's."

"Thanks."

"Will that be all?"

"I notice you have a security system. I'll need to know
the codes."

"Certainly. The password is *sunshine*. And the code is
1720."

"Okay," Jack said. "After I get settled in, I'll need to
ask you a few more questions."

"By all means."

She turned and sashayed across the hall and into her own
room. What was it about her? Jack wondered. He'd seen
women a lot better looking and most certainly with more
appealing personalities, yet he found Peggy Jo intriguing.
Was it because he saw her as a challenge? That had to be
it. He sure wasn't interested in her personally. He preferred
his women a little less cool and defensive.

And apparently Miss Peggy Jo preferred her men—perhaps all men—to be kept at arm's length.

The evening had passed fairly uneventfully, for which
she was grateful. Wendy had been a little too mesmerized
by Mr. Parker, and Hetty had been a little too solicitous.
And Jack, as both Hetty and Wendy were calling him, had
made himself a little too much at home to suit her. By the
time he helped Peggy Jo tuck Wendy into bed, he was

acting as if he were the man of the house. No doubt, Jack Parker was the type who simply took over, regardless of where he was.

As they left Wendy's room, Jack placed his open palm across the small of Peggy Jo's back. His hand was big and warm. And even such an innocent touch disturbed her greatly. She didn't like to be touched. Not by men. And most definitely not by a large, rugged guy who towered over her by nearly nine inches. She rushed ahead of him in order to free herself from that massive hand.

Pausing in the doorway of her room, she waited for him, knowing that they had yet to finish up with their question-and-answer session.

"Do you want to go back downstairs?" he asked as he approached her.

"Not really. Hetty will close up. I'm tired and I'd like to take a long, hot bath and go to bed early."

"Mmm-hmm. Why don't you take that bath while I check things out downstairs and have a look around outside? I'll lock up and arm the security system. Whatever other questions I have can wait until morning."

"Thanks." She took several steps inside her room, then paused and turned around to face him. "Despite my reservations about having a male bodyguard living here in the house, I am glad that you're here. I'll sleep better tonight knowing you're close by. But I haven't changed my mind about replacing you with a female bodyguard as soon as one is available."

"I didn't think you'd changed your mind," Jack said. "But I'll bet if you took a vote, Wendy and Hetty would vote to keep me."

"Wendy and Hetty don't have votes on this issue."

"Pity."

Jack turned and walked off, leaving her standing there staring at his back. As he descended the split staircase, he started whistling. He'd bet money that Miss Peggy Jo was still watching him. He could practically feel her heated glare boring into his back.

Just as he reached the foot of the stairs, the telephone rang. He stood still and waited for someone to answer it. The ringing stopped. He headed down the hallway toward the foyer. Suddenly he heard Peggy Jo's voice calling him.

"Mr. Parker? Mr. Parker?"

He heard a sense of urgency in her voice. Damn, what was wrong? Before he reached the stairs, she called out again.

"Mr. Parker? Jack!"

He ran to the stairs, then took them two at a time. Peggy Jo met him on the landing where the staircase divided. She all but rushed into his arms. He reached out to steady her as their bodies collided.

Grabbing her shoulders, he said, "What is it? Are you all right?"

"It was him. On the phone."

"Damn!"

"He said…he said for me to look on the back porch, that he'd left a present there for me."

Jack felt her trembling, so without giving a thought to his actions, he pulled her into his arms to comfort her. And for just a moment she stayed there in the safety of his embrace, as if she truly liked the feel of his arms around her. But suddenly, when she realized what she was doing, Peggy Jo eased away from him, putting a foot of space between them.

"I'll check the back porch," Jack told her.

"Wait. I want to go with you."

"There's no need."

"There's every need," she said. "Please don't treat me like some weak, helpless female. This is my life, my problem, and I'm not going to back down just because I'm scared."

Damn, he didn't want to like her, didn't want to admire

her spunk. But he did. She was nothing like his mother. Nothing like so many of the women who claimed to be liberated females but in reality were as weak and clinging as their mothers and grandmothers had been.

"Come on, then," he said. "Let's go see what your secret admirer left for you."

# Chapter 4

Peggy Jo absolutely hated the fact that she was glad Jack Parker stood at her side as they opened the back door and walked out onto the porch. The escalating actions of her stalker unnerved her. And the very idea that the man had been to her home, on her back porch, gave her more than enough reason to be scared. Phone calls and letters had been annoying, but recent events—like the ransacking of her dressing room at the station—made her realize her life could well be in danger. Jill had done the right thing contacting the Dundee Agency before she returned to Atlanta last night. And even though Peggy Jo would have preferred a female agent, she wasn't going to complain—ever again—about being protected by a macho hunk. A macho hunk with a gun! When he had gone out to her car for his bag, he'd removed his pistol from his hip holster, then taken a look around the house before he had allowed her to come outside. She'd thought she would never see the day when she would give any man the power to tell her what she could and couldn't do. Yet there she had stood, waiting for Jack to give her the signal, letting her know it was okay. For now, at least.

She might not like being forced to rely on someone else, but she wasn't stupid. Due to no fault of her own, some outside force was wreaking havoc on her peace of mind. She could well be in real danger. The only smart thing to do in a case like this was just what Jill had done. Call in a professional.

"There's a box right beside the steps!" Peggy Jo's heartbeat roared inside her head as she stared at the object plainly revealed by the overhead porch light.

"Just stay right here and let me take a look first." Jack motioned for her to stay put.

She didn't argue, didn't even think about voicing a complaint. Nausea churned in her stomach as visions of all the horrible things that might be inside the box flashed through her mind. A dead animal. A poisonous snake. An explosive device of some sort.

Feeling as if her stomach had just turned inside out, Peggy Jo waited for Jack to examine the shoe-box size container. He took his time, looking at it, listening to it, feeling it. He did everything but lick the damn thing. After he lifted the lid and peered inside, he groaned.

"What is it?" she asked.

"Come see for yourself." He held the box out in front of him.

Squaring her shoulders, she marched bravely forward, then cursed under her breath when she saw the contents of "the gift" her crazed admirer had left for her. She reached down and lifted the shiny jacket from her latest book, *Putting Yourself First*. A beard and mustache had been drawn in black marker on her publicity picture that graced the back of the jacket. And a monologue bubble had been drawn above her head, stating, "Kill all men!" Inside the box the broken spine of the hardback book lay open, and ripped-out pages had been torn in two or marred with black X marks.

"Well, at least it's not a snake or a bomb." Peggy Jo forced a weak smile. "The contents really don't matter half as much as the fact that he was here, at my house. In my yard. On my back porch."

"It seems obvious that this guy doesn't like you. You've pissed him off in some way, and he wants you to know about it."

"So it would seem." Peggy Jo didn't feel half as brave as she was pretending to be. "So, what now?"

"Put the book jacket back in the box," Jack said. "We'll want it all together when we turn it over to the police."

"The police?"

"I believe Detective Gifford is the policeman you've been dealing with on this case. Right?"

Peggy Jo nodded.

"I'll request that they contact him and I'll make sure they understand that I expect them to go over the grounds thoroughly to see if they can find anything that I didn't. They can take this box and its contents and have the crime lab go over everything with a fine-tooth comb."

"I think Detective Gifford and the Chattanooga Police Department aren't 100 percent sure that my stalker even exists. You know they've implied that Jill Lennard, my agent, created an imaginary stalker just to get me some extra publicity."

"If that's what they think, then it's time they alter their opinion." Jack grasped Peggy Jo's arm and hauled her back into the kitchen. Once inside, he released her and laid the box on the table. "Why don't you fix us something warm to drink, while I contact the police."

A refusal danced on the tip of her tongue. She almost told him that she wasn't going to fix him something to drink just because he was the man and she was the woman. But she thought better of the comment. She doubted he had meant anything sexist by his request. At least she could give him the benefit of the doubt. In fact, she wondered why she felt twice as tense around Jack as she did around any other man. Maybe it was precisely because his blatant masculinity was a constant reminder that she was still very much a woman.

"How about hot chocolate?" she asked, shrugging aside her uncomfortable thoughts.

He glanced back at her and grinned as he lifted the receiver off the wall phone. "That would be great. Thanks."

Peggy Jo's stomach fluttered. Reacting to Jack on a physical level surprised her. It wasn't often that she felt attracted to a man in a sexual way. But there was something about this particular man, and her instincts warned her that if she didn't keep up her guard, she'd be in deep trouble. *Oh, girl, get real. What's wrong with you? All the guy did was smile and say thanks. He didn't award you a Nobel Prize or anything.*

By the time she had the milk warming and the cocoa mix and two mugs sitting on the counter, Jack hung up the phone and turned to her.

"They're sending someone over right now," he said. "And they'll notify Detective Gifford."

When the milk came to almost a boil, she took the pot off the hot stove. As she spooned the cocoa mix into their mugs, she said, "I assume you've worked on cases like mine before, haven't you?"

"Yep."

She poured the steaming milk into the mugs, then hurriedly stirred the milk to blend in the cocoa. "What usually happens? Do y'all catch the stalker? Does the stalker—"

"In most cases the stalker is caught and sent to prison. In a few cases the stalker is killed by the police or by the victim. And sometimes...sometimes, the stalker kills his or her victim."

"Things have begun progressing quickly. He's gone

from letters and phone calls to ransacking my dressing room, sending me roses that everyone knows I detest, and now leaving me this little present.'' She eyed the box on the table. ''So, in your opinion, what comes next? Is there a way to predict what he'll do now?''

''You can't accurately predict what a deranged mind will come up with, but his actions are advancing fairly rapidly now, so my guess would be that he's building up to a more personal contact.''

Peggy Jo handed Jack a cup of hot chocolate. He accepted it, nodded and mouthed a thank-you.

''Are you talking about face-to-face contact?'' she asked.

''Not at first. Not yet. But we can expect him or her to do more things to let you know that he or she can get to you. At work. At home.'' Jack sipped the rich, warm drink. ''I think it's time the FBI got involved. The CPD might have been reluctant to contact the Bureau since they suspected your stalker was a publicity hoax, but I'm going to insist the Feds be brought in as soon as possible.''

Peggy Jo pulled out a chair and sat at the table, then set her untouched cocoa on the place mat in front of her. ''I don't understand how a stalking case could be a federal matter.''

''There's a federal statute that prohibits sending physical threats through the U.S. mail.'' Jack pulled out a chair and sat down beside her. ''Ms. Lennard faxed the Dundee Agency several of the letters your admirer sent to you. I think both of the ones I read would qualify as physical threats. Regardless of what they suspected, the police should have already called the FBI.''

''And what can the FBI do that the police and you can't do?''

''We each serve a different purpose. The local police are duty bound to investigate any criminal activities that fall under their jurisdiction. The Dundee Agency provides you constant protection—'' he thumped himself on the chest

"—in the form of yours truly. And our firm can do private investigative work that the police either can't do or won't do. Then the Feds add another element. Just knowing that the FBI is involved might deter the stalker."

"I see."

"And getting a psychological profile on our stalker could help us unearth his identity. Dundee has a psycholinguistics expert, and we can compare his finding with the Bureau's expert. The bottom line is that the more people we have working on this case, the better our odds of finding this person and keeping you safe."

"My life was so simple, so uncomplicated, until six months ago." Peggy Jo stared down into her mug. "I just don't understand why anyone would be doing this to me."

"Believe me, he has his reasons. They may be illogical and totally insane, but to him they're reason enough to come after you, to torment you. It could be as simple as your having said something on one of your shows that he took offense at, or something in your book." Jack eyed the box resting on the table. "Or it could be someone you know. A rejected suitor. A guy with a sick crush on you who has grown to hate you because you haven't responded to his advances. The list goes on and on."

"Chet Compton. Ross Brewster. Buck Forbes," she said. "Each one of them might have reason to hate me."

"And it could be a woman behind the threats, so don't rule out your TV rival, Tia Tuesday. Or a female admirer with a loose screw." Jack gestured by tapping his head. "Your assistant, Kayla. Or if you have a fan club, someone in that club."

"My fan club? Surely, not someone who— The president of my fan club lives here in Chattanooga. Donel Elmore. But she's a sweetheart of a person. She sends me Christmas gifts and birthday gifts. And I trust Kayla completely. I just can't suspect everyone I know."

"You can't afford not to suspect everyone—with the possible exceptions of Hetty and Wendy. And me."

That damn don't-you-just-find-me-irresistible grin of Jack's all but curled Peggy Jo's toes. This is getting ridiculous, she told herself. She didn't even like this man and yet when he smiled at her, her knees turned to Jell-O. The last thing she needed right now, at this time in her life, was some man that made her feel like a woman. A silly, fluttering female in heat!

She cleared her throat. "Does that include everyone at the station? Are you really asking me to suspect people I trust implicitly? People like Kayla and Leda and Burt?"

"I'm not asking you to suspect them. Not exactly. All I want you to do is be careful not to trust anyone too easily. If anyone you know has done or said anything that is suspect, then I want you to tell me. I've begun compiling a suspects list and once we get the profile done on your stalker, we can see if that profile fits anyone on our list."

"Mmm-hmm." Finally Peggy Jo lifted the mug to her lips and drank the lukewarm cocoa. It didn't matter that it wasn't hot. It was sweet and it was chocolate. What else did a woman need during a stressful time like this?

The doorbell rang. Peggy Jo gasped and trembled. Jack reached over and placed his hand on her shoulder. She stared at him for a brief moment and suddenly wanted to throw herself into his arms and cry. Whether she wanted to admit it or not, the strain was getting to her. Her nerves were shot.

"You stay here, and I'll go to the door," Jack told her. "It's probably the police. I told them I'd be timing how long it took them to get here."

"You didn't." Peggy Jo smiled.

"Oh, yes, ma'am, I did."

An hour later, after the police questioned Peggy Jo and Jack as well as Hetty, who'd gotten up and come downstairs shortly after the doorbell rang, quiet descended on the Riverview house. Jack waited until Hetty and Peggy Jo had gone upstairs before he did a final check and armed the security system. As he turned off the last light downstairs, he hesitated a moment. He heard the soft, distant tinkling of music. Something sweet. An old-fashioned tune playing so quietly that at first he'd thought he was imagining the sound. What was it? Where was it coming from? As he climbed the stairs and walked down the hall toward his room, the music grew slightly louder, yet was still hushed and delicate. It sounded like a music box.

He glanced into Wendy's room. She was sound asleep. The music wasn't coming from there. Hetty, wrapped up in her flannel housecoat, stood in the doorway to her room. Her gaze locked with Jack's. She nodded in the direction of Peggy Jo's room. He understood that her gesture was to let him know exactly where the music was coming from. When he knocked on Peggy Jo's door, he glanced back at Hetty. She smiled at him, then turned around and went into her room.

Peggy Jo opened the door just a crack and peered at Jack. "Yes, what is it?"

He grasped the side of the door and forced it open a few more inches. When he got a good look at her face, he saw that Peggy Jo had been crying. He glanced beyond her, inside her room. There in the center of her bed lay a large musical snow globe.

"I heard the music," he said.

"Oh. It's just that." She pointed to the glass globe. "I didn't realize anyone else could hear it, not with my door closed."

"Are you all right?" he asked. Of course, she wasn't all right, he realized. She'd been crying. And in his experience he found that when a strong, in-control woman like Peggy Jo cried, it meant something.

"I'm fine," she replied. "Perfectly fine."

"You wouldn't lie to me, would you?" He could tell she wasn't fine, but she also wasn't going to admit any momentary weakness to him.

"Mr. Parker, I didn't hire you to be my psychiatrist or my counselor. Your job is to protect me, not comfort me."

Acting purely on instinct, Jack shoved the door fully open and then brushed the back of his hand across Peggy Jo's flushed cheek. "My job is to take care of you. And that includes giving you a shoulder to cry on, if you need it."

"I don't need—"

He placed his index finger over her lips, adeptly silencing her rejection. "If you're feeling a little shaky right now, a little out of control, that's to be expected. And if you don't want Hetty or Wendy or any of your friends to see you being just the least bit weak, then turn to me, Miss Peggy Jo. I'm your man."

When she stared at him and for a couple of seconds, he thought she was going to succumb, that she was going to let down her defenses just enough to seek his comfort. But suddenly the barriers came back up, the defensive mechanisms snapped back into place. "You're mistaken, Mr. Parker. You're my bodyguard. Nothing more." She glared at him. "Now, if you'll excuse me, I'd like to go to bed."

"All right." He backed off, but when she started to close the door, he said, "Leave the door open, please."

"I'd prefer it closed."

"I insist that it stays open."

"But—"

"Your choice…either the door stays open or I sleep in your room."

She left the door open.

She wouldn't cry anymore. Not tonight. Not unless she hid in the bathroom so no one could possibly hear her. As she lay in bed, the musical snow globe resting on her stomach, Peggy Jo wondered why she'd obeyed Jack Parker's orders. When he'd given her a choice of either keeping the door open or him sleeping in her room, why hadn't she reminded him that she was his boss, not the other way around? Answer that! she demanded of herself. *Because you knew the man wasn't bluffing. And you knew he was right.*

She lifted the snow globe, turned it over and wound the musical mechanism. The theme from the old movie, *Love Story,* played softly, sweetly, reminding her of her mother. It had been her mother's favorite song. When Peggy Jo had left home at seventeen, fleeing from her angry, jealous step-mother and her weak-willed father, she had taken only a suitcase of clothes and this one precious item—Marjorie Riley McNair's treasured snow globe. Over the years this one possession of her mother's had become a symbol of security and love, just as taking her mother's maiden name had been a tribute to her mother's memory. If only her mother hadn't died when Peggy Jo was seven. If only her father hadn't married Agnes when Peggy Jo was fourteen. If only her father hadn't allowed his new wife to make life a living hell for the teenage Peggy Jo. If only Vernon McNair had given his own daughter half the love and attention he'd given his new wife and stepson. But years ago Peggy Jo had realized the uselessness of wasting too much time thinking if only. She seldom allowed herself to look back, to think about what might have been. Only on rare occasions when she wallowed in self-pity. She had so many regrets that she could spend a week just naming all of them. Of course, the biggest mistake she'd ever made was mar-rying Buck Forbes.

*Don't think about Buck! You have enough to worry about without reliving the three and a half miserable years you were married to that bastard!*

She set the globe on the nightstand to her right, turned off the lamp and pulled the covers up to her neck. As she tossed and turned, adjusting and readjusting to find the most comfortable position for sleep, she started thinking about Jack Parker. And no matter how hard she tried to dismiss the man from her mind, she couldn't. She shut her eyes tight and started silently chanting the words to the theme song of her TV show. Suddenly an image of Jack flashed through her mind. His wide, sexy smile. His broad shoulders. His big hands. His big feet. His big gun!

How had her life come to this? After struggling to become the successful, confident woman she was today, how had she lost control of everything, even her day-to-day living? Her bodyguard had not only invaded her workplace and her home, but her thoughts. He had walked in tonight and within minutes charmed Hetty and Wendy. And if she wasn't careful, he'd charm the pants off her, too.

Oh, dear! Poor choice of words. Charm the pants off her, indeed. Why had that phrase come to mind so readily? she wondered. The sexual implication was undeniable. Okay, so Jack Parker was sexy, and she wasn't totally immune to his sex appeal or his good-ole-boy charm. No big deal. She was human, wasn't she? She had urges just like other women did. But having urges and acting on them were two different things entirely.

Yawning, she checked the time on the lit digital clock on the bedside table. Since she only had to review the edited Christmas shows at work tomorrow, she only had to work half a day. Then she'd be off for a long, four-day Thanksgiving weekend. She wondered if Jack had family who would miss him Thanksgiving day. She and Hetty had planned a quiet meal at home for themselves and Wendy, after which they would get out the Christmas decorations and start preparing for Wendy's favorite season. Maybe Jack could help them bring the tree and other stuff down from the attic. This year, instead of Hetty saying it would be nice to have a big, strong man to lift and carry things, she'd be pointing out to Peggy Jo how handy it was to have a man around the house. And not just any man—Jack Parker. A real Texas cowboy, who made Peggy Jo feel things she didn't want to feel. Made her think about things she didn't want to think about—not now or ever again. As Peggy Jo drifted off to sleep, Jack Parker was still on her mind.

*She could hear him saying her name, calling her darling as he had called Wendy darling earlier in the evening. He was smiling at her, touching her, pulling her into his strong arms. And she loved being there, safe, secure and comforted.*

*He eased her gown off her shoulder, then leaned down and planted a kiss on her warm skin. She shivered as his mouth moved up her neck and to her ear.*

*"Let me take care of you, darling. Let me give you what you need."*

*"Oh, Jack." She lifted her face to his and all but begged him to kiss her.*

*His mouth hovered over hers, tempting her. She sighed as his big hands caressed her, and the moment her lips parted, he took her mouth with his. Her femininity tightened as spirals of desire spread through her body.*

*"Oh, Jack...I want you. Please...please..."*

*"Please what, darling? Say it. Tell me what you want."*

*"I want you to make love to me."*

*He ripped the gown from her body and mounted her. Suddenly he was no longer gentle, no longer considerate. She stared up into his face, into his menacing gray eyes. Oh, heaven help her. This wasn't Jack. The man on top of her, frightening her with his cruelty, was Buck Forbes!*

Jack came out of the bathroom, his hair still damp from his shower, and removed the pajama bottoms from his suitcase. He always kept pajamas for when he was on a case, though he preferred to sleep in the nude. Most clients frowned on having a naked bodyguard running around the place at night.

As he pulled on the navy-blue bottoms, he thought he heard a noise. Moans. Groans. As if someone were in terrible pain. He walked out into the hall and realized the sounds were coming from Peggy Jo's room. From her bed. From her lips.

He rushed into her bedroom. She had thrown off the covers and her gown was twisted around her hips, revealing her legs. She tossed her head back and forth on the pillow, her body flinching again and again, as if she were trapped and unable to move. She appeared to be having a nightmare.

"Don't...don't...don't..." she moaned repeatedly.

Tears seeped out from under her closed eyelids, cascaded off both sides of her face and onto her pillow.

Jack sat down on the edge of the bed, clasped her shoulders and shook her gently. "Peggy Jo, wake up."

She roused slowly, opening her eyes only a fraction. "Please, don't hurt me. Don't..."

He lifted her up and into his arms, stroking her back tenderly. "Shh...hush...it's all right. I'm here. Jack's here. You're safe with me."

"Jack?" She mumbled his name as she eased her arms around his waist and clung to him.

"Nobody's going to hurt you while I'm around. You were just having a nightmare."

She lifted her head from his shoulder and opened her eyes wide. "Jack? It's you, isn't it? It's really you?"

"Of course it's really me," he replied. "Who did you think it was?"

She stared at him as if she were uncertain how to answer his question, as if she were almost afraid to answer him. And then it hit him. She'd probably been dreaming about her ex-husband. Either him or the unknown stalker.

"Who were you dreaming about?" he asked.

She tensed in his arms and tried to withdraw. He wanted to continue holding her but realized the last thing this woman needed right now was for some man—any man—to confine her. So he let her go. But she didn't go far. She simply slipped out of his embrace but stayed close, her hands held in front of her in a protective gesture.

"My ex-husband," she finally said.

"Do you have nightmares about him very often?"

"No. I haven't dreamed about Buck in years."

"It's probably just all this stalker business. You're confusing the danger and fear you once felt about your ex-husband with your feelings about your stalker."

She breathed deeply. Jack tried not to glance at her breasts, but he couldn't seem to keep his gaze on her face. Her peaked nipples strained against the cotton flannel material of her gown. Oh, how he'd love to touch her.

No touching! he reminded himself. She's a client. And she's not paying you to seduce her.

"I'm sorry if I woke you," she said. "I didn't scream, did I? I didn't wake Hetty or Wendy?"

"You weren't screaming. Just sort of groaning. You sounded like you were in pain."

"I learned not to scream when Buck hurt me. If I screamed, he'd just hit me harder, just hurt me more." She turned from Jack, as if she suddenly couldn't bear to look at him because he was a man. "I'm all right now," she said. "You can go back to bed."

His hand hovered over her shoulder, but he didn't touch her. But he wanted to—damn, how he wanted to! He'd never wanted to hold and comfort a woman more than he did Peggy Jo right this minute. But if he tried to take her into his arms again, she would probably protest. And if he made too big a deal of what had happened tonight, come morning she would resent the fact that he'd seen her at a weak moment. Even though he'd just met her today, he already knew one thing about Peggy Jo Riley—she prided herself on being strong and in control. So it had to be killing her that, even though she was self-reliant and independent, she now had to depend on not only the police to help her, but a personal bodyguard to protect her.

Jack rose from the bed. "I'll see you in the morning."

She nodded and tried her best to smile. The effort failed miserably. She slid down in the bed and rested her head on the pillow. Without thinking, Jack reached down and pulled the covers up to her shoulders.

"Thanks." Her voice was a mere whisper.

Before he left the room he picked up the snow globe and wound the music box, then set it back on the nightstand. When he reached the door, he paused and looked back at her.

"If you want me—" he grinned "—just holler. I'm here for you, Peggy Jo."

# Chapter 5

When Peggy Jo made her way downstairs, still groggy from lack of sleep, she heard the sound of Wendy's laughter. It was the sweetest sound on earth. No matter what was wrong in her life, just hearing her daughter's happy giggles banished the blues, at least for a little while. The smell of fresh coffee and Hetty's banana-nut muffins induced her to hurry into the kitchen. There sat Jack Parker in faded jeans, navy-blue sweater and black boots. Simply having him around changed the mood of the entire household. For one thing he took up space. He was a fairly big man. And he made noise. Male noise. Heavy footsteps. Rumbling laughter. A baritone voice. And there was that aura of rugged strength and testosterone-powered energy that surrounded him and seemed to touch everything within a fifty-foot radius. By the way Wendy and Hetty were acting, it was plain to see that Jack had won them over completely. And in less than twenty-four hours!

"Morning, Miss Peggy Jo." Jack rose from his chair,

displaying gentlemanly good manners. "I hope you slept well."

"Do I look as if I slept well?" *Oh, that's it, Peggy Jo, bite the man's head off without any provocation at all.* She sighed. She knew he was trying to be polite and was just making conversation. "Sorry. No, I didn't sleep well, but I'm okay."

"I'll pour you some coffee," Hetty said. "Sit down."

She nodded, then leaned over to kiss Wendy on the forehead. "Good morning, sweetpea. Ready for the last day of school before your big four-day weekend?"

"Sure am." Wendy chomped another bite of muffin, chewed a couple of times and then spoke with her mouth full. "Are we going to—"

"Finish eating first," Peggy Jo said. "Then talk."

After swallowing, Wendy washed her food down with a big swig of milk. "Are we going to decorate the house this weekend? Hetty said that it's sure going to be nice having Jack around to bring the boxes down from the attic and to reach things on the top of the tree and—"

Peggy Jo gave Hetty a scolding glare. "Wendy, I'm sure Mr. Parker—" and she strongly stressed the formal use of his name "—will be of help, but it may not be much fun for him. He'd probably rather be with his family tomorrow for Thanksgiving than work." She pulled out a chair and sat.

"Well, ma'am, as a matter of fact, I'm looking forward to sharing Thanksgiving with three gorgeous gals." Jack winked at Wendy. "Besides, I haven't got much family to speak of, just a few cousins back in Texas."

"It would seem Jack is like us, pretty much alone in this world," Hetty said, then placed a cup of hot coffee in front of Peggy Jo. All smiles, she turned to Jack. "Like you, all I've got in the way of kinfolk are some cousins spread out hither and yon. And Peggy Jo's the same, if you don't count her stepmother and stepbrother. And we don't."

"No, we don't." Peggy Jo certainly didn't consider her father's widow and stepson to be family. They still lived in her father's house and enjoyed a comfortable lifestyle, thanks to her father's hefty life insurance policy. She didn't hate Agnes or Derek anymore, but she was glad they were no longer a part of her life. Of course, there were times when she wished her father was still alive, times when she longed for the chance to make things right with him.

She lifted the cup to her lips and sipped the aromatic brew. Hetty always ground the coffee beans fresh and served only gourmet blends.

"Mommy says that she and Hetty and I are a family," Wendy told Jack proudly. "Hetty's the grandmother and Mommy is the mother and I'm the little girl. Since you don't have anybody else either, would you like to be the daddy in our family?"

Peggy Jo choked on her coffee, the liquid nearly spewing from her mouth. Jack picked up his napkin, reached over to pat Peggy Jo's back and then wiped her mouth.

"Are you all right?" he asked.

"Wendy Sue Riley!" Peggy Jo shouted, once she gained her composure. She could not believe that her child had asked this man, who was little more than a stranger, if he wanted to be her father.

"What did I say wrong?" Tears welled up in Wendy's big blue eyes.

Jack scooted his chair closer to Wendy's, then clasped her little chin between his thumb and forefinger. "Darling, you didn't say anything wrong. It's just that becoming someone's daddy isn't as simple as your asking me and me saying yes. It's a rather complicated matter."

"What's a comp-clated matter?" Wendy sniffed.

Peggy Jo opened her mouth to speak, but before she got a word out, Jack continued, "It's something that isn't easy. You see, before somebody could become your daddy, your mommy would have to marry him."

"Oh. Okay." Wendy looked directly at her mother. "Could we marry Jack?"

"No, we most certainly could not!" Peggy Jo wished the earth would open up and swallow her. And the sooner the better. When she saw the disappointed look on her daughter's face, she felt just awful. Then when Hetty cleared her throat, Peggy Jo glanced at her and saw that I-told-you-so look on her face. She reached over and grasped one of Wendy's small hands. "Don't you remember my telling you that Mr. Parker is an employee. Mommy hired him to work for her. He's not my boyfriend. And he isn't going to be your daddy."

Wendy looked puzzled. "But you hired Hetty to work for you and she's my grandmother. You said so. I don't see why—"

"If you're through with breakfast, young lady, come with me to get your coat and book bag," Hetty said, then glanced at Peggy Jo. "I'll drive her to school this morning since you don't have to be at the studio until ten."

Hetty ushered Wendy out of the kitchen, leaving Peggy Jo to face a grinning-like-a-possum Jack Parker. "I can assure you that it's not a laughing matter. You may think it's amusing to have my daughter ask you to be her father, but I can assure you that I do not find it the least bit amusing."

"Darling, lighten up. Nobody but Wendy took what she said seriously."

"Don't call me darling. I find the use of that word much too familiar."

"Excuse me, Miss Peggy Jo, ma'am. I didn't mean any offense. It's simply a term I use for ladies I like."

Stretching, Jack leaned back in the chair, crossed his arms behind his head and cupped the back of his head with his hands. Peggy Jo tried not to look at his broad chest, at his wide shoulders and big arms, but despite her resolve not to look at him, her gaze settled on his body, scanning him from head to toe.

Jack chuckled. Peggy Jo dodged his head-on gaze.

"Recently Wendy has been talking quite a lot about why she's the only child in her class at the Chattanooga Christian School who doesn't have a father." Peggy Jo removed a muffin from the tray, laid it on her plate, picked up a knife and sliced the muffin in four pieces.

"I'd say it's perfectly natural. She wants what all the other kids have." Jack eyed Peggy Jo in a manner similar to the way she'd raked her gaze over him. "I'd think it would be a simple matter for you to solve. Find yourself a man and get married."

"Been there. Done that. Got the scars to prove it," Peggy Jo said flippantly. She found that distancing herself emotionally from her nightmare marriage helped her tremendously. She preached to other women, through her books, her TV show and her personal appearances, that they could not only escape from their abusers but that they could go on to live normal, happy lives.

"You're a smart woman. You've got to know that all men aren't like Buck Forbes."

"Of course I know that. It's just that I'm not willing to risk screwing up again. I'm perfectly happy with my life exactly the way it is."

"Without a man?"

"Yes, without a man." Peggy Jo popped a quarter of a muffin into her mouth.

"Pity," Jack said. "And such a waste. A woman like you should have a man in her life."

Swallowing hard, she directed her gaze at him. "What about you? You aren't married. Don't you want a wife and kids? Don't you need a woman in your life?"

Jack slapped his knee and guffawed loudly. "Touché, Miss Peggy Jo. Touché. Nope, I don't want a wife, but that doesn't mean I don't enjoy having a woman in my life."

She felt as if a heavy weight had dropped on her chest. Of course a guy like Jack Parker would have a woman. Probably more than one. "Then there's someone special in your life?" *What do you care?* she asked herself. *Damn it, this man's personal life is none of your concern.*

"Not at the moment. But there have been several special ladies, and I'm sure there will be a few more in my future."

"Mmm-hmm." Just as she had figured. Jack was a ladies' man. "You know why I'm opposed to marriage, so want to tell me why you are?"

"No reason," he said. "I just don't think marriage is for me. I like being footloose and fancy-free."

Peggy Jo suspected there was a more complicated reason, one he simply didn't want to discuss. Maybe there was something in his past that was too painful for him to talk about to anyone. Men had a way of denying their true feelings, of hiding behind some outdated macho bravado. Nobody could hurt a tough guy, and she suspected that Jack thought of himself that way.

"Do me a favor, will you?" She popped another muffin quarter into her mouth, then lifted her cup to her lips.

"Anything I can do for you, I will. That's my job."

She nodded, swallowed and licked a crumb from the corner of her mouth. When she did, she involuntarily looked at Jack and caught him staring at her mouth. An odd sensation of sexual arousal shot through her. There was something very carnal about the way he was looking at her mouth, as if he wanted to taste her lips.

This has to stop! she warned herself. She was letting her ridiculous attraction to Jack get way out of hand. Okay, so he was good looking and funny and charming and nice and Wendy adored him. She'd just met the guy yesterday. He could be a total fraud for all she knew. And even if he wasn't, she would be a fool to fall for the big lug.

"Be nice to Wendy, but please, don't encourage her affections," Peggy Jo said. "Don't do anything special to make her care about you. If she becomes too attached to you while you're working for me, it'll break her heart when you leave.''

Jack nodded. A strange look crossed his face. ''Sure. I understand. The last thing I'd ever want to do is break anybody's heart. I'm a love-'em-and-leave-'em sort of guy, but I always try to leave them smiling.''

Heat suffused her body. She couldn't control her reaction to his comment. She would just bet he left them smiling. An unbidden thought came to mind—what would it be like to be Jack Parker's woman, even for just a little while?

Jack pulled the car into Peggy Jo's reserved space at the WLOK studio's parking lot. A crowd of at least two dozen women waited at the front door, all chanting, ''We love Peggy Jo.'' A guy with a video camera stood off to the side taping the cheering throng.

''Wonder what that's all about?'' Jack asked. ''Or is this something you're used to on a daily basis?''

She shook her head. ''I can't imagine what's going on. We don't usually have a crowd unless I'm taping a show. I have no idea what this is about, but that's Watson Stutts with the video cam. He's one of WLOK's News Scene cameramen. He only tapes things for airing on the news segments.''

''Is there a back way we can get into the studio?'' Jack asked.

''Yes, but it's in the opposite direction. If we get out of the car here, they're bound to see us, so we might as well go in the front door. I don't mind talking to my fans.''

The minute she grasped the door handle, Jack grabbed her arm. ''Stay put.'' When she glanced at him in puzzlement, he continued, ''Your stalker just might be in that crowd of devoted fans.''

''But they're all women, except that one—'' Peggy Jo studied the lone male in the group. ''Oh, that's Harry

Vaughan. He's a reporter for the *Chattanooga Times Free Press.*"

"It'll make my job a lot easier, if you don't greet your fans today." Jack tugged on her arm. "Can I drive around to the back entrance?"

"Not from here." She released the door handle. "We'll have to go out of the parking lot and back onto the street." Just as Jack put the car in reverse, Peggy Jo said, "Too late. They've seen us and are heading this way. I'll have to get out and talk to them. I'm sorry."

Jack cursed softly. It was damn near impossible for one agent to protect a client in a crowd. But he'd do it, by God, even if it meant picking up Miss Peggy Jo and carrying her to safety.

"Let me get out first. I'll open the door for you, then you stay right at my side and don't even think about pulling away from me. I'll have one hand on you and the other free for my weapon."

"I hardly think—"

"In this case let me do the thinking." He held up his hand in a stop gesture. "And before you blast me for being a male chauvinist pig, all I meant was that in this situation I have more experience, thus making me the expert. Okay?"

She exhaled a long, agitated huff. "Okay."

He got out of the car and made his way around the hood only moments before the swarm of cheering women reached them. He opened the door and assisted Peggy Jo, who made no protest when he slipped his left arm around her waist. With a warm smile, she turned to greet her fans. While they continued cheering, she shook hands with those closest to her, all the while letting Jack lead her toward the front door. The ladies moved with them, but no one became unruly or caused a problem. When they reached the front door, Harry Vaughan stood beside Ted Wilkes, WLOK's security chief. The crowd didn't try to move inside, probably due to Wilkes's six-four, 270-pound body blocking the entrance.

Watson Stutts followed them inside, still taping. Peggy Jo addressed him first. "What's going on?" Then she turned to the newspaper reporter. "And what are you doing here, Harry?"

"You're big news now, Peggy Jo," Watson said. "The station's going to want an interview for tonight's six-o'clock newscast."

Harry Vaughan managed to get right in her face when he said, "And I'm here to ask you questions about what it feels like to have a stalker invade your privacy and frighten you so much that you hire a bodyguard to be with you twenty-four hours a day."

"How did you know?" Peggy Jo all but gasped the question, then groaned as if she'd figured out the answer on her own.

Jack leaned over and whispered in her ear, "Want me to put an end to this right now?"

"No," she said softly. "Let me handle things."

"Your call," he replied, but kept his arm around her waist and his right hand free.

The women outside continued their chanting praise. Peggy Jo shoved open the door that led into the reception area. Jack stuck to her like glue. When she stopped abruptly, he pivoted with her, their bodies moving as one. She pointed her finger at Watson.

"Turn that camera off."

He hesitated, then did as she had requested.

"Harry, if you print anything about my being stalked, you could well be giving this person what he...or she...wants. Publicity. I've tried to keep this under wraps for that very reason. So, would you mind telling me where you got your information?"

"Can't reveal my sources." With a sly grin on his face, Harry shrugged. "But I hear some of the letters you've been sent are really threatening and downright sleazy in sexual content. Is that right?''

"No comment," she said.

Jack felt, as much as saw, the tension in Peggy Jo. Her back stiffened suddenly and her jaw tightened.

"Ah, come on," Harry said, following her as Jack led her down the hall. "Everybody in Chattanooga will be fascinated by this story. I want to follow it through to the end. Until y'all catch this guy or..."

Jack growled. Harry skidded to a halt, then swallowed hard.

"I'm taking Ms. Riley to her office." Jack didn't bother making eye contact with Harry or Watson. "And if anybody follows us, I'll see to it personally that he'll be talking funny the rest of his life."

With that pronouncement, Jack escorted Peggy Jo through the maze of hallways within the WLOK building and straight to her office. Kayla jumped up from behind her desk the moment they entered.

"You have more mail," Kayla said. "I've already opened it and sorted it. There's no message from the stalker."

Peggy Jo sighed. "Anything else I need to take care of right now?"

"No, just this—" Kayla lifted a small package off her desk and held it out to Peggy Jo. "It's from Donel Elmore."

Peggy Jo reached for the box, but Jack grabbed it. She glared at him and said, "What are you doing?"

"My job. You don't open anything yourself. Especially not any packages."

"But this is from Donel, the president of my fan club. She sends me stuff all the time. Pot holders, refrigerator magnets, hand knitted hats and scarves. You name it, she's sent it to me."

"Humor me. Let me open this package."

"You better watch him, Peggy Jo," Kayla said, amusement in her voice. "He'll be wanting to open all your Christmas presents, too."

Jack set the box on Kayla's desk, pulled a pocket knife from his pants pocket and flipped open the blade. "Ladies, would y'all stand back, please."

"Good grief, do you think it might be a bomb?" Kayla asked. "Surely not from sweet Mrs. Elmore."

After adeptly using the knife to slice through the sealing tape, Jack parted the cardboard flaps, then looked inside and gradually removed the thick bubble wrap from around a ceramic turkey-shaped serving platter.

Peggy Jo blew out a sigh, then giggled. "You almost had me believing Donel had sent me something deadly."

Jack grinned sheepishly. "Better safe than sorry."

He handed the plate to Peggy Jo, who hoisted it under her arm and headed toward her desk.

She sat down, then said, "Kayla, get me Jill Lennard on the phone immediately. I have a feeling my agent knows something about who leaked the story of my being stalked and hiring a bodyguard."

Jack crossed the room and braced his hip on the edge of Peggy Jo's desk. "You think your agent was Harry Vaughan's secret source?"

"Yes, I'm afraid so." Peggy Jo laid the turkey platter down on her desk. "Months ago, after I'd received a bunch of letters and a few phone calls, she mentioned to me what great publicity this thing would be for my career. But when Detective Gifford all but accused Jill of inventing the stalker for that very purpose, she let the matter drop."

"Got Ms. Lennard on line one," Kayla said.

Peggy Jo lifted the receiver. "Jill, did you phone anyone at the *Chattanooga Times Free Press?*"

Jack could tell by the expression on her face that Peggy Jo was mighty unhappy. He suspected that her agent had just confirmed Peggy Jo's worst fears.

"Damn it, Jill, you've just made my life more complicated. For two cents, I'd fire you right now."

Jack stuck his hand into his pants pocket, pulled out a handful of change, picked out two coins and laid the pennies on Peggy Jo's desk. She looked at the two cents, then glanced up at him and smiled.

"If you ever again do anything that is contrary to my wishes—friend or no friend—I'll be looking for a new agent. Do I make myself clear?"

Peggy Jo hung up the phone. "She's the one who contacted Harry. And she apologized profusely. She defended herself by saying that she thought getting publicity for me would not only be great for my career, but would make the stalker aware that everyone in Chattanooga was concerned about me and that might make him back off."

"Yeah, sure," Jack said. "Once we get a profile on this person, my guess is that Ms. Lennard's theory will be shot to hell and back."

"Look, I have work to do this morning, so—"

"Excuse me, Peggy Jo," a man said.

The voice came from the person who had just opened the door to the office. Jack recognized him as the security chief.

"Yes, what is it, Ted?" she asked.

"Well, there's a person—a sort of delivery person—here to see you. He's legit. Showed me his driver's license and his work ID, too. His name is Van," Ted said. "So, should I let him in?"

"What sort of delivery does he have?" Jack stood and crossed the room in two seconds flat.

Ted opened the door all the way. There in the hallway stood a guy dressed like a cowboy. His outfit was cartoonish, with plastic chaps and an enormous white Stetson made of molded plastic. He sported a couple of six-shooters on his hips. Jack stepped out into the hall, lifted both guns from their plastic holsters and saw immediately that his guess was right. Toys.

"I work for Balloons, Ballads and Baskets," Van said. "You can call the store and ask them to vouch for me. I'm just here to deliver a singing message to Ms. Riley."

"Oh, for goodness sakes, let the man sing his song and leave." Peggy Jo crossed her arms over her chest and leaned back in her swivel chair, awaiting the performance.

The singer looked to Jack for approval. Jack nodded. The guy sang a brief rendition of "You Are My Sunshine." Actually, his voice wasn't half bad. Kayla even applauded.

"There's a message, too," Van said and once again looked at Jack. "It's sort of personal."

"Go ahead," Peggy Jo said.

"All right, but don't say I didn't warn you." Van cleared his throat. "'If I'd known you wanted a cowboy in your life, I could have been your cowboy. You're my sunshine, and I don't want to share you with anybody. So, why don't you tell him to ride off into the sunset without you.'"

"Is that it?" Jack asked.

"Yes, sir, that's it."

"Escort Van outside," Jack told Ted. "And give him a nice tip, then contact his boss. See if they can ID the guy who paid for this performance."

"I'll get right on it," Ted said, then led Van down the hall.

The minute the two men exited the office, Jack glanced at Peggy Jo. She uncrossed her arms, shoved back her chair and stood.

"Kayla, go get us some coffee," Jack said.

"Yes, sir. Sure thing."

The minute Kayla left, Jack closed the door. Peggy Jo paced the floor in front of her desk.

"He knows about you," Peggy Jo said.

"Yeah, it seems he does, but that shouldn't come as a surprise to you."

"No, it doesn't. But sending a singing messenger here to make the announcement does surprise me. For six months all he did was write letters and make phone calls. Then two days ago he somehow got into the studio and ransacked my dressing room. Then last night he left a box on my back porch. And today... He's suddenly getting closer."

"He's escalating his attacks," Jack said. "He's getting braver. Taking more chances."

"Sometimes I wish he would try to attack me. At least that way I'd know who he is."

"Mmm-hmm. I can understand." Jack paused a moment, then said, "What significance does the word *sunshine* have for you?"

"Oh, you're wondering if there's a connection between my security code word being *sunshine* and the song that guy sang to me being 'You Are My Sunshine.'"

"Was it only a coincidence?"

"Maybe, but...well, sunshine was my mother's pet name for me."

"And how many people know that?" Jack asked.

"Anyone who's read one of my books."

"You need to change your code word for your security system."

The phone rang. Peggy Jo jumped.

Jack picked up the receiver. "Ms. Riley's office."

The dial tone hummed.

"It was him, wasn't it, checking on me after his latest stunt." She balled her hands into fists and shut her eyes. "Damn him!"

Jack eased over and gently placed his arm around her shoulders. She shivered. He rubbed his cheek against hers.

"While you're doing whatever you need to do here, I want to take a look at those letters this guy sent you," Jack said. "Then I'll contact Dundee and the FBI. I want a profile on this guy as soon as possible."

"I'll get the letters," Peggy Jo said. "The police returned them to me when they didn't get any fingerprints or DNA samples off them."

Jack sat down behind Kayla's desk. "Just put them on the desk here."

Peggy Jo opened the door to the storage closet and removed a large box, then set it on the desk. "Here they are. He's written over fifty letters in the past six months."

Jack whistled. "The FBI should have been called in on this sooner."

"I told you the local police thought Jill was pulling a publicity stunt."

"Do you think there's even the remotest possibility that they were right?" Jack lifted a handful of letters from the box.

"No. Jill would use the situation to get me publicity, but she'd never pull a hoax."

"Yeah, I agree. Besides, things are becoming a little too complicated for a simple publicity stunt."

Peggy Jo came around to stand at his side, her gaze resting on the letters he held. "After the first few I quit reading them. They were so...so filled with sex and violence."

Jack dropped the letters onto the desk, reached up and grasped her hand. "We'll get this guy. He's going to make a mistake, and we'll nab him. But until then I'm going to keep you safe. I want you to trust me, Miss Peggy Jo."

She squeezed his hand. "I...I trust you, Jack."

## Chapter 6

Peggy Jo put on a pair of old jeans and an oversize orange and white UT sweatshirt. At work she dressed for success. At home she dressed to please herself. Her natural style was casual and comfortable. She didn't bother with any makeup except a little blush on her cheeks and some clear gloss on her lips. She pulled her long hair back into a ponytail and slipped a pair of small gold hoops through the holes in her ears. If she were more the femme fatale type, she would take more time with her appearance this morning. After all, there was a man around the house now. An incredibly attractive man. And unless she missed her guess, that man found her equally attractive. Some men found her plumpness a turnoff. More men found her aggressive personality a threat. But there were men who actually liked their women with some meat on their bones, and most guys who were confident in their masculinity weren't threatened by a strong woman. She figured if ever a guy was confident about being a he-man, that guy was Jack Parker. He all but swaggered with self-confidence and sex appeal.

Ever since yesterday morning in her office, when Jack had asked her to trust him, and she had, somewhat to her surprise, told him that she did, Peggy Jo had been berating herself for being such a pushover. And that was something she hadn't been in a long time, something she had thought she'd never be again. She shouldn't have told him that she trusted him, even if she did. At least, she shouldn't have told him so soon. He should have had to work a little harder to gain her trust. But darn it all, there was something about Jack that made her instinctively know she could trust him, at least on a professional level. Trusting him on a personal level was a different matter altogether. Of course, Hetty and Wendy didn't seem to have any problems trusting Jack on every level. Both her housekeeper and her daughter had taken to Jack instantly, and despite her having talked to Wendy again last night about Jack being only a temporary fixture in their lives, Wendy continued being fascinated by the big, tall Texan.

Peggy Jo left the sanctuary of her bedroom and bounded downstairs. The moment she reached the open hallway, she heard giggles and male laughter coming from the den and the clatter of pots and pans in the kitchen. Making a quick decision, she opted for kitchen duty with Hetty rather than joining the gaiety in the den.

She swung open the kitchen door. "Morning. What can I do to help?"

Hetty rose from where she'd been bent over the open oven door. "I've got everything under control in here. Why don't you go watch the parade on TV with Wendy and Jack?" Hetty closed the oven door, wiped her hands off on her white apron and instantly went to the sink and began peeling the potatoes waiting there in a large steel bowl.

"I'd prefer making myself useful in here," Peggy Jo said.

"Why?" Hetty asked. "You usually let me take care of

meal preparations. You hate to cook. What's different about today? Has Jack Parker got you running scared?''

''What!'' Peggy Jo rushed toward Hetty. ''Will you please keep your voice down. He's right over there in the other room.''

The kitchen opened up into the den area, with a couple of wooden columns at each end of a wide ceramic tile bar that served as a divider for the two rooms. Years ago the kitchen had been larger, but a former owner in the Sixties had divided the room into two spaces, forming a separate den.

Hetty continued peeling potatoes with the expert ease of an experienced cook. ''Why don't you just admit that you find Jack attractive and that you feel a lot safer with him around.''

''Of course I feel safer with him around. He's a trained bodyguard. That's his job—to keep me safe.'' Peggy Jo kept her voice low.

''He's a mighty fine looking man.'' Hetty rinsed the peeled potatoes, then began slicing them and dropping the slices into a pot of water. ''And he's a nice man, too.''

''All right, I agree, he's good-looking. But we hardly know him. How can you be so sure he's nice?''

''Take a look in yonder at him with Wendy.'' Hetty nodded toward the den. ''That man's a born daddy if ever there was one. He likes kids, that's plain to see. He's good with Wendy. They've been inseparable since breakfast, watching TV, playing games, telling stories.''

''Hetty, you've got to stop this, right now.'' Peggy Jo glanced into the den to make sure the twosome on the sofa was still engrossed in the Thanksgiving day parade on TV. ''Jack Parker is my bodyguard. Nothing more. Once the stalker is arrested, Jack will leave and we'll never see him again. Beginning and end of story.''

Hetty lifted the pot from the counter and placed it on the front right eye of the stovetop, then set the heat on high.

"It's not as if I'm asking you to marry the man. But you haven't dated anybody seriously since I've known you. You haven't even shown any real interest in a man before now. So, why not go with what you're feeling and enjoy getting to know our houseguest?"

"I have no real interest in Jack," Peggy Jo said, her voice a whispered hiss. "That's what I'm trying to tell you."

Hetty shrugged as she walked to the refrigerator. Before opening the door, she looked right at Peggy Jo. "Fine. Waste a golden opportunity. That's up to you. But get out of my kitchen. If you're afraid of temptation, then go back upstairs to your room and I'll call you when lunch is ready."

"I am not..." Peggy Jo realized the fruitlessness of defending her position yet again. She couldn't win with Hetty. "Fine. I'll join the others in the den."

When Hetty opened the refrigerator, Peggy Jo grabbed a canned diet cola, popped the lid and walked toward the den. She hesitated to the right of the sofa and sipped on the carbonated beverage. Jack glanced over at her and smiled. Without giving her response any thought, she returned his smile.

Jack patted the sofa cushion beside him. "Come join us. You haven't missed much of the parade."

"Yeah, Mommy, Santa Claus hasn't put in an appearance yet," Wendy said.

Jack tapped his finger playfully on Wendy's nose. "That's what I'm waiting for—Santa Claus. I'm hoping I've been good enough this year to get a really nice present under the tree from ole Kris Kringle."

Peggy Jo held her breath, wondering how her daughter would respond and how Jack would react to Wendy's pronouncement, whatever it might be.

"Jack, you don't have to pretend for me," Wendy said. "I know there isn't a real Santa Claus." Wendy positioned herself on her knees and moved across the sofa to Jack's side, then slipped her arm around his neck. "Did you believe when you were a little boy?"

"Heck, ma'am, I still believe in jolly ole St. Nick. Whoever told you there's no Santa Claus was sadly mistaken."

Wendy's gaze collided with Peggy Jo's. "Mommy told me there is no Santa Claus, no Easter Bunny, no Tooth Fairy and—"

"Well, sugar plum…" Jack put his arm around Wendy's waist. "I suppose that's just a matter of opinion. And I'm of the opinion that little girls have the right to believe in magic and fairy dust and never-never land."

"What's fairy dust?" Wendy asked. "And what's never-never land?"

Peggy Jo cleared her throat. Jack met her gaze head-on. "Hasn't your mommy ever read to you about Peter Pan?"

"No, we don't read fairy tales and stuff like that. Mommy says that there is no Prince Charming and that fairy tales are a bunch of hooey. We girls have to take care of ourselves."

"Oh, I see." Jack's brow wrinkled when he frowned. "Maybe Mommy will let me buy you a copy of Peter Pan and read it to you. There's no Prince Charming in the book, but there is a little girl named Wendy."

"There is?" Wendy's blue eyes widened with surprised delight.

After placing her canned drink on a coaster atop a side table, Peggy Jo sat down on the sofa between Wendy and Jack. "Wendy, honey—"

Wendy jumped into Peggy Jo's lap. "Mommy, please, can Jack buy me that book and read it to me? Mrs. Clement has read us some stories with happily-ever-after endings at school and I know better than to believe that they're true."

Peggy Jo felt about an inch high. What must Jack think of her parenting skills, depriving her child of bedtime stories filled with sentimental hogwash? Her own mother had read those happily-ever-after tales to her once upon a time, and she had believed them with her whole heart. Someday my prince... Oh, yeah, sure. Buck Forbes had swept her up into his white pickup and taken her straight to hell.

Damn it, she didn't care what Jack thought or what anyone else thought for that matter. She had done what she believed right—she was protecting her child from the disillusionment and hurt that she had felt when she realized the truth. Her main goal was to be a good mother to Wendy, but how could she be a good mother if she didn't protect her child? Perhaps now, as a six-year-old Wendy might miss out on the delights of daydreams that could never come true; but as an adult, she would thank Peggy Jo. Wouldn't she?

*Don't let Jack Parker make you doubt yourself, make you doubt that you're a good mother!*

Okay, so what would it hurt if she let Jack buy Wendy a copy of Peter Pan? She would just have to remind her child that the story was make-believe and that no one, not even Peter Pan, can live in never-never land and remain a child forever.

"Mommy!"

"Oh, sorry, sweetpea." Peggy Jo lifted a stray curl off Wendy's cheek and tucked the silky, black strand behind her ear. "If Mr. Parker wants to buy a copy of Peter Pan and read it to you, he may. If you're sure you want to hear it."

"I do, Mommy. I do." Wendy threw her arms around her mother's neck and hugged with all her might. "Can we go buy the book today?"

"Not today," Peggy Jo said, "but—"

"How about we make a trip to the bookstore tomorrow?" Jack suggested. "You and your Mommy and me."

"Yippee!" Wendy cried. "Mommy, can I call Martha Jane and tell her that Jack's going to buy me a book and we're all going together tomorrow to buy it?"

"Well, yes, I suppose..."

Before Peggy Jo could finish the sentence, Wendy jumped off the couch and flew into the kitchen, where she shoved a chair up to the wall telephone. Within minutes she had dialed her friend's number and was chatting away like mad.

Jack leaned back into the soft, overstuffed sofa, spreading his big body into a comfortable position. He studied Peggy Jo, looking her up one side and down the other.

"Do you think you've been fair to Wendy, denying her the magical world of imagination?" Jack asked.

"I don't consider it denying her something," Peggy Jo replied. "I see it as protecting her from future hurt and disappointment. My mother fed me all that garbage about Prince Charming and magical worlds where everyone lives happily ever after. And when I learned it was all a lie, it hurt me more because I had once believed in it."

"Once again, we have a difference of opinion. My father taught me to believe in all the same bunk. I was told there was a Santa Claus and a Tooth Fairy." Jack avoided her direct gaze. "When I learned some of life's hard lessons, I found it rather comforting to remember a time when I'd believed in magic, when life had been fun and easy and anything was possible."

"Good for you," Peggy Jo said, then realized how sharply she'd spoken. "I'm sorry. I didn't mean to snap at you."

"Have you really lost all your faith in those magical, mystical things you believed in as a child?"

How could she answer him without exposing more of the hurt and anger that never quite went away, that stayed buried deep inside her? She was saved from responding by Wendy, who came racing back into the den and plopped down between Peggy Jo and Jack.

"Martha Jane asked me if Jack's your boyfriend," Wendy said. "And I told her he was our friend. Yours and mine. Was that okay?"

Peggy Jo laughed. "Yes, that was okay."

Wendy reached out both arms in opposite directions and latched on to Jack's neck and then Peggy Jo's neck. Her little hands encouraged them to draw closer, bringing them together, with only her small body between them.

"Oh, boy, this is the best Thanksgiving ever," Wendy said.

Peggy Jo glanced at Jack who was staring at her. Their gazes locked and held, a silent, sensual message passing between them. For the life of her, Peggy Jo couldn't break eye contact, and when Wendy slipped down and off the sofa, leaving only a narrow space between the two adults, Peggy Jo couldn't move. Couldn't breathe.

"Friends kiss friends sometimes, don't they?" Wendy rubbed her hands together, her wide-eyed expression hopeful.

Peggy Jo sucked in a deep breath. Jack's lips spread into a wide grin, then he leaned over and kissed her on the cheek. Her face flushed with embarrassment. And her body warmed with sensual heat.

Wendy clapped her hands as she jumped up and down.

"That had to be the best meal I've ever eaten," Jack said, rubbing his full stomach as he lounged on the den sofa. He hadn't shared Thanksgiving with a family in several years. Not since he'd spent his mother's last Thanksgiving with her and her fifth husband in their Dallas penthouse. Before her death four years ago, Libbie Reid had buried two husbands and divorced three. She had gone through mates as if they were disposable tissues.

He'd asked Peggy Jo's permission before putting his feet on the coffee table and had been surprised when she had plopped down beside him and put up her feet alongside his.

"Thanks for the help in the kitchen," Hetty said. "Y'all enjoy your football game. I'm headed upstairs to my room. Got a good book waiting for me."

"I'm going to stay down here with Mommy and Jack," Wendy said as she crawled up into Jack's lap. "Jack's going to teach me about football."

"Oh, he is, is he?" Hetty chuckled as she walked out of the kitchen.

"Sure you don't mind me monopolizing the TV this afternoon?" Jack asked.

"If we get tired of football, Wendy and I both have sets in our rooms," Peggy Jo replied. "But for now, I think we'll just stay put. I want to watch you teach Wendy about the game."

Jack sensed that Peggy Jo wanted to see how long his patience lasted with a six-year-old. Every time he turned around, it seemed that she was testing him, scrutinizing how he would react in any given situation. She had reluctantly admitted that she trusted him, but he figured that trust went only so far. She trusted him to do his job, to protect her, but in every other way she saw him as just another man. And she believed that men in general were not trustworthy. He figured that a woman had to have been mighty disillusioned to bear such strong resentment toward the entire male sex. He wondered if she made every man in her life jump through hoops to prove himself worthy.

Jack snuggled Wendy comfortably on his lap. "Now, let's see where to begin. Hmm. Okay, there are two teams. The members of one team are all wearing red jerseys and the members of the other team are all wearing blue jerseys."

"What's jerseys?"

"Shirts," Jack and Peggy Jo answered simultaneously.

Wendy studied the burly players, then glanced over at Peggy Jo. "They're all men. Don't girls play football?"

Peggy Jo lifted her eyebrows, tilted her head and stared straight at Jack, as if daring him to answer the question without coming off sounding like a total chauvinist.

"Girls don't play high school, college or professional

football," Jack said. "Take a look at those guys. They're mighty big. Not too many girls grow up to be that large, so if they played football with those big ole bruisers, they'd be at a disadvantage."

"What's dis-vantage mean?" Wendy frowned.

"Well, it just means it wouldn't be fair to girls if they played a sport with boys that are twice their size." Jack spoke to Wendy, but kept his gaze fixed to Peggy Jo's face. She was just waiting for him to slip up, to say something politically incorrect, so she could jump on him with both feet. Well, he had no intention of proving her right about men. He planned to be the most charming, easygoing good ole boy she'd ever known. Why, by bedtime tonight, Miss Peggy Jo just might find herself liking her bodyguard.

"Oh, I see." Wendy yawned. "Okay, so tell me some more about football."

Jack winked at Peggy Jo, then began again, doing his best to explain in simple, six-year-old-girl language the basics of the game. By the time the game got into full swing, Wendy's eyes blinked open and shut and instead of commenting on what he was telling her, she just made little affirmative noises. And by halftime, Wendy was sound asleep.

"Want me to take her upstairs and put her in bed?" Jack asked.

"Yes, thanks," Peggy Jo replied. "She doesn't usually take a nap in the afternoons, but she's had a big day today."

Jack rose to his feet, the sleeping child in his arms, and headed for the hallway. As he made his way upstairs, the warm, cuddly weight of Wendy's little body held close to his heart, Jack's mind filled with some rather unfamiliar thoughts. Thoughts about a home and children. And a wife.

He laid Wendy in the center of her canopy bed, then covered her with a hand-crocheted afghan of pink roses. A lock of unruly dark curls fell across her cheek. Jack eased the curls back into place, then leaned over and planted a kiss on her forehead.

Hell, who'd have thought that spending two days with a precocious six-year-old would have him yearning for hearth and home, for pipe and slippers. Maybe his age had something to do with these unbidden thoughts. After all, he was thirty-eight, an age when most men were married and raising a family.

But he'd never wanted marriage and was too old-fashioned to bring children into this world outside the bonds of holy matrimony. He figured kids had it hard enough as it was, why burden them with the extra problem of having unwed parents? He had sworn when he'd been thirteen and his father had killed himself—put a gun in his mouth and pulled the trigger—that he would never let a woman have enough power over him to send him into a suicidal tailspin if she left him.

Libbie had been a beautiful woman with the ability to reduce men to blithering idiots. His father had been the first of many who had succumbed to the lady's irresistible charm. There had been a time when even Jack had been under her spell. He'd thought she was the most fabulous lady on earth and had loved it when people compared him to her. His father had said many times, "Jack looks like his old man, but he's got his mother's charm."

But everything changed the day his father died. The day Jack discovered the suicide note lying beside Jeb Parker's body. He had memorized his father's final words:

Libbie, my dearest love, I know I must set you free to be with another. But I cannot bear the thought of living without you. Be happy, and if you ever think of me, think of me kindly. And try to help Jack remember me as a good man and a good father.

He hadn't cried for his father ever again, not since that day. He had loved the guy! Why hadn't his father lived for him? Even if Libbie had left them, they could have made it all right without her. Why'd he have to go and kill himself?

Jack took his time going back downstairs. Peggy Jo was probably wondering what was taking him so long. He had no intention of telling her his thoughts—not his laments about his parents nor his foolish thoughts about a family of his own.

When he returned to the den, he found it empty. The halftime show was still on TV. Where was Peggy Jo? If she had gone upstairs, he would have met her on his way down. Surely she hadn't gone outside for some reason. He moved into the kitchen, scanning the area thoroughly. The back door stood wide open. Damn! What had she been thinking? Didn't she know that if her stalker could leave a box on her back porch, he could just as easily be there himself, waiting for her. Jack's Glock 9 mm—that had a safety lock on it—was upstairs. Peggy Jo had asked him not the wear the gun in the house around Wendy, and he had reluctantly agreed.

He eased carefully toward the door and looked out on the porch. There she was, kneeling over something on the ground. He surveyed the backyard and saw nothing unusual. Trees, shrubs, winter-dead grass, Wendy's small playhouse, which was attached to her wooden gym set. As he stepped out on the porch, Peggy Jo rose to her feet and turned sideways. She held a scruffy orange-and-white kitten in her hands and spoke to it in a low, soothing voice.

"Hello, there little fellow. Are you lost or did someone just toss you out with the trash. Huh?" Peggy Jo brought the dirty ball of fur close to her face, but wisely kept enough distance so that if the kitten lashed out, it couldn't strike her.

He watched as she continued talking to the stray animal. Cooing to it. Stroking it lovingly. Suddenly she snapped her head around, apparently sensing his presence. An odd expression crossed her face, as if she'd been caught doing something she shouldn't.

"Hi," she said. "I heard a crying sound coming from the backyard and when I looked outside I saw this little fellow. He's just a baby, probably only a few weeks old."

Jack came down the steps and out into the yard. "You don't suppose he belongs to a neighbor and just wandered away."

She shook her head. "No, I don't think so. I think maybe somebody dumped him. Look how skinny and dirty he is."

Jack reached out carefully to pet the kitty's head, but the tiny animal didn't react. Poor little ratty-looking thing was practically lifeless. "Well, why don't you bring him inside and let's see if he'll drink some milk. I have a feeling he's half-starved."

"I can't bring him inside."

"Why not?"

"If Wendy sees him, she'll want to keep him."

"So?" Jack shrugged.

"You don't understand. I've never allowed her to have a pet."

"Why not?"

Peggy Jo avoided looking directly at Jack, instead, she studied the kitten. "If I got her a pet and something happened to it, she'd be devastated. I just couldn't risk—"

Jack groaned. "Okay, why don't you tell me about it?"

"About what?"

"About the cat you loved and lost."

"It wasn't a cat. It was a dog. My mother's dog," she said. "Buster was the most adorable little Boston terrier you've ever seen. He'd been given to my mother as a sixteenth birthday present, so she loved him like a baby. When Mama died, I was seven. Buster was fourteen. After we lost her, he grieved himself to death."

"That must have been rough for you." Jack felt an overpowering urge to pull Peggy Jo—and kitten—into his arms. She had no idea how adorable she looked standing there holding that damn scraggily, half-dead cat.

"The worst part was that my father refused to allow me to have another pet." She paused, as if considering carefully her next words. "When he remarried, he and his new wife bought her son a little bulldog their first Christmas together."

"Son of a bitch," Jack cursed under his breath. "Come on—" Jack put his arm around Peggy Jo's shoulder. "Let's take Fur Ball into the kitchen and find him some cream to lap up."

He was halfway surprised when she didn't jerk away from him. So, with the first hurdle successfully jumped, he moved on to the next and urged her into motion, leading her up the steps and onto the back porch.

"Something tells me that I'm going to live to regret this," Peggy Jo said as Jack opened the back door and they took the kitten inside to the warm kitchen.

Once inside, Jack closed the door behind them. "Darling, don't you know it's not the things we do in life that we most regret, it's the things we didn't do."

# Chapter 7

Only the inducement of a trip to the bookstore to purchase a copy of *Peter Pan* pried Wendy away from Fur Ball. The two had taken to each other instantly, and the bedraggled kitty had slept on a pillow beside Wendy's bed last night. By morning the weak feline had roused enough to drink more milk and licked a paste of cream and oatmeal from Jack's finger. Hetty had promised Wendy to keep a close watch on the household's new pet and to give him more milk whenever he woke from napping.

Jack had tried his best to be subtle in his efforts to do his job, not wanting to alarm Wendy or spoil the outing for her. But despite how much he was enjoying himself with Peggy Jo and her daughter, he couldn't help feeling a bit uneasy just having them out on the crowded downtown streets. After they'd left the car in a parking garage, Peggy Jo had suggested taking a shuttle to the bookstore and the restaurant, but Wendy had pleaded for them to walk. Of course, if they'd gone to Hamilton Place, the problem would be even greater. The day-after-Thanksgiving sales were in full swing at the mall. As Peggy Jo had requested, he'd made sure his weapon was out of sight, the holster hidden beneath his pullover sweater. He understood why she didn't want Wendy exposed to the gun.

As they came out of The Children's Hour bookstore on Broad Street, Wendy clutched the bag that held her new book close to her chest. Peggy Jo clasped her child's other hand tightly.

"After lunch you're going to read this book to me, aren't you, Jack?"

"You bet I am. And if you like it a lot, I'll read it to you again as a bedtime story. How does that sound to you?"

"It sounds good," she replied, her pretty little face alight with happiness.

Jack extended his left arm over Wendy's head and rested his open palm on Peggy Jo's back, bringing them closer together, Wendy just slightly in front of him. The threesome walked up Broad Street, probably appearing to passersby as the ideal American family.

Jack didn't make a big production out of staying alert to his surroundings or being constantly aware of every stranger. Who was to say whether Peggy Jo's stalker might be some innocent-looking person or a weirdo he could spot a mile away. However, Peggy Jo and he had agreed that locking her daughter and her away in the house until her crazed admirer was caught simply wasn't an option. So far the person hadn't made any threats against Wendy, only Peggy Jo. Often just the presence of a bodyguard deterred an amateur criminal, and that was what most stalkers were—amateurs. But they were also more often than not mentally unbalanced, which made them less predictable than the regular, run-of-the-mill criminal.

Jack had shipped off the box of "love" letters to Dundee late Wednesday. And he'd put in a call to Sawyer McNamara, the FBI agent Dundee had worked with on several cases. Sawyer had promised two things: that the FBI's psycholinguistics expert would also take a look at the letters and come up with a profile and that Sawyer would come to Chattanooga next week to meet Peggy Jo, once this case became an official federal matter.

"You're awfully quiet," Wendy said. "Is something wrong?" She tugged on the hem of Jack's denim coat.

"Sorry, I was just thinking about lunch," Jack replied. "Your mom tells me that this restaurant has some mighty good food."

"You sure do like to eat, don't you?" Wendy giggled.

Jack slowed his gait. "It's one of my favorite things to do," he said, then glanced over Wendy's head to catch Peggy Jo staring at him. "I'm a man with a healthy appetite."

He could tell that Miss Peggy Jo understood his meaning. That creamy skin of hers flushed pink as she turned up her cute, freckled nose, hurriedly looked away and began walking faster. He chuckled softly. Heck, it was so damn easy to rile her that he found himself doing it just for the fun of it.

"What's your hurry?" Jack asked.

"Mommy must be hungry, too." Wendy stared up at her mother.

"It's forty-six degrees today and I'm cold. Besides, the restaurant is still five blocks away, and I want to eat and get home in plenty of time to bring the Christmas things down from the attic."

"We'll have plenty of time to get everything done," Jack told her. "I'm looking forward to getting the tree set up and stringing outside lights and—"

"You sound genuinely excited, as if you've never put up Christmas decorations before," Peggy Jo said. "Believe me, it can be a major chore. Last year I hired Ross to help me get the icicle lights put up outside."

"You've got me this year. I am, as you've guessed, a novice, but I'm willing to follow orders," Jack said.

"You really haven't ever helped put up Christmas decorations?" Peggy Jo asked. "Didn't you help your parents get ever—ing ready when you were at home?"

"Nope. My mother always oversaw things like that, and she most certainly didn't allow my father or me to get involved."

Libbie had always hired a decorator to design the perfect Christmas atmosphere, with fancy, glittery items not suited for a child to touch. His mother had been a great one for pomp and circumstance, for showing off what his father's money could buy. And later on what his succession of stepfathers' millions and multimillions could buy.

"Mommy always lets me help," Wendy said. "I'm her best helper. And every year we always buy a new ornament for each of us to put on the tree. One for me, one for Mommy and one for Hetty."

"So that's why you bought those tree ornaments at the bookstore." But unless he had counted wrong, Wendy had chosen four brightly painted wooden ornaments, and Peggy Jo had laid the four items on the checkout counter.

"Yep, that's why," Wendy replied. "And we bought an extra one this year—for you!"

"Wendy, I thought that was suppose to be a secret, until later," Peggy Jo said.

"Oops, sorry. I let it slip."

Jack felt as if a hard fist had punched him in the gut. It wasn't that he hadn't been given gifts; he had. Perhaps he'd been given too many gifts as a young man. A horse. A sports car. Expensive trips. Gifts from his mother to make up for the time she hadn't spent with him. Sometimes he wondered if those gifts had been bribes to keep him from warning off her potential husbands. Had Libbie been afraid he'd tell each new man in her life that she was a black widow spider? And sometimes lady friends gave him gifts, usually flirtatious little items like silk boxer shorts or speciality condoms. He'd had women cook meals for him, give him back rubs and one even flew him down to St. Croix in her private plane. But a simple ten-dollar Christmas tree ornament had him going all soft and sentimental. And why was that? he wondered. Because Wendy had chosen the gift or because Peggy Jo hadn't vetoed the idea?

"We thought that since you might still be with us at Christmas, you should have your own memento to put on the tree." Peggy Jo didn't even glance his way as she continued walking as briskly as Wendy's short stride could accommodate.

They reached the Big River Grille and Brewing Works at five minutes after twelve. The renovated warehouse on Broad Street housed a family-style restaurant and a brewery. The waiting line for seating was relatively short considering the time of day, so they managed to find room inside, out of the crisp November wind. Jack surveyed the others in line, then the restaurant itself, packed with customers. Wendy kept peeking inside the plastic bag she held tightly to her, checking on her new book. And Peggy Jo smiled and spoke to several people who recognized her.

A burly guy with curly gray hair, who was several feet ahead of them in line, turned around and glared at them. "Hey, you're that Peggy Jo Riley who's on TV, aren't you?"

Red warning lights went off inside Jack's head. His hackles bristled. The man's tone was downright unfriendly. "Can I help you?" Jack moved from Peggy Jo's side to stand directly in front of her. "I'm Ms. Riley's personal bodyguard."

"Is that so?" The man's tone didn't soften any as he gave Jack the once-over, then glanced around at the other people in line. "It's a good thing she's hired herself a watchdog. If she keeps spouting off that feminist garbage and making good wives start questioning the right a man has to be the head of his own household, then somebody's bound to try to shut her up.''

Every muscle in Jack's body tightened. His hands instinctively curled into fists, and without conscious thought, he eased toward the loudmouthed man, who stepped out of the line.

Peggy Jo grabbed Jack's arm, leaned over and whispered in his ear, ''Please, don't make a scene.''

The man came toward Jack, who hadn't moved a muscle. He couldn't pull his weapon in a restaurant filled with people. With families. Wives and children.

The guy glared at Jack, then walked past him and said, ''I've lost my appetite,'' as he exited the restaurant.

The people around them murmured and stared, and all of the women smiled at Peggy Jo. Jack willed his body to relax, to switch from defensive mode to observation mode. Some people could be such idiots and men like that loudmouth gave all men a bad name.

''That man wasn't very nice, was he?'' Wendy looked to her mother for a response. ''He doesn't like you.''

''No, sweetpea, he wasn't very nice. And no, he doesn't like me,'' Peggy Jo said. ''But he's gone now, so let's just forget about him and enjoy our lunch. What do you say?''

Wendy nodded, then looked up at Jack. ''You like Mommy, don't you? You'd never be ugly to her the way that bad man was, would you?''

Jack gently popped his index finger on Wendy's nose, then squeezed her chin playfully. ''You bet I like your mommy. She's a very interesting lady. Very smart. And pretty, too.'' Jack lifted his gaze in time to catch Peggy Jo watching him.

The hostess came up to Jack and said, ''Sir, your table is ready.''

As they followed the young woman, Wendy chatted away about what she wanted to order for lunch, about decorating the house for Christmas and about Jack reading her new book to her. Peggy Jo kept a tight hold on Wendy's hand, and Jack brought up the rear.

"Peggy Jo!" a man's voice called from behind them.

Jack grabbed Peggy Jo's arm, effectively halting her, while he snapped around to search for the man who had spoken. Chet Compton came rushing out of the bar area. Jack had seen the guy both days he'd been with Peggy Jo at WLOK, and there was something about the station manager that rubbed Jack the wrong way. He couldn't quite put his finger on it, but he sensed that Chet was bad news.

"Mind if I join, y'all?" Chet asked. "I just got here and went straight to the bar. The wait for a table is up to twenty-five minutes now, so it would help me out if I could share a table."

Jack would like to have told the guy to get lost, but it wasn't his call. Not about this.

"Sure," Peggy Jo said, then glanced at the waitress. "This gentleman is with us."

When they reached the table that seated four, Jack helped Peggy Jo and Wendy off with their coats and held out a chair, first for Wendy and then for Peggy Jo.

"Do you have to pay him extra for that?" Chet asked Peggy Jo.

"What?" she stared at Chet in puzzlement.

Chet laughed. "I was making a joke. Just asking if you had to pay this guy extra to be a gentleman."

Before Jack could speak for himself, Peggy Jo replied, "I'm finding that being a gentleman is part of Jack's nature." She turned to her daughter. "Wendy, you remember Mr. Compton, don't you?"

"Yeah, sure." Wendy pointed at Chet. "You're the man my mommy doesn't want to date anymore."

Jack couldn't suppress a chuckle. *Out of the mouths of babes!*

"Yeah, that would be me," Chet said with a grimace, as he accepted the menu the waitress handed him.

* * *

Peggy Jo had never been so glad to have a meal come to an end. Chet had tried to be pleasant, but he kept making little digs at Jack, and Jack reciprocated in kind. Once or twice she actually thought Jack might ask Chet to step outside. And to make matters worse, Chet had caught the same shuttle and ridden back to the same parking deck where they had parked. On the drive home Jack had commented that he thought it rather odd that Chet had just happened to park in the same garage and had shown up at Big River right behind them.

"If I didn't know better, I'd think your old boyfriend might have been following us," Jack had said.

"Chet is not my old boyfriend," she'd replied quite adamantly.

But in retrospect it did seem a bit too coincidental that Chet just happened to show up for lunch moments after they arrived at the restaurant. He often ate lunch at the studio. She'd heard him complain more than once about how he hated waiting in lines at restaurants, so he seldom ate lunch downtown during a weekday.

Peggy Jo sat at the kitchen table helping Hetty fold a load of towels fresh out of the dryer. They could hear Jack reading to Wendy. The twosome sat together on the den sofa, Fur Ball curled up asleep in Wendy's lap.

"This is turning out to be quite a good holiday weekend for our Wendy," Hetty said. "She's adopted a kitten and a man."

"The kitten we can handle," Peggy Jo said. "It's the man who worries me."

"Afraid you can't handle him?" Hetty kept her gaze focused on the towels, never once glancing up at Peggy Jo.

"I *know* I can't handle him."

"That's the kind of man you want, honey. The kind that's his own man. Despite what you think—and what you sometimes imply to others—you don't really want some easily manipulated guy who'd let you run over him like a steamroller.''

"Well, I certainly don't want another Neanderthal jerk like Buck.''

"No, you don't,'' Hetty agreed. "But there's a happy medium to be found in men like Jack.'' She inclined her head toward the den. "I'd say he's that perfect combination of strength and gentleness.''

"My, my, my. You're certainly singing his praises.'' Peggy Jo folded one last towel, scooted back her chair and stood. Lowering her voice to a whisper, she said, "If you like him so damn much, why don't you…adopt him or something? Because, believe me, that's the only way he's going to become a member of this family.''

Hetty placed a stack of towels in the laundry basket. "I think you're kicking up too big a fuss about it. You like him just a little bit more than you want to.''

"I've heard enough of this. I'm going upstairs to put on my old clothes and then head up to the attic and go through the Christmas boxes.''

"All right.'' Hetty lifted the basket. "After I put these away, I'll start looking for the extra extension cords. I think they're in the hall closet.''

Fifteen minutes later Peggy Jo climbed the narrow steps that led from the upstairs hall to the attic. She reached out on the wall and flipped the switch that controlled the two attic lights. When she stepped out into the large open space, she realized that the lightbulb that lit the right side of the attic had burned out, leaving that part of the room in shadows. A small attic window allowed the afternoon sunshine to add enough illumination to see all the boxes of stored Christmas items.

She had a few memories of the holidays before her mother died, and although she cherished those sweet memories, she tried not to think about them often. Her mother's death had irrevocably changed her life forever. What was that old adage? Something about a child without a father is half an orphan, but a child without a mother *is* an orphan. For some children that might not be true, but in her case those words had proven prophetic.

In the beginning it hadn't been that way. She and her father had clung to each other after her mother's death, becoming closer than ever—until he met Agnes. Of all the sweet, loving women her father had dated during the years after her mother's death, Peggy Jo couldn't figure out why he'd married Agnes, who wasn't as pretty or smart or nice as the others. Sometimes she wondered if Agnes's young son had been as much an attraction for Vernon McNair as the woman herself had been. Vernon had been one of those old-fashioned men who valued male children more than female children.

Such a pity that Agnes hadn't been able to give him a son of his own. After four miscarriages, the doctors had told them not to try again. Things had been strained between Peggy Jo and her stepmother from the very beginning, but once Agnes learned that there would be no babies, she had made it her mission in life to make Vernon accept her son, Derek, as the son she couldn't give him. And the more her father doted on Derek, the more he neglected her. And the stronger the bond grew with his stepson, the more miserable Agnes made life for Peggy Jo.

No, she tried not to think too much about the past, about her childhood. Even the good memories had somehow become tainted by the bad ones.

Pushing thoughts of long-ago holidays from her mind, she set to work checking the labels on the boxes and moving them toward the stairs, one heavy box at a time. When she had half the large cardboard cartons in place, she managed to ease the box which contained the Christmas tree from beneath several other containers. But the long, narrow tree box was heavier than she'd remembered and as she tugged on the end, she lost her balance and fell backward—right into Jack's arms.

She screeched when he grabbed her, breaking her fall. "Oh, my God, you scared me half to death," she gasped. "I didn't hear you come up here."

"Good thing I arrived when I did or you'd have wound up flat on your...backside."

He brought her closer to him and tightened his hold. Her body clenched with awareness, spreading tingles from her core to every nerve ending. She didn't want this. Couldn't deal with it. If she succumbed to her attraction to this rugged cowboy, she'd be in way over her head. What was wrong with her? Why couldn't she just ignore the fact that Jack was good-looking, sexy as hell and a really nice guy? Ever since her divorce from Buck, she'd been able to resist combinations like that, so why did she feel as if Jack Parker just might be her own personal Waterloo?

"You should have waited for me to lift all these boxes," Jack said, his face only inches from hers, his voice deep and low. "I'd say this was man's work, but you don't like dividing chores by gender, do you?"

She swallowed nervously as his mouth came closer and closer, until only a hairbreadth separated his lips from hers. "Hetty and I have never had a problem getting these boxes downstairs." Her voice squeaked slightly.

"Let me make it easier for you this year. I can do the heavy work, and you can oversee the job."

She found herself caught like an insect in a spider's web, trapped by the desire she saw in Jack's golden-brown eyes, eyes the color of dark topaz. He was going to kiss her. All she had to do was turn her head to avoid the kiss. But she waited, her breath caught in her throat, and didn't voice a protest when his mouth made contact with hers. Just a soft brush of his lips, his breath warm. The tension inside her eased slightly. She hadn't been expecting this sweet tenderness. He played with her mouth, gentling her with an expertise she knew had come from years of practice. But at this very moment she didn't care how many women he'd kissed. All that mattered was that he was kissing her. And she was kissing him back.

The moment she responded, he slid one of his hands down her back and splayed it across the base of her spine, then lifted his other hand to cup the back of her head. She whimpered as pure sexual pleasure roared through her body like a freight train. She opened her mouth for his invasion, inviting him in, her need as strong as his.

Jack released her abruptly, leaving her bereft, her dazed mind wondering what had happened. He clutched her shoulders.

"Did you hear that?" he asked.

"Hear what?"

Hetty's cry rose to the attic, the panic in her voice obvious. "Come downstairs right now! Hurry!"

"Oh, Lord, Wendy!" Fear seized Peggy Jo.

Jack squeezed her shoulders, then released her. He turned around and headed downstairs, taking the steps two at a time. Peggy Jo rushed after him, into the second-story hallway and down the stairs to the foyer. Hetty stood guard over Wendy, who clung fiercely to the housekeeper.

"What is it?" Jack asked. "What happened? Are you two all right?"

"In there—" Hetty nodded toward the living room. "And we're fine. Just scared. Darn thing took us by surprise."

Peggy Jo rushed forward, knelt on her knees and pulled Wendy into her arms. Then she glanced over Wendy's head to look into the living room. She gasped.

One of the windows facing the front of the house had been broken. Glass fragments lay scattered over the wooden floor and colorful oriental rug. Lying almost dead center in the room was a large object the size of a small cannonball.

"Nobody touch it," Jack ordered as he rushed past them

to open the front door. He ushered them out onto porch and into the yard.

Wendy cried, "Somebody broke our window."

"Yes, I know. But it's all right. Jack's here and he'll take care of everything." Odd how she was able to say that so easily, so confidently and without any reservations.

A car parked across the street revved its motor and sped away. Jack cursed loudly, then removed his cell phone from his pocket and tossed it to Peggy Jo.

"Call the police," Jack said. "See if you can contact Detective Gifford. Tell him to come over here pronto. I didn't get the license plate number off that car—if he was even our guy—but I recognized the make and model."

She nodded.

"Y'all go around to the backyard and stay out of the house until I come and get you," he said.

Peggy Jo's heartbeat drummed inside her head. "Why? What do you think—"

"I've got to check things out inside. Understand?" He looked point-blank at Wendy, indicating why he wasn't speaking bluntly.

"Yes, I understand." Peggy Jo grabbed Jack's arm. "Please be careful."

He cupped her chin, then raked his thumb across her lips. "I'm always careful, darling."

Peggy Jo tugged Wendy's hand and motioned for Hetty. They did just as Jack had told them to do and went straight to the backyard, all the way out to the gym set in the far back corner.

"Why did Jack want us to come out here?" Wendy asked. "It's cold and we don't have our coats."

"We won't have to stay out here long, sweetpea," Peggy Jo said and prayed she was right. "Jack will come get us in few minutes." She took off her sweater and wrapped it around Wendy. "Why don't you go inside your play-house?"

The five minutes that passed seemed more like five hours to Peggy Jo. She realized that Jack thought as she did—that the object hurled through her window might be some sort of bomb. *Please, God, please, don't let anything happen to Jack.* Just the thought of him getting hurt was more than she could bear.

"Hetty, keep Wendy out here," Peggy Jo said.

"Jack won't like it if you go in there with him," Hetty told her.

"I can't stay out here wondering what's going on."

"You can and you will. Let the man do his job. He's an expert."

"What on earth did I ever do to deserve this kind of harassment?"

Hetty opened her mouth to speak but halted as she stared toward the house. That's when Peggy Jo realized Jack's presence on the back porch had distracted Hetty.

Peggy Jo ran toward the porch. Jack met her in the middle of the backyard. He held up an innocent-looking baseball.

"This was at the core of the ball that shattered the window. There were layers of paper wrapped around it. You need to take a look at those papers." Jack lifted his arm and waved at Hetty. "You can bring Wendy inside now. You two stay busy in the den while Peggy Jo and I check out the mess in the living room."

After he escorted her inside, they went straight to the living room. He took her by the arm and led her to sofa.

"Take a look at those." Jack pointed to the wrinkled pictures glued to newspaper that he had spread out on the sofa cushions.

"Don't touch them," he advised. "I picked them up using Hetty's plastic gloves I found in the pantry. There probably aren't any prints on these, but our guy could have slipped up and left just one print or even left a clue we can't see with the naked eye."

Peggy Jo studied the pictures. Pictures of her. Of Wendy. Of Jack. Pictures taken earlier today: going into the Children's Hour Bookstore; going into the Big River restaurant; on the front porch of the house.

"Oh, my God, he was following us, taking pictures and we didn't even know it." Salty bile churned in Peggy Jo's stomach. "How could we not have seen him?"

"He wasn't close by," Jack told her. "These were probably taken with a telescopic lens. Know anybody who's an amateur photographer?"

The blood ran cold in her veins. "Yes. I know two people."

"Who?"

"Ross Brewster. He wants to be a professional photographer someday," Peggy Jo said. "He has several cameras and is always snapping shots of me and the guests on my show. Several of the pictures on the wall in my office are ones Ross took."

"Let's hope Ross has an alibi for today." Jack put his arm around her shoulders and pulled her away from the photographs. "Who else?"

"What?"

"You said you knew two shutterbugs. Who's the other?"

"My ex-husband. Photography was one of Buck's hobbies."

"Do you still think he doesn't make a prime suspect?" Jack asked.

"I don't know. Maybe. But I still don't understand why he'd come after me now when we've had no contact in thirteen years." She realized it was time to admit the possibility, however remote, that Buck might be her stalker. The very thought terrorized her, but she knew she had to face the truth. "Maybe you should put Buck on your suspects list and—"

"I already have," Jack told her. "The Dundee Agency

is going to do some investigating into his whereabouts and I'm going to insist that the local authorities stop dragging their feet. It's past time they took your predicament seriously.''

# Chapter 8

Hoyt Gifford had the look of rumpled newspaper and reminded Peggy Jo of a middle-aged private eye from an old forties film-noir mystery. He'd brought along a crime-scene investigator, a rookie no doubt, at least by the looks of him. A wide-eyed, twenty-something kid named Sterling. But at least Detective Gifford was actually investigating, which was more than he'd done in the past. The police had been convinced that Jill Lennard was staging all the stalker incidents, but now that they'd had to deal with Jack a few times, the detective seemed to be giving her the benefit of the doubt. She wondered if Jack had said something to Gifford, perhaps even issued him a warning. Despite his good-ole-boy charm, Jack could be rather intimidating. And besides that, he had the prestigious Dundee Agency backing him. And from what Jack had told her, the agency had all the right connections with various federal agencies.

Sterling looked over the broken window and the debris in the living room, then bagged the baseball and the photographs. He continued gathering whatever evidence he could find around the place, while Gifford asked more questions.

"I've called in your description of the vehicle," the detective said. "But I doubt anything will come of it." He turned to Peggy Jo. "You're sure you don't know anyone with a car of that make, model and color?"

Peggy Jo shook her head. "No, I don't."

"Looks like your admirer is getting closer with each new stunt," Gifford said.

"And more dangerous," Jack added.

"Yeah," Gifford agreed. "Ransacking Ms. Riley's dressing room, leaving a package on her back porch, following her and taking pictures and now breaking a window in her house." He scratched his balding head, making the fluffs of gray hair stick straight up. "Now that he's moved beyond just letters and phone calls, it's not likely that he'll go backward. I'd say y'all can expect more destructive acts and perhaps even personal violence."

Peggy Jo was glad that Wendy and Hetty were out of earshot, safely ensconced in the den, watching one of Wendy's *The Land Before Time* videos. She wanted her child protected from this ugliness as much as possible. What worried her the most about the whole situation was the effect it might have on Wendy.

"Do you think my child or my housekeeper is in any danger?" Peggy Jo asked.

Gifford gnawed on his bottom lip while he considered her question, then said, "Maybe. Maybe not. It's hard to tell with these weirdos. Sometimes the only person in any danger is the one the guy is obsessed with. So far he hasn't threatened anyone but you, has he?"

"No, only me." Peggy Jo wrapped her arms around her waist.

"We'll do what we can do on our end, but I'll have to tell you that in cases like this, the odds are against us. We might not know who this guy is until he's ready to show himself, and by then it might be too—''

Jack cleared his throat loudly. Gifford froze to the spot as his gaze met Jack's. The detective wiped his mouth with the back of his hand and then rubbed his jaw.

"Parker here thinks we need to look into the whereabouts of three men in particular, so I'll check with Ross Brewster and Chet Compton to find out where they were this afternoon," Gifford said. "And we'll run a check on your ex-husband to see if we can find out where he is and what he's been up to lately."

Well, at least this was progress, Peggy Jo thought. The police were finally taking the situation seriously.

As she and Jack walked Gifford and Sterling to the front door, the detective paused in the foyer. "By the way, when's the last time you heard from your ex-husband?"

"I haven't seen or heard from Buck since our divorce thirteen years ago. Why do you ask?"

"Just a thought, ma'am. Wouldn't it be odd for a man who hadn't been a part of your life for that long to suddenly begin stalking and harassing you?"

Before Peggy Jo could respond, Jack said, "Odd as it might be, I want you to run a check on the man. Find out where he's living, where he works, if he's married and if he's been in any trouble since Ms. Riley divorced him."

"Yeah, sure," Gifford said. "But we'd probably do better to concentrate our efforts on finding out if Brewster and Compton have alibis."

Jack walked to their car with Gifford and Sterling. Peggy Jo waited on the front porch. Even though it wasn't quite seven o'clock, the crescent moon appeared in the black sky, and the temperature had fallen a good ten degrees. As soon as Gifford slammed the door on his midsize sedan, Jack hurried up the sidewalk and bounded onto the porch.

He put his arm around her shoulders and turned her toward the closed front door. "Let's go inside. It's getting downright chilly out here."

Halting in the foyer, Peggy Jo gazed into the living room. "We'll have to do something about the broken windows. That ball destroyed the storm window, too."

"I'll need a big piece of plastic, a hammer and some nails," Jack said. "I'll do a patch job tonight, and in the morning we'll put in a call to see if we can get somebody out to replace the glass."

"I'll ask Hetty about the plastic. The hammer and nails will be in the pantry. I have my own toolbox. That's something I preach to my audience—learn how to fix little things around the house without depending on a man to do it for you."

"For now, with this project, you can depend on this man—" he pointed to himself "—to fix it. Tell Hetty that if she doesn't have anything sturdier, a couple of large garbage bags will do."

"I'll get the things you'll need," Peggy Jo said. "And while you're covering the window, I'll sweep up the glass and put things back in order in the living room."

Working as a team, he and Peggy Jo finished the repair and cleanup job in record time. After he hammered in the last nail to secure the layer of black garbage bags over the broken window, she loosened the tie-backs and drew the damask curtains to cover the ugly plastic.

"Now that we've got that done, how about I bring down the Christmas boxes and we put up the tree?" Jack suggested.

Peggy Jo let out a long, low sigh. "I'd like to forget about Christmas, the tree, the decorations…everything." Propping her hands on the broom handle, she looked at Jack and forced a weak smile. "You don't have to say it. I know. I can't let today's incident affect the way I live my life. If I do, then I'll give my stalker power over me, and that's just what he wants.''

"That's true, too. But it wasn't what I was going to say. I was going to say that, for Wendy's sake, you have to continue your life as usual, including your annual holiday rituals.''

Wendy deserved a normal holiday season, and it was up to her to see that the annual traditions she had started when her daughter was a toddler continued this year. Despite any and all outside interference. "You're right.''

"Did I hear you correctly? Did you actually tell me—a mere man—that I'm right?'' Jack teased.

She grinned at him. "Okay, so maybe I deserved that comment. I have given you a difficult time. And I do tend to let my low opinion of some members of the male sex cloud my vision occasionally.''

With the hammer in one hand and the extra nails in the other, Jack crossed the room, came up to Peggy Jo and brought his arms down on top of her shoulders. He lowered his head just enough so that they were nose to nose. "Darling,'' he said in that incredibly sexy Texas drawl, "don't you know by now that I'm not like any other man you've ever met?''

His nearness took her breath away, but despite warning bells going off inside her head, she didn't move away from him. "I'm well aware of that fact.'' She drew in a deep, steadying breath and willed herself not to succumb to his charm. And Lord knew he practically oozed charm from the pores of his skin. "And I'll bet you're aware of the fact that I'm not like any woman you've ever known.''

His lips hovered over hers, taunting, tempting. "That's for sure.''

Just as he moved in for the kiss, Peggy Jo tightened her hold on the broom, gave it a little shove and tapped Jack in the center of his chest with the handle. "You'd better start bringing the boxes down from the attic. The one marked Tree has the Christmas tree in it.''

Jack chuckled, removed his arms from her shoulders and leisurely backed away from her. ''So, where do you want the boxes? I suppose you set the tree up in here, don't you?''

''Yes.'' As she studied the closed drapes covering the dark plastic garbage bags that covered the broken window, she clicked her tongue against the roof of her mouth. ''We always put it in front of the windows, but I'm not sure how it'll look there now.''

''We'll set it up where you usually do. By Monday you'll have new glass in the window.''

''Fine, then.'' She picked up the dustpan and put it on top of the garbage can filled with broken glass. ''I'll get rid of these, check on Hetty and Wendy and meet you back in here in a few minutes. We'll set the tree up first, then open the other boxes.''

Peggy Jo headed for the kitchen while Jack went upstairs. After putting the garbage can on the back porch, she returned the broom and dustpan to the pantry. When she entered the den, Hetty glanced up from where she sat on the sofa with Wendy and Fur Ball, who lay sleeping on a pillow in Wendy's lap.

''Get everything taken care of?'' Hetty asked.

Peggy Jo nodded. ''Jack's gone up to the attic to bring down the tree.''

Wendy's vision moved quickly from the television screen to Peggy Jo's face. ''Are we still going to put up the tree?''

''Of course we are,'' Peggy Jo said.

Wendy tenderly stroked the sleeping kitten's back. ''I thought maybe since somebody broke our window and the police came and—''

''No, no, don't be silly, sweetpea.'' Peggy Jo rushed over to the sofa and sat beside Wendy, then took her daughter's hands in hers. "We're not going to let some mean person who likes to break out people's windows ruin things for us. We're putting up the tree tonight. And tomorrow we'll finish decorating the house, just like always."

Hetty rose to her feet. "Well, it sounds as if we've got a big job on our hands tonight. I'd better see about putting together a bite of supper for us."

"Thanks, Hetty. Supper would be nice," Peggy Jo said. "In all the hurry-scurry, I'd forgotten about supper."

"Why don't you two go help Jack set up the tree. Then after supper we can get started on the decorations." Hetty went into the kitchen, immediately opened the refrigerator and began pulling out covered bowls.

"Oh, Mommy, we mustn't forget what we bought today for the tree." She glanced down at Fur Ball. "I want to get him a present before Christmas. Maybe a little play mouse. And a stocking to hang over the fireplace beside mine."

"We'll go shopping soon," Peggy Jo said, but wondered what Jack would say about another outing, this time to one of the local malls.

As Hetty continued busying herself in the kitchen, she asked, "What did you buy for the tree—this year's new ornaments?"

"Yes," Wendy replied. "We bought one for all of us. Jack, too."

"Oh, Jack, too, huh?" Hetty gave Peggy Jo a don't-tell-me-that-means-nothing look.

"You're going to love yours," Wendy said. "It's a teapot. And mine is a silver bell. Well, it looks like a silver bell, but it's made out of wood. And you'll never guess what I picked out for Mommy and Jack. I got Jack a wooden horse and Mommy a tiny TV set."

"You can show them to Hetty later," Peggy Jo said. "Turn off the TV and go see if Jack has brought the tree down from the attic. Tell him I'll be there in a minute. I need to talk to Hetty about something.''

''Okay.'' Wendy lifted Fur Ball from his pillow as she got up, then she left the room and disappeared down the hall.

Peggy Jo marched into the kitchen. ''Do not read anything into the fact that I let Wendy buy Jack a Christmas tree ornament. It doesn't mean anything.''

''Did I say that it did?'' Hetty measured out coffee beans and put them into the electric grinder, then turned on the machine.

The minute Hetty completed the job and the noise stopped, Peggy Jo said, ''If I'd told her we couldn't buy an ornament for Jack, she wouldn't have understood.''

''Probably not.''

''Will you please stop this silliness right now!''

Hetty ceased preparing the coffee immediately and looked Peggy Jo square in the eye. ''I'm not doing anything. And I didn't say anything. But I know what's wrong with you and why you're assuming I've come to the wrong conclusion.''

''Don't say it.''

''Don't say what?''

''Oh, all right. I like Jack Parker. He does seem to be a really nice guy. Nothing like my father or Buck.'' Peggy Jo glowered at Hetty. ''There, I said it. Are you satisfied?''

Hetty just smiled and returned to preparing the evening meal. Peggy Jo huffed, shook her head and stomped out into the hall. Why had she bothered trying to explain the way she felt about Jack, when her feelings confused her so? Yes, she liked the man. And yes, she was terribly attracted to him. And yes, she was glad to have him around to protect her. But she didn't want to like him, didn't want to be attracted to him and hated the very thought that Jack Parker was prepared to kill to protect her—that he was even prepared to die to protect her. Dear God, what kind of person did that make her, having these fluttery, feminine needs, these primitive reactions to this particular man?

*Those feelings make you human, Peggy Jo,* an inner voice told her. After all these years, after reinventing herself and teaching other women to do the same—to stand alone, to not rely on a man—she suddenly found herself very much in need of Jack Parker. And not just on a professional level.

When Peggy Jo reached the living room, she found Wendy assisting Jack in setting up the tree. Fur Ball lay undisturbed on a cushion, which rested in the center of the sofa.

Before adopting Wendy, she hadn't bothered with putting up a tree or celebrating the season. After escaping from Buck's clutches, she'd been too busy surviving, too busy working twelve hours a day, seven days a week, to even think about holidays. But having a child had changed all that. She had purchased the seven-foot spruce tree for Wendy's first Christmas and had begun holiday traditions for herself and her child.

"Mommy," Wendy called to her. "Come see. Come see. We got it put up."

For her child's sake, Peggy Jo breezed into the living room as if she didn't have a care in the world. She paused just inside the doorway and inspected the bare tree. "Y'all did a great job."

"Jack got it straight the first time," Wendy said. "See."

"Yes, I see."

"Jack knows how to do everything, just like a real daddy." Wendy smiled at Jack as if he'd been the one who had set the moon and stars in the sky.

"Wendy, whoever gave you the idea that daddies can do everything?" Peggy Jo asked.

"Martha Jane said so." Wendy eased closer to Jack's side. "She said it was too bad I didn't have a daddy of my own, 'cause real daddies can do everything that mommies can't do.''

Peggy Jo felt like screaming. "Well, I've never heard such—"

Jack cleared his throat several times.

"Martha Jane is mistaken," Peggy Jo said, realizing she'd been on the verge of blasting six-year-old Martha Jane's opinion to smithereens.

Wendy reached out and clasped Jack's hand. "But Martha Jane should know, shouldn't she? She's got a real daddy."

"What your mother is trying to say is that no one can do everything," Jack said as he squeezed Wendy's hand. "But there are some things that men can do better than women, just like there are things women can do better than men. But for the most part, mommies and daddies work together, and working together is the best way to be good parents."

"Is that what you meant, Mommy?"

Peggy Jo could not—would not—disillusion her daughter any more than she'd already disillusioned her about life and love and men in general. Had she made a mistake by teaching Wendy not to believe in magic and fairy tales and daddies who could do everything? Just because she didn't believe in happily-ever-after, didn't mean such a thing was impossible for Wendy. She'd never questioned her judgment in this matter. Not until lately. Not until Jack Parker came into their lives and started putting all sorts of nonsense into her head. The damn man made her want to believe, to trust, to dream.

"Yes, that's what I meant."

The phone rang. Peggy Jo gasped but instinctively picked up the receiver from the telephone on the table just inside the living room door.

"Hello?"

"Did you get my pictures?" The voice was muffled, as it had been in previous calls.

"Yes."

Jack picked Wendy up and set her on the sofa beside Fur Ball. He put his index finger to his lips, cautioning her to be quiet. Peggy Jo looked right at Jack, who mouthed the question, "Is it him?" She nodded. He took out his cellular phone and hurriedly punched in a number.

"I know where you are every minute of the day and I know what you're doing. You're messing around with that cowboy, and I don't like it. You ruined my life and I'm not about to let you be happy."

Jack motioned to her to continue talking, and that's when she realized that Jack had the police on his cell phone. Was he hoping they could trace the phone call? All the previous calls had shown up on her Caller ID as either pay telephone or unknown, as this one had. Would it be possible for the police to locate the caller?

"What did I do to ruin your life?" Peggy Jo asked.

"The same thing you've done to all the husbands who expect their wives to do what they're told to do," the man said.

"Then your wife watches my television show?"

"My woman used to watch it, but I put a stop to that!"

"Did you ever watch my show?"

"Yeah, I've watched it, and I've read your books, too! You're a real piece of work, a first-class bitch, but not for much longer."

The dial tone rang in Peggy Jo's ears. She replaced the receiver and looked at Jack. He said something softly into his cell phone, then hit the off button, looked at her and shook his head.

"Not long enough," Jack said. "The guy knows just how long he can talk. We're not going to catch him this way."

He came over, bent down and pulled the plug that connected the phone line to the wall jack.

"Why did you do that?" Peggy Jo asked.

"I'm unplugging all the phones in the house tonight,"
he told her. "There's no point in changing your number
again, since you've already done it twice. From now on
we'll use only my cell phone. That should put a stop to his
calls. And come Monday, we'll get your cell phone number
changed, and you can let everyone know that they can leave
a message with your answering service and you'll get back
to them."

"Are we playing a game with our telephones?" Wendy
asked.

"Yes, ma'am, Miss Wendy Sue, that's just what we're
doing," Jack said.

Jack helped Hetty clean up in the kitchen while Peggy
Jo took Wendy upstairs for a bath. He'd promised Wendy
to come up soon and read *Peter Pan* to her again. She'd
been so excited when he'd read to her earlier today about
the little girl with her name who had traveled to never-
never land and had all sorts of wild adventures.

"Tonight you can read to me and Fur Ball," she'd said.
"He was asleep in the chair in the corner when you read
it to me the first time."

Wendy Riley had somehow managed to wrap him around
her little finger in only a couple of days, and he wasn't sure
how it had happened or why. He hadn't spent much time
around small children. He'd grown up an only child, born
so that his father could have an heir and his mother could
secure her right to her husband's money in case of a divorce. Of course, Libbie had found herself several men
even richer than Jack's father had been. Ironic thing was
that all her millions had never made Libbie happy, and in
the end she'd had no one who cared about her. Not even
her own son.

"Penny for your thoughts," Hetty said as she placed the last pot on the drainboard.

"They're not worth a penny," Jack said. "I was thinking about my mother."

"Ah, I see." Hetty wiped her hands off on her apron.

"Just what do you see?"

"I see why you're still single at the ripe old age of…what?…forty?"

Jack clutched the dish towel to his heart. "You wound me, Miss Hetty. I'm only thirty-eight."

"Close enough. My point is that you haven't settled down because your mama did something that made you scared of marriage. And don't tell me I'm wrong."

Jack laid the kitchen towel on the counter. "You're not wrong."

"Peggy Jo's daddy was the first man in her life who broke her heart. If Vernon McNair had been the kind of father he should have been, she never would have run off and married Buck Forbes when she was seventeen."

"Peggy Jo's experiences made her dislike and distrust all men," Jack said. "My mama's actions didn't do that to me. I love the ladies. I realize there are a lot of good ones in the world. And I've known my share of them." He winked playfully at Hetty.

"Humph! You may love the ladies, but have you ever really trusted one?"

She had him there. He couldn't truthfully say that he'd ever completely trusted a woman. Certainly not enough to commit his heart and his life.

"You haven't, have you?" she asked.

"You know what, Hetty, my darling? You're a wise woman. If I'd had a mother like you… But I didn't."

"That was my loss as well as yours," Hetty said. "If I were your mother, I'd be asking you why you weren't married and giving me some grandchildren."

"If you were my mother, I'd probably already be married and have a houseful."

"It's not too late, you know. I could always adopt you."

Jack burst into laughter, then hugged Hetty affectionately. She returned his hug.

"Get out of here and go on about your business," she told him.

"I'll do just that." After kissing her cheek, he left the kitchen.

When he arrived upstairs, he paused outside Wendy's bedroom. Holding the newly purchased *Peter Pan* book in her hands, Peggy Jo sat on the edge of the bed staring at her sleeping child. Fur Ball lay curled on his pillow on the floor beside Wendy's canopy bed. In that moment Jack was forced to admit to himself that he was not only enchanted by the child, but also by the mother. The more he learned about Peggy Jo, the more he longed to know. She was a puzzle he wanted to figure out, a riddle he wanted to solve.

Just as he started to turn and leave, to head down the hall to his own bedroom, Peggy Jo glanced up and saw him. She smiled. His stomach knotted. The woman had a smile that created wickedly delightful thoughts in a man's head.

She stood, laid the book on the nightstand, then adjusted the covers around Wendy. Jack knew she was coming to him. And even though his rational mind told him that all she wanted was to say good-night, his male libido had ideas of its own.

As she came out into the hall, she half closed Wendy's bedroom door. "I started reading to her, waiting for you, and she fell asleep on page three."

"She's had another full day."

"Yes, she has. And so have we."

"Mmm-hmm." He'd never been so at a loss for words with a woman. So what the hell was wrong with him now? Peggy Jo Riley had him practically tongue-tied.

"Before I started reading to her, Wendy told me that she was glad you were here to look after us."

Jack stared into Peggy Jo's eyes. Cat-green eyes. Oh, Lordy, how he wanted to kiss this woman. One good taste of her lips earlier in the day just hadn't been enough. He wanted a lot more.

"I told Wendy that I was glad, too. Glad that you were here."

"That's some admission, coming from you." Jack's body betrayed him. His sex hardened. And it was all he could do not to grab Peggy Jo and carry her off to bed. Instead he simply stared at her.

Peggy Jo flushed. "Well, good night, Jack. I'll see you in the morning."

When she turned to leave, he called to her. "Peggy Jo?"

She whirled around to face him. "Yes?"

Jack grasped her face with his hands, leaned over and covered her mouth with his. When her lips parted on a gasping sigh, he deepened the kiss, delving inside, claiming her completely.

## Chapter 9

Peggy Jo didn't know what hit her. Jack had taken her by surprise. The small part of her mind that was still capable of rational thought told her she had to put a stop to this madness, that she could not enjoy his moist, devouring mouth on hers. But her body overruled such commonsense thoughts. Her body wanted Jack, needed him, longed for more. Why weren't alarm sirens and red flashing lights going off inside her head the way they always had in the past when a man got too close, became aggressive and all macho with her? *Help!* her self-protective instincts screamed. But those cries were drowned out by the deafening turbulence taking place in every feminine fiber of her being.

She was fast losing control, edging closer and closer to surrendering herself to these luscious feelings. She couldn't remember ever feeling this way, ever wanting a man's touch the way she wanted Jack's. His possession was powerful and yet at the same time gentle. And it was that very combination of strength and tenderness that seduced her.

Her knees weakened. Her stomach fluttered. Her femininity moistened. And she reciprocated passionately, consuming his mouth in the same fashion he was hers. A mutual hunger dominated their actions. The kiss went on and on, until they broke apart in order to take some deep breaths. Jack slid his hands down either side of her neck to grasp her shoulders. They stared into each other's eyes, hot passion pulsating between them.

"No," she finally managed to say, then repeated the word several times, for her benefit as much as his. "No. No. No."

"Yes, Peggy Jo." He tightened his grip on her shoulders. "Say yes."

She shook her head and jerked free. Staggering backward, she almost lost her balance, but reached out and laid her open palm against the wall to steady herself.

"I can't handle this," she said. "Don't you understand that this wasn't supposed to happen. I haven't been able to feel anything for a man since…since—"

*Heaven help me!* She turned and ran away from Jack. Once inside the safety of her room, she closed the door, then leaned against it and breathed deeply, over and over again. She waited, her breath ragged, her heart beating like crazy. Afraid Jack would come after her. Equally afraid that he wouldn't.

She listened to his footsteps drawing closer and closer. She held her breath, waiting for the knock, but also wondering if he might simply burst through the door. His footsteps moved away, passing her door. She sagged with relief, but a part of her was disappointed.

*You fool! You stupid idiot! What did you want? Did you want him to knock down the door and come after you?*

Peggy Jo walked across the room and halted at the foot of her bed. She hurriedly stripped out of her clothes, socks and shoes, down to her underwear. Then, carrying the clothes with her, she went into the bathroom. What she needed was a long, hot soak in the tub, to soothe her nerves and clear her head. She dumped the clothing into the hamper, then removed her bra and panties and tossed them on top of the other items. After turning on the water faucets and pouring in some scented bubble bath, she looked at herself in the mirror. Her lips were rosy and slightly swollen. She most definitely had the look of a woman who had been kissed quite thoroughly. Trying to ignore the evidence Jack had left of their shared passion, she squirted toothpaste on her toothbrush and began her nightly ritual. This was followed by flossing, gargling with mouthwash and then cleansing her face with a moisturizing liquid.

When she stood on tiptoe to reach the top shelf of the medicine cabinet, where she kept the cucumber face mask gel, she caught a glimpse of her breasts in the mirror. Her nipples were still puckered and pebble hard. An image of Jack flicking his tongue over her breasts flashed through her mind. She gasped as pure sensation flooded her body, pooling at her feminine core.

*Forget the damn cucumber mask! Just get in the tub, relax and put Jack Parker out of your mind.*

But ten minutes later, surrounded by an abundance of floral-scented bubbles, she realized that putting her bodyguard out of her mind was easier said than done. No matter how hard she tried to think of something else, he kept invading her thoughts. His devilish smile featured prominently in the images she couldn't banish, as did his firm, demanding mouth.

Okay, she told herself, enough of this. You have other things to think about. You need to finish your Christmas shopping. And make plans to take Wendy to Betsy's farm outside of Spring City for a visit. Of course, there were plans to be made for the new show, the nationally syndicated, new-and-improved version of *Self-Made Woman.* Jill had told her that she needed to seriously consider moving to Atlanta and taping the show there, because Atlanta had become a major U.S. city, a city known around the world these days. She hadn't given the idea much thought, hadn't even mentioned it to Wendy or Hetty. How would they feel about leaving Chattanooga?

Tension drained from Peggy Jo's body as she pushed thoughts of Jack to the back of her mind, concentrating on everything and anything other than the hunk sleeping down the hall. By the time the bath water became lukewarm and all the bubbles had dissolved, Peggy Jo was feeling more like her old self. In control. In charge. Whatever had gotten into her out there in the hall had been an aberration, a temporary deviation from sanity. She had no intention of letting herself fall for some Texas cowboy who had nothing more than a good time on his mind. She was too smart to ever allow herself to be manipulated by a man. Any man. Not even one as devastatingly appealing as Jack.

Jack stood under the showerhead, his face turned upward to accept the full force of the spray. He wanted the water to wash away his thoughts about Peggy Jo Riley. The woman had done a number on him, but how she'd accomplished that feat he didn't know. She had sneaked up on him and caught him off guard. That had to be it. Inch by inch, minute by minute. A smile here. A laugh there. A tentative touch. A hesitant stare. Her womanly wiles hadn't been obvious, nothing blatant, nothing a man could see coming straight at him. This gut-wrenching need to march down the hall and into her room had taken him by surprise. He had made the mistake of thinking Peggy Jo was like every other woman he'd known. She *had* warned him, hadn't she? How stupid could a guy be?

Pretty damn stupid, the reply came from the Jack Parker who knew how to charm the ladies, enjoy their company and yet keep them emotionally at arm's length. So how the hell had Peggy Jo gotten close enough to get under his skin?

And why her? It wasn't as if she was the most beautiful

woman he'd ever known. She was pretty enough, in a clean, wholesome sort of way, but no breathtaking beauty. And she was a bit on the plump side, maybe even fat by today's standards of bone-thin females. Peggy Jo was definitely no cover model. And that personality of hers! She certainly wasn't nice, sweet and demure. And she wasn't overtly sexy. But there was a sensuality about her that intrigued him, that made him want her. Despite all her flaws, she was quite a woman, his Peggy Jo.

His Peggy Jo! His woman?

As he began to scrub his body, Jack imagined what it would be like if he weren't showering alone, if she were here with him, her soapy hands lathering him from head to toe. Just the thought of her touching him aroused him. His sex swelled and throbbed.

Damn! He didn't like this turn of events. He didn't like it at all. Oh, it wasn't that he hadn't lusted after a particular woman before—he had. More than once. But this time it was different. This was something more than lust, and that's what bothered him. When a man let himself become emotionally involved, he was in trouble. And heaven help him, he had begun to care about Peggy Jo in a very personal way. She had already become more to him than just a client.

*Get her off your mind,* he told himself. *Stop thinking of her as a woman and start thinking about her as nothing more than a job.* He was in her life to protect her, to guard her night and day. He needed to concentrate on how he could best keep Peggy Jo safe from now until her stalker was caught and put behind bars.

She turned and twisted. She pulled the covers up to her neck, then flung them to her hips. She punched her pillow, then grabbed another and shoved it under her head. Now her head was too high. She jerked the second pillow out from under her head and tossed it on the floor.

She glanced at the lit digital clock on the bedside table. Twelve twenty-seven. Why was she still awake at this hour of the night? She should have been asleep two hours ago. She had tried counting sheep, but the woolly creatures had suddenly turned into hundreds of Jack Parkers jumping over a fence and coming straight at her. Then she had tried meditating and began chanting a one-syllable word, trying to erase all thoughts from her mind. She had made the mistake of choosing the word *oh*. The more she repeated the word in her mind, the slower the repetition became, until she was moaning the word while visions of Jack's big hands caressing her body tormented her unbearably.

Her entire body ached with need, unlike anything she'd ever experienced in her life. She'd never had desire drive her crazy. Not like this.

*You can control it,* she told herself. *Get up, go downstairs and do something. Fix yourself some hot cocoa. Watch a movie on TV. Eat a piece of German chocolate cake.*

She jumped out of bed, slid her feet into her house slippers and grabbed her robe lying at the foot of the bed. Visions of delectable chocolate cake swirled about in her head as she made her way along the hall, tiptoeing, being careful not to disturb anyone. She forced herself not to glance at Jack's open bedroom door, but she did pause momentarily to sneak a peek at her sleeping daughter. Then she rushed downstairs.

Moonlight illuminating the kitchen let her see well enough to make her way to the sink, where she immediately turned on the small fluorescent light fixture beneath the window cornice. A diffused glow of cream-white light washed over the small area. Trying to be as quiet as possible, she took a plate from the cupboard and a knife and fork from the silverware drawer, then crept over to the crystal cake plate. Relief was only a moment away. Chocolate. Sugar. Coconut. Pecans. A foodaholic's quick fix to any problem. Even now, after years of retraining herself, the guru of "love thyself, help thyself" sometimes fell off the wagon.

She lifted the crystal dome, set it aside and sliced a huge piece of cake, then put the slice on her plate and replaced the dome. Maybe she could find something to watch on TV while she indulged herself. After she cuddled up on the sofa, her feet tucked under her, she turned on the television but quickly muted the sound. She found a home-shopping program that was selling jewelry. She didn't have to hear the saleswoman in order to enjoy looking at the gold, silver and gemstone items.

First she sniffed the cake, savoring the aroma. Then she cut into it with her fork and quickly brought the bite to her mouth. The first bite was good, the second even better. The third was scrumptious. And every bite after that was sheer heaven.

Food was better than sex, wasn't it? And a whole lot less dangerous. A piece of cake or pie never broke a girl's heart. A candy bar never punched a woman in the nose or gave her a black eye. An ice cream cone never disappointed anyone or led a person to expect more from it than it was willing to give.

She didn't need a man! What woman needed a man when she could give herself pleasure when she needed it? Peggy Jo chuckled at her own cleverness.

Tears sprang into her eyes quite suddenly. Unexpected tears. What was wrong with her? Why wasn't the chocolate cake working its magic? Why wasn't she feeling better?

Why couldn't she stop wanting Jack Parker?

Jack opened the den door quietly, not wanting to startle Peggy Jo. He had known the minute she left her room, but had waited a couple of minutes before going out into the hall and following her. He had stopped a moment at Wendy's door to check on her and Fur Ball, then made his way downstairs. He knew where Peggy Jo was because he saw light coming from beneath the door.

He stopped dead still in the doorway the minute he saw her. She sat on the sofa, curled up, her feet tucked under her, her long, wavy hair falling freely below her shoulder blades, as she stared at the silent television. She held an empty plate in her hand. Huge teardrops glistened on her eyelashes. And a smear of chocolate smudged the corner of her mouth. She was, without a doubt, the sweetest temptation he'd ever seen.

*You must be losing your freaking mind!* he told himself.

The edge of her yellow-and-white-striped flannel gown hung a couple of inches below the bulky, yellow terry cloth robe, and the tips of her fuzzy yellow house shoes peeked out from beneath the hem. This woman was no sexy, alluring babe. But she called to him on every level a woman can speak to a man. To his mind, his heart, his body. And yes, even his soul. Something inside him recognized her, knew her, wanted her more than life itself.

*Get real, Jacky-boy, what you want is to get laid.*

Okay, so he wanted that, too. But right now he was satisfied just to look at her. Maybe he should go back upstairs and let her have her privacy. She'd obviously found satisfaction in eating a piece of Hetty's German chocolate cake and in having a good cry. Too bad there wasn't a six-pack in the fridge. He wouldn't mind finding a little oral satisfaction himself.

Ah, hell, why had he used that word? Oral. It conjured up images he was better off without at the present moment. He had to stop thinking about Peggy Jo as a desirable woman and remember she was a client in jeopardy, whose very life could be in danger. But try as he might, looking at her right now, all he could see was a lovely, vulnerable, compelling lady in need of his comfort. The one question—the only question—was, could he comfort her without his solace turning into something more?

*Close the door quietly,* he told himself. *Turn around and leave her alone. She's a big girl. She can take care of herself. She doesn't need you or any man. Wasn't that what she preached on her television show and in her books? She was self-sufficient. So, leave her the hell alone.*

Just as he started to take his own good advice, he realized that she must have sensed his presence. She glanced away from the TV screen and looked straight at him. Her soft, full lips parted in a surprised gasp, and he could tell by the wistful look in her eyes that she didn't want him to leave. Whether she realized it or not, Peggy Jo needed something from him. A shoulder to cry on? A pal to listen to her troubles? A little friendly concern or even sympathy? Or maybe just a pair of strong arms to hold her? Whatever she needed, he was her man.

Damn! He didn't like the sound of that, even if it was only a figure of speech. He wasn't her man. Jack Parker was his own man. No woman had ever owned him.

"I hope I didn't wake you when I came downstairs," she said, that please-don't-leave-me expression still on her face.

"Nope. I was awake." The truth was he'd never been asleep. He'd been lying in bed with a hard-on, thinking about her.

Jack stayed in the doorway, as a wise inner voice tried to talk him out of going into the den. *You'll regret it if you do.*

"You didn't need to check on me," she told him. "And you don't have to stay with me. I'm fine."

Ah, hell! As he entered the den, he closed the door behind him, then walked across the room and sat beside her on the sofa. She stared at him with those incredible green eyes, and he suddenly felt as if he'd been poleaxed in the gut.

*You're beyond saving, Jacky-boy. This little lady's got a hold on you.*

He licked his thumb, then reached out and slid his damp thumb across the corner of her mouth, washing away the dab of chocolate. She inhaled deeply and held her breath for a moment, releasing it in a nervous, sensual sigh when he put his thumb to his lips.

"Jack…I…we…" She stammered, as if searching for the right words and unable to find them.

Okay, so bringing this sexual tension thing between them out in the open was going to be up to him. No need to try to put a pretty face on this mess or sidestep the issue. "How about we both lay our cards on the table? Let's just be up-front with each other about what's going on here. I'll go first if you want me to."

She nodded her head with quick, jerking movements. "Yes, you go first, please."

"All right." He now realized that he shouldn't have sat beside her, and he damn well shouldn't have touched her. Jack eased to the opposite end of the sofa. "Plain and simple—we want each other." When she opened her mouth to comment, he lifted his hand in a stop gesture. "Let me finish."

She nodded again, then waited.

"I don't like what's happened between us any more than you do," he said. "And I've got to be honest with you, I sure as hell don't understand it. We've known each other only a few days, and although I've…er…bedded a woman on shorter acquaintance, I've never felt—" He cleared his throat. "It's not just sex, you know. I like you. I like you a lot. And I care about you. About what happens to you. And not just because you're a client."

She stared at him, her eyes shimmering with tears. Heaven help him if he said the wrong thing. Despite her tough-gal facade, Peggy Jo had a soft underbelly that most of the world didn't see. She was a woman who had been brutally hurt in the past. The last thing he wanted was to ever cause her more pain.

"The truth is, I want to have sex with you, and I shouldn't because you're a client," he told her. She didn't so much as blink an eye. "And you should know that it would be only a temporary thing for me. I'm not the kind of guy for long-term commitments. I don't want a ring on my finger or in my nose. Do you understand what I'm saying?"

"Yes, I understand." She slid her legs off the sofa and let her feet touch the floor, then straightened her shoulders and tilted her chin. "You want us to have sex, but you don't want to marry me."

"Yeah." Man, hearing her say it made him sound like a womanizing jerk. Okay, so he was a womanizer. But he'd never been a jerk. "Believe me, as a general rule I don't sleep with my clients. Heck, usually I'm not even attracted to them. But, Peggy Jo Riley, there's something about you that I can't resist."

As she swiped the tears from her eyes with her fingertips, she laughed softly. "You're a real sweet-talker, Jack. I bet you've been able to get any woman you ever wanted, just by telling her what you thought she wanted to hear."

"Ah, shucks, ma'am, you flatter me," he said. "But I've got to admit that there have been a couple of ladies I wasn't able to charm." He laid his hand across the back of the sofa and leaned forward, closer to her. "You, for one."

A sad smile replaced her temporary laughter. "Don't beat yourself up about it. I'm different from most women, so you shouldn't consider your attempt to charm me a failure. I find you charming, even likable. And as Hetty keeps pointing out to me, you're a good man. But I don't need a man. Any man. Not even you."

Instinctively he moved closer, spanning the distance that he had only minutes before placed between them. "Needing and wanting aren't the same thing. Don't lie to yourself. You may not need me, but you want me."

"I want a lot of things I can't have, but—"

"Darling, you can have me. Anywhere. Anytime."

A smile played at the corners of her mouth. She found him amusing. *That was good, wasn't it?* he asked himself. He grinned at her as he eased his arm from the back of the sofa to drape her shoulders.

She stiffened the moment he touched her. "Back off, Jack," she said. "I can't breathe when you get this close."

*Oh, Peggy Jo, my darling, do you have any idea what that simple admission told me about your true feelings?* He lifted his arm from her shoulders and returned it to the back of the sofa, but he didn't move away from her.

"Thank you," she said.

"Sure. No problem."

"Since neither of us can sleep, would you like some decaf coffee or some hot cocoa?" she asked.

"No, nothing for me," he replied. "But if you want—"

"I don't. I was just trying to make conversation, to be polite."

Jack placed his hands on the top of his thighs and patted his fingers up and down against his pajama bottoms. "So, what do we do now? Watch TV? Play cards? Swap war stories?"

"Swap war stories?" she asked. "Are you suggesting we spend our sleepless night getting to know each other better?"

"Sure. Why not? That is, if you're sure you're totally opposed to our fooling around a little."

"I'm sure," she replied.

"So, who goes first this time?"

"You went first before, so I suppose it's my turn."

"Start in the beginning, with 'I was born a precious little redheaded doll' and go from there."

His amusing comment gained him one of her smiles. "I was born a precious redheaded doll, with parents who adored me. I lived a happy, normal life until I was seven and my mother died. My father seemed to dote on me after that and we became closer than we'd ever been. I adored my daddy.'' She paused, took a deep breath and continued. ''When I was thirteen, my father met a woman named Agnes, who became determined to become the next Mrs. McNair. Agnes put on a good show of liking me, until after she and Daddy married when I was fourteen. Then she became the proverbial stepmother from hell. When I was seventeen, I ran away from home and wound up marrying the first guy who came along.''

''Buck Forbes?''

''Oh, yeah. Buck. Good ole Buck.'' Peggy Jo stiffened her spine, as if arming herself to do battle. ''Agnes tormented me and made my life unbearable, but I didn't know anything about misery until Buck took over every aspect of my life. He told me when to get up, when to go to bed. How to dress, what I could say, what I could and couldn't do. And if he thought I'd disobeyed him, even in the most inconsequential way, he'd use me as a punching bag.''

''Oh, Peggy Jo…darling…'' Jack longed to take her in his arms, to promise her that he'd be around from now on to make sure nothing and no one ever hurt her again. Why was it that she brought out all the protective, possessive instincts within him?

''I was young and scared and had nowhere to go,'' she said. ''The only relative I had—other than my father—was my mother's sister's daughter, but Betsy was just a few years older than I was, and she was working her way through college and…afterward, when I was honest with her about my life with Buck, she told me I should have come to her, that she'd have found a way to have helped me.''

''You told me the first day we met that you miscarried a child, and after that happened you decided to leave Buck.''

''No, that's…not…exactly right.'' Her voice cracked with emotion. ''I'd decided to leave Buck a dozen times before that, but I'd never had the courage. After I lost my baby, I felt I didn't have anything else to lose. At that point I didn't care if he killed me.''

"That's when you went to a women's shelter?"

"Mmm-hmm. And while I was there, I took out a restraining order on Buck and filed for divorce. I was twenty-one, and I thought my life was over. It took me six years to reinvent myself. I went back to school, worked two jobs, put myself on a diet and took a couple of self-improvement classes. Then one day I realized that I could do a better job of teaching women how to like themselves and take care of themselves than anyone teaching those classes.

"I had learned to stand on my own two feet and I knew that I'd never be at the mercy of another man as long as I lived," she explained. "Not my father. Not Buck. Not some new man who might want to control me." Her gaze connected with Jack's and held fast. "I'm not willing to risk losing who I've become. Especially not for a short-lived affair with you."

"Darling, you've got it wrong," he said. "I don't want to control you. All I want to do is love you."

# Chapter 10

Had she heard him right? Peggy Jo wondered. Had Jack said that he wanted to love her? He couldn't mean that in the truest sense of the word. Not love her, as in *in love* with her. He meant he wanted to have sex with her, right? Yes, that had to be it. Men usually didn't realize that, for many women, love and sex didn't mean the same thing. For Peggy Jo the two words belonged together, but they were not interchangeable. There was sex and then there was love. To her way of thinking sex and love went together, like bacon and eggs, like winter and cold, like a rhinestone-studded white jumpsuit and Elvis Presley. Sex was physical gratification. But love was more. Love encompassed more than the physical. Love involved the heart and the soul. Love was caring and giving, commitment and marriage and kids—and growing old together.

"You mean you want to have sex with me."

"Yeah, isn't that what I just said?" Jack looked at her hopefully.

She heaved a sigh of relief. She could handle Jack putting the moves on her, couldn't she? All she had to do was keep reminding herself that if she succumbed to her own desire and gave Jack what he wanted, she would surrender more than just her body to him.

"I thought we agreed to share war stories instead of giving in to our baser instincts." Peggy Jo turned halfway around, pulled one leg up and set her foot on the sofa cushion, then cupped her knee with her hands. "I've told you my sad tale, leaving out my usual humorous and sympathy-grabbing line that I've shared with my television audience on several occasions."

"And just what would that line be?" he asked.

"Oh, the one about the only thing worse than being a freckle-faced, redheaded stepchild was being a fat, freckle-faced redheaded stepchild."

Jack chuckled. "The world isn't always kind, is it?" His good-natured smile melted away, replaced by a somber expression. "At best, children can hope they're lucky enough to have parents who'll protect them for as long as possible. But sometimes it's our parents who land the most deadly blows."

She inspected him, noting the tension, the barely concealed anger. And the hurt. "So, you didn't have an Ozzie and Harriet childhood, either, huh?"

"My old man was the best. We spent a lot of time together. He let me start helping him around the ranch as soon as I was big enough to sit in a saddle. I loved him and I loved being with him."

"So, you grew up on a real ranch?"

"Yeah, a big spread that my father had inherited from his father."

"And do you still own the ranch? Have you kept it in the family?"

"No, I don't still own the ranch." His voice held a cold, deadly edge. "My father left the ranch to my mother, thinking she'd keep it for me, but she sold it after he died, then shipped me off to military school and moved to Dallas with her new husband.''

Poor Jack. Did he, too, have a stepparent from hell? ''I'm sorry. I know what it's like to be despised by a stepparent.''

''Oh, my stepfather wasn't the problem.'' Jack laughed, but there was no mirth, no sincerity in the sound. ''Actually none of my stepfathers ever caused me a problem. They all liked me and I actually liked a couple of them. I felt sorry for all the unlucky saps.''

''Just how many stepfathers did you have?''

''Four,'' Jack replied. ''My mother buried two husbands and divorced three, and with each subsequent marriage, she got richer and richer. She started out with my father, who owned a big spread and a nice house and gave her everything he could afford and then some, but it was never enough. Husband number two was actually a millionaire businessman. She wound up with a nice divorce settlement from him.

''It turned out that husband number three had some dirty little secrets and paid Libbie a ton of money to keep her mouth shut after their divorce. Husband number four was a bit smarter and made her sign a prenuptial agreement, but when they split after five years, he let her keep all her jewels and furs and the Dallas penthouse.''

''Your mother sounds like an old movie star, marrying and divorcing again and again.''

''Libbie liked to think of herself as a Dallas socialite, but until she married Orson Reid, she had never actually made it to the top. But old Orson, bless him, finally gave her everything she'd always wanted.''

''Which was?''

''More money than she could spend in ten lifetimes and a position at the top of the social register.''

Peggy Jo had studied his expressions while he'd been talking about his mother's marriages. She had seen a myriad of emotions. Humor. Pity. Sympathy. But those feelings had been for his numerous stepfathers. Whenever he had referred specifically to his mother, there had been no warm emotions evident in either his facial expression or his voice.

"You hated her, didn't you?"

"Oh, yeah, darling, I hated her till the day she died."

The whole time he'd been talking, he hadn't once made direct eye contact with Peggy Jo, but he did then, and his gaze pleaded with her for understanding.

"Some people would think you're awful for saying such a thing about your mother, but I don't. A part of me hated my father as much as I loved him. I blamed him for so much of the bad in my life. But once I was able to stop hoping that he'd be a real father to me again, the hatred gradually went away and I was able to forgive him. We spoke on the phone from time to time, and he even drove to Chattanooga from Cleveland once a year for us to spend the day together. It was only an hour trip. We could have seen each other more often, but... Vernon McNair died several years ago, but my daddy died in my heart a long, long time before then."

"I'm glad you were able to forgive your father before he died," Jack said. "Maybe it meant something to him. But you see, my mother never regretted anything she did. She didn't think she needed forgiveness for the horrible things she did, not even murder."

"Murder?"

Jack clenched his jaw. The pulse in his neck throbbed. Peggy Jo sensed the rage inside him. When she reached out and touched his arm, he flinched.

"Yeah, she might as well have put a bullet in my father's heart. It would have saved him the trouble of putting one in his brain."

Shadows created by the small fluorescent light over the sink played with the semidarkness in the den to create shadows. A hushed silence permeated the area as Peggy Jo sat beside Jack. She was speechless. He was all talked out. She curved her hand over his forearm and squeezed gently. When he didn't look at her, she wondered if it was because he couldn't.

He cleared his throat loudly, swallowed hard and got to his feet. Without saying another word, he walked out of the den and into the kitchen, then stood at the back door and stared into the yard. Peggy Jo gave him a few minutes alone in the other room before she joined him. She chose not to speak as she went straight to the man whose pain had captured her heart in a way his charm never could have. Her only thought to comfort Jack, she slipped her arms around his waist, hugged him to her and laid her head on his back. That simple, consoling gesture told him what her words alone could never say. Slowly, almost as if he were fighting an inner battle, Jack turned to her, then grabbed her and held her close, burying his face against her shoulder.

"Ah, darling, what is it about you?" he whispered the words against her neck as he lifted his head.

"Jack, I—"

He covered her mouth with his in a hungry, devouring action that took her breath away. She didn't even think about resisting. She couldn't have, even if she'd wanted to. Somehow they had connected on a deeply emotional basis while sharing stories of their pasts. Each had allowed the other brief glimpses into their souls and in doing so had shared an intimacy as profound on a spiritual level as love-making was on physical level. It seemed only appropriate that one would lead to the other, that the physical would simply be an affirmation of the spiritual.

She realized that Jack would probably laugh if she told him what she was thinking. He'd say something typically male, like "Darling, all I want is to get into your pants." But she knew better. And if he were completely honest with himself, he did, too.

Peggy Jo had known, in her heart of hearts, that this day

would come. Despite all her denials of never wanting another man in her life, of preferring to avoid the complications sexual relationships brought into a person's life, she had feared that someday some irresistible man would tempt her beyond reason. She had gone through years of therapy after her divorce from Buck, learning by slow degrees how to recover emotionally from having endured three and a half years of brutality from a man who had once vowed to love and cherish her. So, she was years beyond being ready for lovemaking. She usually didn't like to be touched, didn't really trust men enough to allow one the simple intimacy that seemed so natural and right with Jack. Her body ached with a need so desperate that she almost cried when his big hand slid inside her robe, covered her breast and kneaded softly.

She whimpered with longing when he removed his mouth from hers, then kissed a trail across her jaw and down her neck. His mouth halted at the top button on her gown. He brought his hand up from her breast to undo every button, from neck to belly. With that accomplished, he eased the robe from her shoulders and it dropped to the floor behind her. His other hand clamped down on her hip and pulled her toward him. She drew in a deep breath when she felt his erection thrusting against her. Before she could do more than lay her hands on his chest, he rubbed himself against her, wordlessly asking her to separate her thighs so he could settle himself against her mound.

Like a madwoman she grabbed the hem of his T-shirt and jerked it up to his armpits, revealing his hairy chest and stomach. When she tugged on the thin cotton garment, he released her long enough to lift his arms into the air to assist her in removing it. She flung the white T-shirt aside and placed her hands on his naked chest. He was a beautiful sight. Wide shoulders, muscular arms and thick swirls of dark brown hair covering his chest. She wanted to see all of him, every rock-hard inch. And she wanted to touch him everywhere.

While she caressed his upper torso, familiarizing herself with his neck, shoulders, chest, belly and tiny male nipples, he spread apart her gown, just enough to reveal her left breast. He cupped and then lifted the full, soft globe and at the same time lowered his head until his lips met her breast. He flicked the nipple with the tip of his tongue and groaned deep in his throat. When fierce sucking replaced the tantalizing flicks, she cried out as her body vibrated with preparatory shock waves and moisture flooded her femininity. And all the while his other hand caressed her buttocks.

Peggy Jo explored Jack's back, lovingly at first, then she raked her nails over his flesh, her actions those of a woman in need. He returned to her mouth, devouring, while he crushed her naked breast against his bare chest and pressed his arousal against the cradle of her thighs.

When she reached out and slipped her fingers inside the fly of his pajama bottoms, he grabbed her hand and stilled it over his crotch. "Be very sure this is what you want," he told her. "Once you touch me, there won't be any going back. Do you understand?"

She nodded, her breath quick and ragged with desire.

"Say it," he demanded. "Tell me that you want me, so there'll be no doubts later that this was what you wanted."

"I want you, Jack."

That was all she had to say. He not only released her hand, but he shucked off his pajama bottoms and stood before her totally naked. She gasped at the sight of him. Big. Bold. And ready.

"It's just sex, isn't it?" she asked, half-afraid he'd say yes and equally afraid he'd say no.

"It's whatever you want it to be, darling."

While her mind tried to control her sex-starved body long enough to make a rational decision, Jack walked her backward toward the den, his hands caressing her arms, his lips nipping at her neck. She bumped into the kitchen wall, which halted their return to the den. Jack pinned her there against the wall, then swept down to consume her mouth with his. He deepened the ravenous kiss when she parted her lips, invited him inside and put her own tongue into play. Heat spread through her like a wildfire, burning her from inside out. This sexual frenzy was an unknown element, one she had never before experienced. It was gloriously exhilarating and at the same time frightening in its intensity.

When she realized that Jack felt what she felt, that uncontrollable desire dominated his actions just as it did hers, she should have been afraid of him, of all that raw, masculine power. But she wasn't. Because this was Jack. And Jack would never hurt her.

He cursed softly as he shoved her gown up her leg until he could grab her naked buttocks with both hands and grind his sex against her. "You need a bed," he told her. "I should wait...but I want you now."

Her body wept with need, begging for release, longing for a fulfillment that it somehow knew only Jack could provide. She grabbed his shoulders to keep her weak knees from buckling and gave herself over completely to the urgent, age-old message encoded in her female brain. This man was her mate. She must take him into her body and procreate.

*Procreate!*

Peggy Jo gasped. What was she thinking? She was on the verge of having unprotected sex with a man she'd known only a few days.

"Jack!"

His fingers slid up and inside her. She cried out with pure pleasure. "Ah, darling, you're so ready."

"No, I'm not," she said breathlessly. "I mean, you're not...we're not."

"You can't change your mind. Not now." He all but whimpered.

"I haven't changed my mind. Not exactly. It's just...I'm not on the pill. And...and you don't have a—"

"Damn!" He heaved a deep sigh. "Yeah, I do have something. Upstairs. In my duffel bag."

"Oh."

"Now, Peggy Jo, don't go getting the wrong idea," he said. "I do not make a habit of having sex with my female clients. It's just I'm the type of guy who is always prepared. I'm always careful to protect myself and the lady I'm with. It's just that tonight...with you...I got a little more carried away than usual."

She shoved him, just enough to put some space between them, then she looked him over from head to...but her gaze never made it to his feet. It stopped on his erection. Merciful heavens, he was standing there in the middle of her kitchen, stark naked with an impressive arousal, and he seemed totally nonplussed by the fact. Obviously, he was a man quite comfortable with his own body.

Peggy Jo burst into laughter. The situation somehow struck her as funny.

"What the hell's the matter with you?" he asked. "Why are you laughing?"

"I'm not laughing at you. I'm laughing about us."

"Well, darling, I'm not in a laughing mood." He eased toward her, closing the minuscule gap between them. "I'm in the mood for loving." He brushed the back of his hand across her cheek and down her throat.

She closed her eyes, savoring his touch. Where she had only recently shied away from a man's touch, she now longed for Jack's hands on her body.

"Let's go up to my room." He indicated the direction with his head.

She kissed his nose. "Don't you think you'd better put

on your pajama bottoms first, just in case we wake Hetty when we go upstairs.''

He glanced down at his nakedness and chuckled. ''Damn, woman, you've got me so hot and bothered that I'm not thinking straight.''

''Then it's a good thing I am.'' She adjusted her gown, covered her naked breast and redid several buttons.

''You won't be, once I get you in my bed.'' Jack left her long enough to find his pajama bottoms and T-shirt. He put them on, then picked up her robe off the den floor and motioned to her. ''Let's go.''

When she came to him, he draped the robe around her shoulders, then slid his arm around her waist and led her out of the den. They walked side by side up the wide stairs that creaked softly with each step they took.

''Old houses creak and groan,'' she whispered. ''Hetty and Wendy are used to the sounds. They won't wake up.''

He nodded but didn't slow his pace. He ushered her upstairs and into his room, then locked the door behind them. He took a long, hard look at her, raking his gaze over every inch of her.

''Would you take off your gown and let me look at you?'' he asked.

*Oh, gee, I can't do this,* Peggy Jo thought. He was asking an awful lot of her, to expose herself completely for his inspection. It wasn't that she was ashamed of her body or thought herself ugly. Counseling and years of struggling with self-esteem issues had convinced her that all the horrible, cruel things Buck had said to her and about her were unfounded. No, she wasn't slim and she wasn't the most beautiful woman in the world, but men found her attractive. She could have had her pick of quite a few admirers.

''You aren't getting shy on me now, are you, darling?''

''You first, okay?''

He grinned. That sinfully enticing grin that heated her blood. ''No problem.'' He removed his T-shirt and pajamas and tossed them aside. Without the least bit of modesty and totally without embarrassment, he stood boldly, proudly before her.

*He's waiting for you,* she reminded herself. "Turn the overhead light off first."

He did as she requested, which left only the bedside lamp still burning. She knocked the robe from her shoulders and let it fall to the floor. His gaze met and locked with hers.

"Shouldn't you get the…the…protection out of your duffel bag?" she asked.

"Sure, I'll do it now, if that's what you want."

He went straight to the closet, opened the door and reached inside to remove his bag. She listened but didn't watch while he unzipped the bag and rummaged around inside.

"What now?" he asked as he came over to her.

"You're asking me?" She made herself look at him. "You're the one with all the experience, the one who carries a—" She just then noticed the box of condoms he held in his hand. "That's a whole box of condoms."

He grinned sheepishly. "You never know, we might need more than one."

More than one! Did he mean that he planned to make love to her more than once? Of course that's what he meant. She let out a long, low sigh, not realizing until that moment that she'd been holding her breath.

"Jack, I'm having second thoughts about this," she said. "I shouldn't be doing this, not with Hetty and Wendy in the house."

"They'll never know."

"And you and I just met a few days ago."

"What better way to get to know each other," he countered.

"I haven't had sex since…not in a long time. And when I had sex, I didn't like it all that much."

"You'll like it with me."

That's what she was afraid of. More than anything else. More than revealing her naked body. More than compromising her principles. More than taking a chance Hetty might suspect what was going on. She was terrified that she might like sex with Jack. She already had feelings for him. Strong feelings that she couldn't control. If the sex was good...ah, damn!

Jack held out his hand, and for just a minute she thought he was going to grab her. But instead he beckoned to her as he backed up toward the bed. When he sprawled out in the middle of the bed, he wiggled his index finger in a come-to-me gesture.

With a courage born of desire, Peggy Jo grabbed either side of her gown and lifted it up and over her head. She closed her eyes and prayed that Jack would like what he saw, that she hadn't been wrong to put her trust in this man. She had never been this exposed, this vulnerable with a man since her divorce. But this man wasn't Buck. He was Jack. And Jack was a good man.

*Jacky-boy, you'd better say and do all the right things,* he cautioned himself, as his gaze slowly scanned Peggy Jo's body. His sex grew harder and heavier in response to the visual stimulation of her nakedness. She was round and voluptuous. Womanly. And beautiful. Very beautiful.

"Disappointed?" she asked defensively.

"Darling, I'm practically speechless."

"Oh?"

"Looking at you makes me glad I'm a man."

"Mmm..."

"Peggy Jo, you take my breath away you're so beautiful."

Tears glistened in her eyes. Her round, firm breasts rose and fell with her labored breaths. She all but ran to him, then hesitated for one, long, heart-stopping moment. He grabbed her arm and pulled her down into the bed with him.

Jack was determined to make it right for her. To show her how good it could be between a man and a woman.

# Chapter 11

Peggy Jo knew that she'd probably regret what she was doing. Later. In the morning. In the harsh light of day when reality returned. But this was now, in the moment, and her mind wasn't in charge. Her body was. And her body yearned for Jack, demanded his touch, longed to become one with him. All the reasons she shouldn't be doing this didn't seem important. She was thirty-four years old, and this was the first time in her life that she'd ever wanted a man with such desperate passion. She didn't know what to say or do. Confusion threatened to dampen her ardor. During sex, Buck had wanted her to lie still and keep quiet until he finished. Only when he was beating her did he want a response.

Seeming to sense her uncertainty and sudden reluctance, Jack took charge. He removed a condom from the box and ripped open the individual packet. Peggy Jo watched in fascination as he prepared himself for their lovemaking. For a split second she allowed the sight of his overwhelming masculinity to intimidate her.

Easing himself up on one elbow and cradling his head with his open palm, he reached out, lifted a long lock of hair from her chest and placed it over her shoulder. His hands were huge, his fingertips slightly rough. But there was such gentleness in his touch that she trusted him not to hurt her.

She looked up at him and smiled. "I want it to be good, Jack. Please. It was never—"

He silenced her with a kiss. Tender at first. Warm and soft and sweet. She became so involved with the kiss that she barely noticed he was caressing her shoulder. But when his tongue sought entrance into her mouth, he skimmed his hand down to her elbow and his arm that draped across her body raked over her breasts. She gasped. The sensation shot through her as if she'd touched a live wire. He ravaged her mouth. She lifted one arm up and around his neck, then grabbed his biceps with her other hand. His arm bulged with steely muscles. Hard. Strong. Powerful.

When his fingertips danced between her breasts and down over her belly, she whimpered. Her nipples peaked with aching awareness. Touch me there, she wanted to scream. But his hand moved south, covering her stomach, smoothing over first one hip and then the other before easing down her right thigh and back up the left. Her feminine core throbbed, and a gush of moisture flooded the area between her legs.

Her hand tightened around his upper arm, her nails biting into his skin. She lifted her hips, seeking his hand. He forked his fingers through the triangle of curls as he shoved his other hand beneath her head to bring her mouth closer to his in a crushing kiss that robbed her of breath and all coherent thought. Feelings took over completely, and she became totally body conscious, aware of new and incredibly pleasurable sensations. Being with Jack seemed oddly familiar, as if this wasn't the first time for them, as if they had been together before. Many times. Maybe that was the reason it seemed so right. His body didn't seem like a stranger to hers.

They responded to each other with equal passion, neither the aggressor. Or perhaps both were aggressors. While the kiss continued, he familiarized himself with her body, but with the utmost tenderness. His ragged breathing, his flushed face and sweat-dampened flesh revealed to her that he was holding back, at a great sacrifice to himself. And that fact alone made her want him all the more.

Suddenly she realized that she wanted more than his gentleness, more than his restrained touches. She wanted Jack Parker unleashed, unbound and free to take her with the need that seemed to be tearing him apart inside. Her own hunger had driven her to the point of near madness. For only madness could have erased the haunting memories from her past and liberated her so completely.

With boldness born of passion, she shoved him onto his back and came down over him, straddling his hips. When she bent down and licked his tiny nipples, he groaned and reached up to thread his fingers through her hair. But she escaped his clutches as she moved downward, her fingertips gliding over his chest and belly. When she reached his sex, she lifted her head and smiled at him before raking a fingernail ever so gently from tip to shaft. Jack tensed. His erection jerked involuntarily. She encompassed him with her hand and pumped him slowly, carefully.

"Ah, darling, I'll give you to the count of a million to stop that."

She continued to caress him, loving the feel of his strength in her hand, but within minutes he halted her.

"I'm only up to a thousand and five," she said.

"Screw counting." His voice was ragged, indicating he was on the verge of losing control. "I can't wait any longer."

"About time," she told him and eagerly participated when he lifted her and brought her down over his sex.

She adjusted her hips, situating herself to accept him. He rammed up and into her with a force that rocked her to the core. No half measures. No slowly easing into her. When he took her, he took her completely, burying himself deeply inside her.

Her moisture cushioned him, and her body stretched to accommodate his size. Peggy Jo had never felt as complete, as whole, as she did at that very moment. She loved the feel of Jack inside her. Every fiber of her being reacted favorably to his possession.

And then he began to move. She gasped when he lifted her up and down, forcing her body to absorb the friction. With one hand on her hip, caressing softly, he guided her into action, and within minutes she set the pace. While she rode him, he concentrated on her breasts. The moment his mouth encompassed one tight nipple and sucked, her body exploded with release. Fast and furious. And unexpected. It happened so quickly, she hadn't had time to prepare herself. She went wild, riding him frantically, draining every last ounce of satisfaction from the moment. Then she went limp on top of him, her energy spent. He soothed her. Rubbed her back. Kissed her temple. Whispered her name.

And then he flipped her over onto her back and hammered into her. His big hands brought her hips upward to meet each hard, demanding lunge. She felt him tense, heard the harshness of his breath, saw the strain on his face. Realizing she had brought him to this point, her sheath clenched tightly and when he drove into her again, he groaned as if in pain. The power of his release racked his body with intense shudders.

He collapsed on top of her, big, hot and sweaty. But his weight was a delicious burden. She wrapped her arms around him and nuzzled his neck. A low, satisfied moan hummed from his throat. Without saying a word, he rolled off her, then pulled her to his side, cradling her in his arms.

They lay there, neither speaking for endless moments.

She wondered if he was as astonished by what had happened between them as she was. Had it been as extraordinary an experience for him as it had been for her or was sex always such an overwhelming event for him? When the cool night air chilled her, she remembered that she was naked. As if he had read her mind, Jack grasped the edge of the sheet and blanket which lay at the foot of the bed and dragged the covers up and over them.

"Are you all right?" he asked.

"Mmm-hmm." She didn't want to talk. All she wanted was to lie in his arms and have the moment last forever.

He lifted his head, folded his arm beneath his neck and looked at her. "We're pretty good together, aren't we, darling?"

"Unbelievably good."

"It had been a long time for you, hadn't it?"

"Since I'd had sex? Yes." She wished he wouldn't talk, wouldn't analyze what had happened between them. Reality was fast encroaching on this surreal affair. "And it was never like that before, never fulfilling for me."

"Peggy Jo—"

She pressed her hand over his mouth. "No, don't. You mustn't tell me that it was special for you, that it had never been that good for you either. I know that's not true."

"You don't know anything if you think this wasn't different for me, too."

She shoved away from him and scooted off the bed. He reached out to grab her hand, but she slipped away. Before he could get out of bed, she had picked up her gown and pulled it over her head. As she reached down on the floor for her robe, he came up behind her and wrapped his arms around her waist.

"What's the matter, Peggy Jo, can't you stand to hear the truth?" He rubbed his beard-stubbled jaw against her smooth cheek. "We've got chemistry, darling. The kind that sets the sheets on fire. You don't get that with just anybody.''

"Jack, please.''

"I thought I'd already done that,'' he teased. "Pleased you. I know for a fact that you sure did please me.'' He turned her around to face him.

"I'm glad you liked it, too,'' she said.

"Liked it? I loved it. Didn't you?''

"You know I did, but—''

"What's wrong?'' he asked. "You're not having regrets already, are you?''

"No. No regrets.''

"Then, what is it?''

"This was just sex. That's all.'' She paused, giving him time to deny her statement, to jump right in and tell her that it had been more than sex for him, as it had been for her. When he didn't speak, she continued. "We were hot for each other. We were curious what it would be like if we made...if we had sex. Now we know. Curiosity satisfied.'' She inhaled deeply, then released her breath slowly. "So, that's the end of it. We defused the time bomb ticking between us.''

When she tried to pull away from him, he held her all the tighter. "We didn't defuse the bomb. We let it explode.''

"Okay, so we let it explode. Same thing. We did it. It's over with. We can move on.''

"Ah, I see.''

He loosened his hold on her enough that she easily escaped from him. She walked across the room but paused at the closed door and glanced over her shoulder.

"I need to get back to my room.''

*Ask me to stay. Tell me you want to hold me in your arms all night. I'll have to refuse you, but please, ask me, anyway.*

"Yeah, sure. Go.''

"Okay." Her hand hovered over the doorknob. "I...I feel as if I should say thank you."

"You already did, darling," he told her. "In every way that matters."

Heat rose up her neck and flushed her face. "I'll see you in the morning."

He grinned, but it wasn't that cocky, flirtatious grin she had become so accustomed to. It was a soft, almost sad grin.

Peggy Jo forced herself to open the door and leave his room. Once outside, she tiptoed across the hall to her own bedroom. With each step she took, she prayed she wouldn't turn around and run straight back into Jack's arms.

He stood in his open doorway and watched her until she disappeared inside her bedroom. It took every ounce of his willpower not to go after her and drag her back into his bed. With most women, it didn't matter to him whether or not they spent the night in his arms. But Peggy Jo was different. He couldn't think of anything he'd like better than to hold her close till morning. Already he was thinking about making love to her again. But she had told him in no uncertain terms that once had been enough.

*Go to bed,* he told himself. *Get some sleep. And put on your damn pajamas!*

After slipping into the pajama bottoms, he flopped in the middle of the bed, on top of the tangled sheets. He could smell Peggy Jo's unique scent. He ran his hand over the pillow where she'd rested her head.

*Jacky-boy, you underestimated the lady and overestimated yourself.* He had thought he could pleasure her and find release for his own sexual tension without becoming emotionally involved. He had done it so many times before, he'd thought it would be easy. But he hadn't counted on how responsive she would be, how completely she'd fall apart in his arms. And he sure as hell had no idea that one taste of her wouldn't be enough to satisfy him. It hadn't been ten minutes since he had her and he already wanted her again.

The way he saw it, he had two choices. One, he could stay on as her bodyguard and keep his damn hands off her. Or two, he could call Ellen first thing in the morning and ask her to send a replacement immediately.

He'd sleep on it and make his decision in the morning.

Peggy Jo stared at the clock through half-closed, bleary eyes. She rubbed her eyes, opened them fully and took a second look. My heavens, was it really ten forty-five? She seldom slept this late. When she tossed back the covers and started to get up, she moaned as the soreness in her body reminded her of why she'd overslept this morning. She had exhausted herself in Jack's bed. The man's powerful love-making had worn her out.

She couldn't stifle several more groans as she rolled out of bed. Every muscle in her body ached. And why shouldn't they? Jack's brand of lovemaking took a lot out of a woman. The smile came involuntarily to her lips. Oh, great, she was probably smiling like an idiot, like some lovesick fool. As she made her way into the bathroom and turned on the shower, she avoided even glancing at herself in the mirror. She knew what she'd see—a satisfied woman.

After stripping out of her gown, she paused for a minute. She could smell Jack's scent still on her skin, as if he had embedded himself in her flesh. A shudder of remembrance passed through her. Shaking her head to dislodge thoughts of what she'd done last night and with whom, she opened the linen closet to remove towels and a washcloth. She stepped into the tub and pulled the shower curtain closed. Standing there, with the water pelting down on her, she shut her eyes and enjoyed the steady stream of hot water.

What would she say to Jack this morning? How should she act? What would he expect? Damn! She wasn't used to having to deal with the morning after. She'd just wait and take her cue from him.

Twenty minutes later, with her hair dried and put into a ponytail, a pair of comfortable, baggy gray sweats covering her clean body, Peggy Jo went downstairs, dreading more and more with each step having to face Jack.

She found him sitting beside Wendy at the computer desk, the two of them engrossed in a computer game. Hetty sat in the corner rocking chair, knitting away on an afghan, a sleeping Fur Ball on his pillow beside the chair. The moment Peggy Jo entered the room, three sets of eyes focused on her.

"Well, if it isn't our sleeping beauty," Jack said, his gaze skimming over her leisurely, the perusal implying a certain familiarity with her body.

"Hi, Mommy," Wendy said. "Did you get your nap out? Jack and me checked on you twice, but you were still asleep both times. One time you were snoring and Jack said that was because you were so tired." Wendy giggled.

Jack winked at Peggy Jo. When her cheeks flamed with heat, she cupped her face with her hands.

Hetty glanced up from her knitting. "Are you feeling all right? You looked flushed to me. Do you have a fever?"

Oh, she had a fever all right. A fever in her blood named Jack Parker. "No, I'm fine. Really." She patted her cheeks, slid her hands down either side of her neck and said, "It is rather warm in here, isn't it?"

"Same temperature it is every day in the house," Hetty said. "What's the matter with you? You're acting mighty peculiar."

"Nothing is wrong with me." Peggy Jo glared at Hetty. "I guess I missed breakfast, so I'll just fix myself some fresh coffee and toast some bread."

"Mommy, Jack and me—"

"Jack and I," Peggy Jo corrected as she headed into the kitchen.

"There's sausage biscuits in the oven," Hetty said. "Want me to make the coffee?"

"Jack and I want to go to town today," Wendy said. "We want to see *The Nutcracker* and then talk to Santa and go by the bakery and buy chocolate fudge."

"What?" Peggy Jo stopped dead in her tracks.

"Those two have had their heads together all morning," Hetty said. "Wendy told Jack that you had tickets to take her to see *The Nutcracker* at the Tivoli, and I told him he was welcome to take my ticket. They have the whole afternoon plotted out, so you might as well not put up a fuss. We can work on Christmas decorations here at the house tomorrow and all next week."

"Oh, I'm sorry, sweetpea. I'd forgotten all about the play at the Tivoli. Of course we'll go." Peggy Jo purposely avoided even glancing at Jack. She was afraid if she looked at him, Hetty would figure out exactly what was wrong with her this morning. "But what's this about your wanting to go see Santa?"

"That was my idea," Jack said. "I talked her into it. At least once in their life, every kid should sit on Santa's lap and tell him what they want for Christmas."

"Do you really want to do that?" Peggy Jo asked her daughter.

"Yes, Mommy, I do. Jack said it would be fun and that I could pretend he was the real Santa—if there is a real Santa—and tell him my secret Christmas wish."

Peggy Jo smiled at her daughter, enjoying the excitement that glowed in the little girl's eyes.

When Wendy turned back around to the game she was playing, Peggy Jo's gaze met Jack's head-on. Her stomach knotted. Her nerves quivered. Her body instantly recalled the pleasure he had given it last night.

She swallowed as she continued staring at him. He smiled. She returned his smile. Hetty cleared her throat loudly. Peggy Jo jerked around and scurried into the kitchen.

As she removed the coffee beans from the refrigerator, Hetty came up beside her. She tried to ignore her housekeeper's presence, but when she reached for a measuring cup, Hetty grabbed her arm.

"Are you going to tell me what's going on, or do I make an educated guess and tell you?"

"Please, Hetty, leave it be. Nothing's going on," Peggy Jo said.

"Don't give me that, missy," Hetty said quietly. "Something's happened between you and Jack. And don't even think about denying it."

She'd have to tell Hetty something, anything to stop her from delving too deeply. "All right," Peggy Jo whispered. "He kissed me. There, are you satisfied?"

"And you kissed him back, didn't you?"

"Oh, all right. We kissed each other." Peggy Jo measured the coffee beans and dumped them into the coffee grinder. The sound of the machine prevented further conversation, at least temporarily.

The minute Peggy Jo removed the ground coffee from the grinder and poured it into the filter already in the coffee maker, Hetty took the pot, filled it with water and then emptied the water into the reservoir.

"Is that all that happened?" Hetty asked.

"You're being awfully nosy."

"You're being awfully secretive."

"What I did or didn't do with Jack is none of your business."

"I knew it!" Hetty's voice rose just a fraction.

"Shh. Please, lower your voice."

"Peggy Jo Riley, you slept with him, didn't you?"

No, no, a thousand times no! It wasn't possible that Hetty knew for certain what had happened. She'd just have to lie her way out of this one. No way was she going to confess to the matchmaker of the century that she and Jack had made love last night.

"Whatever gave you such a ridiculous idea?"

"Because I came downstairs to fix me some warm milk in the middle of the night. I'd woke up and couldn't go back to sleep. And I just happened to notice that Jack's bedroom door was closed. So, I checked in your room to see if you were all right, and you know what I found?"

Peggy Jo shook her head.

"I found your bed was empty and came to the logical conclusion that you were in Jack's bed with him."

Peggy Jo groaned. "It was just sex."

"Mmm-hmm."

"It was. And it isn't going to happen again. We defused the bomb. Or we exploded the bomb." Peggy Jo shook her hands in front of her in a frustrated gesture. "Oh, whatever. The point is the bomb won't go off again."

"Oh, missy, if that's what you think, you're kidding yourself. With a man like Jack, once wouldn't ever be enough. You'd just better prepare yourself for another explosion."

# *Chapter 12*

Jack hadn't voiced a protest when she'd told him she intended to drive herself to work this morning and every morning this week. She realized that doing the driving herself was a minor thing, but these days she needed to feel in control of something, even if it was only the little things. Jack had gone out ten minutes ago to start the car and let it warm up. She assumed that he also wanted to inspect the vehicle, as well as check for anything vaguely suspicious in the neighborhood. There was no point in denying the fact, even to herself, that having Jack around made her feel infinitely safer. And not just because he was a man, but because he was a professional.

Peggy Jo had successfully avoided being alone with Jack most of Saturday and Sunday. She didn't trust herself to be alone with him. Even in small doses, he was lethal to her iron-willed resolve. She still couldn't believe she'd had sex with him. But what disturbed her even more was the fact that she didn't regret what she'd done. Knowing that she could not allow it to happen again didn't immunize her against the desire that simmered below the surface, just waiting for the right moment to heat up again. Having Wendy with her as much as possible had helped keep things nonthreatening between Jack and her. But Hetty hadn't been any help at all. In fact, she had tried to find ways to put Peggy Jo and Jack alone together every chance she got.

Busying herself with constant activity had been crucial to keeping her bodyguard at arm's length. Saturday afternoon they had attended the play at the Tivoli, gone to the Northgate Mall to visit Santa and on the way home stopped by Panera Bread Bakery & Cafe. That night they had decorated the tree. On Sunday they'd spent the afternoon finishing the decorations throughout the house, and Jack had even put up the icicle lights outside. She'd been able to use Wendy as a buffer during the days, and each night she'd sought the solace and safety of her room. Jack didn't come to her, didn't bother her in any way. When he'd said goodnight Saturday and Sunday nights, he'd gone to his room and stayed there until morning.

Fortunately, her stalker didn't strike again, but she suspected he was simply lying in wait, letting her relax just enough that when he pulled his next stunt, she'd be all the more terrorized by the experience. In a rare moment when they were alone in the den last night, she had run her theory by Jack, who had agreed with her and at the same time tried to reassure her. She had pretended not to see the questions in his eyes, knowing full well that he wanted to talk to her about more personal matters. But he had not pressed her, and for that she was thankful.

Finding out from the police that neither Ross Brewster nor Chet Compton had alibis for Friday afternoon made her dread going to work this morning. They both had to know that Jack suspected them, otherwise why would Detective Gifford have questioned them? Ross had told the police that he'd been alone in his apartment studying, but there was no one who could corroborate his story. And Chet had sworn he'd left work early on Friday to do a little Christmas shopping, but he couldn't name a single person who might be able to swear to his whereabouts.

And as for the police running a check on Buck Forbes—Detective Gifford had promised Jack a report by Monday. And today was Monday. She wasn't sure she wanted to know anything about her ex-husband. Where he was living or what he was doing. The man hadn't been a part of her life in thirteen years and she wanted to keep it that way. After all, Detective Gifford was probably right when he'd asked what reason Buck would have to come back into her life to torment her now, after all these years.

Hetty rushed out into the driveway, waving her arms. Peggy Jo stopped the car and rolled down the window.

"What's wrong?"

"Nothing's wrong," Hetty said. "Mrs. Pullman just called and said you could pick up Missy's angel costume this morning since her house is right on your way."

"Okay, thanks." Peggy Jo closed the window, then glanced into the back seat at Wendy. "Can't this wait until Hetty picks you up this afternoon?"

"No, Mommy, please, let's go get it now." Her big blue eyes pleaded. "Today everybody's going to be in their costumes so we can do the play all dressed up. If I don't have Missy's angel outfit, I'll be the only one—"

"Enough said. We'll stop by the Pullman's." Peggy Jo's concession ended Wendy's pitiful whining.

When she backed the Sebring onto the street, Jack turned toward the back seat and said, "So, when's the play? You've been talking about it, but you didn't say what night it was."

"It's this Thursday." Wendy's voice held that edge of excitement and anticipation that usually only children experienced. "I'm so glad you're staying with us now, so you can come to the play. I wish Fur Ball could come, too."

"I've told you that we can't carry Fur Ball with us to the play," Peggy Jo said.

"We'll take lots of pictures and show him," Jack said. "Isn't that right, Mommy?"

"Yes, of course. And if you're very good this week and do everything you're told without a fuss, I might get one of the WLOK cameramen to come to the school Friday night and videotape the play for us."

"Oh, Mommy!" Wendy squealed. "I promise I'll be very good.

Five minutes later, they drove into the Pullmans' driveway. Before Peggy Jo even opened the door, Mrs. Pullman came outside, the angel costume in her hand. She hurried toward the car, her unbuttoned plaid flannel housecoat flapping against her as she walked into the early morning wind.

Peggy Jo got out and met her. "I'm sorry Missy has the flu. I appreciate your letting us borrow her costume. It certainly saved us from having to come up with one at the last minute."

"No problem. And I don't think you'll need to make any adjustments since our girls are almost the same size. They're both little petite dolls."

"Yes, they are." Peggy Jo grabbed the clothes hanger holding the outfit. "Thanks so much."

"You're most welcome." Mrs. Pullman glanced beyond Peggy Jo and into the car. "Is that your bodyguard? I heard he was from Atlanta, but he looks like a cowboy."

"Yes, that's him." Peggy Jo began backing away, trying to make her escape.

"Must be just terrible having to be protected night and day."

Mrs. Pullman followed Peggy Jo toward the car, her gaze riveted to Jack. Peggy Jo didn't want to be rude, but she didn't have the time to indulge this nosy woman's curiosity any more than she already had.

"We're running late," Peggy Jo said, then opened the

car door. "I have to get Wendy to school. Bye. And thanks again."

She opened the back door, hung the costume on the clothes hook, then hopped in the front seat and started the engine. As she backed out of the drive, she caught a glimpse of Mrs. Pullman still standing in her driveway.

"I love this dress," Wendy said. "And look at these wings!"

"You're going to be the most beautiful angel that ever made an appearance in a school play," Jack said. "Right, Mommy?"

"Right. The most beautiful ever."

Stopping by the Pullmans to pick up the prized costume ran them late. Peggy Jo hated being late. She prided herself on always being on time. Whenever something unexpected came up, like this morning, it tended to color the rest of her day—gray and gloomy.

"I'll go in and explain why you're late." Peggy Jo unbuckled her seat belt.

Jack hopped out of the car, opened the back door and helped Wendy out, then he removed the white diaphanous angel gown and papier-mâché wings that hung on the clothes hook above the door. Together the threesome entered the building. Wendy clasped Jack's hand tightly, and when they walked down the hall, she tugged on his hand and motioned for him to bend over so she could tell him something.

When he paused and leaned down, she whispered, "Some of the kids may think you're my daddy. I told them just because they'd never seen my daddy, didn't mean I didn't have one."

Peggy Jo pretended not to hear what her daughter had just confessed. Instead she said, "Why don't you let Jack walk you to your class while I go to the office and explain why you're late."

Wendy's little face lit up. "Oh, gee, yes, that'd be great."

Later would be soon enough to talk to Wendy and clear up, once again, any notions she had about Jack taking over the role of daddy in their household. But for now she simply didn't have the heart to reprimand her child or deny her the pleasure of letting some of the other children wonder if the man holding her hand was her daddy.

Jack remained quiet on their drive to WLOK, hoping that Peggy Jo would say something to him. But she remained silent. Apparently, she wanted to pretend that nothing had happened between them Friday night. He realized that she'd avoided being alone with him over the weekend and had kept Wendy with her as much as possible. She had to know that he wouldn't try to talk her into doing something she didn't want to do. If Friday night had been a one-night stand, then he could accept that fact. All she had to do was just tell him.

He had thought seriously about contacting Ellen and asking her to replace him with another Dundee agent, but he just couldn't bring himself to turn over this case to someone else. Besides, there were only a handful of top agents whom he'd trust to take care of Peggy Jo, and all of them were on assignments, including Dundee's three female agents. Matt O'Brien was on the west coast. Domingo Shea was in the Caribbean. Frank Latimer and Jed Tyree had both been assigned the duty of being instructors for the new Dundee recruits. Every new agent, regardless of his background, had to go through six weeks of specialized training.

If he hadn't allowed this case to become personal to him, he might find it easier to walk away. But by the same reasoning, if he hadn't let it become so personal to him, he'd have no need to walk away. He couldn't help wondering if Peggy Jo might call Ellen and ask if one of the female agents was free now. When they had met, less than a week ago, she'd been adamant about wanting him replaced as soon as possible.

The minute they parked, Jack got out and quickly came to her side of the car. She accepted his assistance, but didn't make direct eye contact with him. He stayed at her side until they reached her office, then he posted himself in a chair and watched her as she began her workday routine. Kayla had already made coffee, and she hurriedly brought Peggy Jo a cup, then glanced at him.

"Want some coffee, Mr. Parker?"

"Thanks. I can help myself."

"Kayla, have you seen Chet or Ross this morning?" Peggy Jo asked.

"Ross called to say he couldn't come in this morning," Kayla replied. "But Chet is here. He's in an awful mood, too. And he asked me to let him know when you arrived."

"He's probably really ticked off," Peggy Jo said. "I'm sure he didn't like having Detective Gifford question him."

"Why did the police question Chet?" Kayla asked. "They don't suspect him of being your stalker, do they?"

Jack could tell that Peggy Jo felt reluctant to respond, so he thought it best to do it for her. "The police are keeping tabs on several men who know Peggy Jo. Just as a precaution. No one has been accused of anything. Not yet."

"Then should I or should I not let Chet know that Peggy Jo is here? I'm going to pick up the morning mail and I might run into him."

Peggy Jo finally looked at Jack. "I think I should talk to Chet myself. Otherwise, he's going to take his frustration out on everyone else at the studio today."

"Fine," Jack told her. "Whatever you think best."

She turned to her assistant. "Stop by Chet's office and tell him I'm here and I'll come by his office before I go on the set."

"Sure thing."

The minute Kayla left, Peggy Jo entered her dressing

room. Jack followed, and when she sat down in front of the mirrored wall and began going through her supply of makeup, he walked up behind her.

"Are we ever going to talk about it?" he asked.

"About what?" She chose lipstick, eyeliner and blush, laying each item on the vanity table.

"About what happened between us on Friday night."

Without so much as blinking an eye, she said, "We wanted it. We did it. It's over. What's there to talk about?"

He clamped his hands down on the back of her chair. "That's it? That's all you have to say?"

"What do you want from me? I warned you that I'm not like the other women you've known. I'm not going to fall apart on you and beg you to—"

Jack whirled the chair around so fast that she was forced to face him. Gasping loudly, she glared up at him. For a split second he saw fear in her eyes. Damn! He hadn't meant to frighten her.

"Nobody's asking you to do any begging." He leaned over her, his gaze linking with hers as he grabbed the chair's wide armrests. "But don't pretend with me that Friday night didn't mean something to you. You may be too tough to fall apart emotionally after the fact, but you came apart in my arms when we made love."

"We had sex!"

"Is that what this is all about? You think it wasn't anything more than sex for me?"

"Just shut up about it, will you? There's no point in discussing it." She tried to force the chair to turn, but Jack wouldn't allow her to budge.

"If you're not upset about it for some reason, then why not talk about it?" He released his fierce hold on the armrests and whirled her around to face the mirror again, then brought his face down beside hers. "Take a good look, darling. You're blushing."

Shutting her eyes, she refused to look into the mirror.

She didn't want to see the two of them together. Cheek-to-cheek. "Please, Jack, just go in the other room and leave me alone for a few minutes. I'm not going to discuss what happened Friday night. As far as I'm concerned, we're both better off to forget it ever happened."

"Is that what you really want?"

She nodded her head. "Yes."

"Fine. Have it your way."

Shaking her until her teeth rattled wasn't an option. Neither was kissing her into submission. If anything happened between them again, she would have to instigate it. Never let it be said that Jack Parker got down on his knees and crawled to any woman.

He went into her office and sat in the chair behind her desk, leaving her alone in the dressing room. He watched her through the open door. She finished laying out her makeup, then got up and started to close the door.

"Leave it open," he said, his tone sharp.

"I want some privacy while I change clothes."

"I've already seen it all," he reminded her, then could have kicked himself for such a crass remark. Okay, so he was pissed at her, but that didn't mean he had to act like a jackass.

Peggy Jo slammed the door.

Why the hell did he feel as if she'd just slapped him? And why did he have the overwhelming urge to keep after her until she admitted that she would never forget their night together, that she wanted to be with him again? Because he wanted her and was having a damn difficult time accepting the fact that she apparently didn't want him.

But she did want him, didn't she? Otherwise why would she be fighting so hard to keep a barrier between them?

Kayla opened the office door and came in carrying a box of mail, which she set on her desk. "Is she getting ready?" Kayla nodded toward the closed dressing room door.

"Yeah. She wants her privacy."

Kayla nodded, then sat down behind her desk and picked up a letter opener. "I gave Chet Peggy Jo's message, but he nearly bit my head off. I've never seen him so upset. Well, maybe one other time. Right after Peggy Jo dumped him."

Jack glanced at the closed dressing room door. "How long does it usually take her to get ready?"

"Not long. Why? You aren't concerned about her being in there alone are you? Don't be. The only other door into that room stays locked."

"Who has a key?"

"Who has a…well, I do. And of course, Peggy Jo does. And security does. I guess that's it."

Jack heaved a sigh of relief, then got up, crossed the room and poured himself a cup of coffee. Afterward, he propped his hip on the side of Peggy Jo's desk, lifted the coffee to his lips and while he sipped on the hot liquid, he stared at the closed door. Damn stubborn, infuriating woman!

Peggy Jo changed into a dark-purple wool suit and applied the makeup that would cover most of her freckles and give her plain features a more glamorous look. As she picked up the tube of lipstick and brought it to her lips, her hand trembled. Damn, Jack Parker. He had turned her world upside down. Now he wanted to discuss what had happened between them Friday night. There was no point in talking about the situation, because there was no situation. She had allowed herself to become just one more woman in a long line of women who had succumbed to Jack's charm. She had prided herself on being smarter, on being much too smart to fall for a sexy smile and a pair of broad shoulders.

Just as she steadied her hand enough to put on a coat of plum lipstick, the side door of her dressing room opened. She gasped in surprise because she always kept that door locked. Chet Compton stood in the doorway, his eyes narrowed to slits and his jaw tight.

"I was hoping I'd find you alone in here." Chet entered the dressing room, then closed the door behind him and pocketed the key.

"Jack is outside in my office," she said.

"No need to involve him," Chet told her. "This is between you and me."

"I want you to leave now. Otherwise I will call Jack."

Chet rushed her, and before she could say more, he grabbed her, pulled her out of the chair and slapped his hand over her mouth. She squirmed, but he held her securely.

"Hell, Peggy Jo, why'd you have to sic the police on me? You know I'd never do anything to hurt you." He nuzzled her neck with his nose. "You know how I feel about you. I'd be so good to you. If you'd just give us a chance, honey, we'd make a great team."

She maneuvered her mouth just enough so she could bite down on his hand. The minute her teeth sank into his skin, he yelped and jerked his hand away from her mouth.

"Jack!" she screamed.

"Damn it! There's no need to call him."

"You're right." Peggy Jo elbowed Chet in the stomach, then followed that move by kneeing him in the groin. "I just called him for backup."

Growling in pain, he released her immediately as he doubled over, then cursed loudly. Before Chet recovered from Peggy Jo's attack, Jack stormed into the room, assessed the situation and, just as Chet lifted his head, Jack landed a hard right blow directly to his jaw. Chet hit the floor with a thud. Kayla rushed through the door.

"What happened?" She looked down at Chet. "How did he get in here?"

"He had a key," Peggy Jo said, then walked over and

looked down at Chet. "He was upset about being questioned by the police."

Jack bent down and helped a moaning Chet to his feet. "Kayla, call Ted Wilkes and ask him to come help Mr. Compton back to his office."

"I can get...back to...my office.." Stunned and slightly winded, Chet jerked away from Jack. "Without any help."

"Should I call the police, too?" Kayla asked, then when Chet growled, she jumped and eased backward, out of the dressing room and into the office.

"No, don't bother," Peggy Jo said.

"Are you sure you don't want to file charges against him?" Jack glowered at Chet.

"I'm sure." Peggy Jo focused her gaze on the station manager. "As long as you stay away from me and don't pull another stunt like this, I won't press charges. Do I make myself clear?"

"Yeah," Chet said. "Very clear."

As Chet left the dressing room through Peggy Jo's office, he grumbled the word bitch quite clearly. When Jack made a move to go after him, Peggy Jo grabbed Jack's arm.

"Let him go."

Jack glanced at her hand on his arm. Realizing the intimacy of a mere touch between two lovers, Peggy Jo released him immediately.

"We'll get the lock on that door changed today," Jack said. "Two keys only. One for you and one for me."

"That's not a bad idea." Peggy Jo checked her watch. "I'm running late. I should have been on the set five minutes ago. I can't seem to catch up this morning." She hurriedly reapplied her lipstick and ran a brush through her hair. "That'll have to do. Let's go."

Jack followed her out of the dressing room and into her office, where she picked up a copy of the questions she planned to discuss with today's guests on *Self-Made Woman*. She had booked two child psychologists with different views on celebrating Christmas and how parents should deal with children's demands for more and more presents. Then she would end the show with a segment on a theme that she was carrying through from a week before Thanksgiving until the final episode of the year—how to eat well but wisely during the holidays.

As she walked past Kayla's desk, she paused. "Call Dr. Harper and Dr. Herbert and remind them to be here at eleven o'clock sharp. And please, when they get here, stay with them and keep them apart. I don't want them using up all their energy on a preshow argument."

"Will do." Grinning, Kayla continued opening the morning mail and sorting it into stacks.

Jack escorted Peggy Jo out of her office and down the hall. They had gotten less than ten feet away when Kayla let out a bloodcurdling scream.

Peggy Jo turned to run back up the hall, but Jack grabbed her arm. "Stay here," he said. "I'll see what's wrong."

Kayla's continued cries echoed through the corridor as Jack ran toward Peggy Jo's office.

# Chapter 13

Jack found Kayla standing up behind her desk, her eyes watering and her nose streaming as she coughed uncontrollably. When he approached her, she whimpered but seemed unable to speak. He grabbed her shoulder.

"What's wrong? What happened?"

She pointed toward her desk as she continued coughing. Jack surveyed the desktop, noting the stacks of opened mail had been scattered. Lying in the middle of the disarray was a small pile of a finely ground, brown substance. Suddenly Jack's eyes and nose began burning. Damn! He tightened his hold on Kayla and dragged her out of the office. The minute she saw them, Peggy Jo came running.

"What's wrong?" She looked frantically from Jack to Kayla.

"Take her in the ladies' room and help her wash her face. Make sure she splashes water into her eyes and up her nose. I'm fixing to do the same. We've both breathed in some sort of poison."

"Oh, God!"

"Go. Now!" Jack bellowed the order, then raced to the men's room. As soon as he washed his face, he realized the water wasn't helping any. He managed to make his way out of the rest room and up the hall to the next office. The local news anchor's secretary looked up from her desk.

"Call security and have them close off Peggy Jo Riley's office," Jack said. "And tell them not to go inside. Then bring Ms. Riley's car around to the back entrance and have one of the security guards meet us there. After that, call the police."

"Sir, you're Ms. Riley's bodyguard, aren't you?"

"Damn right. Now stop wasting time and make that call!"

"Yes, sir."

By the time he got Peggy Jo and Kayla outside to the car, Ted Wilkes was waiting for them. Good thing, too, Jack thought, because his eyes were watering like crazy and he was coughing his head off. He wasn't in much shape to protect anybody at the moment.

"Wilkes, I need one of your men to go with us to the emergency room," Jack managed to say between coughs. "And make sure Detective Gifford has been contacted. I want him to meet us at—" He glanced at Peggy Jo. "What's the name of the damn hospital?"

"Erlanger," Peggy Jo said. "Jack, get in the car. Now!"

"Wilkes," Jack called as he crawled into the back seat, while Kayla got in the front. "Don't let anybody near Peggy Jo's office."

"I've got Phil stationed by the door, and I'm going with y'all," Ted Wilkes replied. "We've already called the police. Gifford is meeting us at the E.R. and he's sending somebody over here."

"Fine. Get in," Peggy Jo said as she slid behind the wheel.

The minute Ted hopped into the back seat with Jack, she shifted the car into gear and roared out of the back parking area. Jack held his breath as Peggy Jo pressed her hand down on the horn and raced through downtown Chattanooga traffic, running a couple of stop signs and several red lights.

Detective Gifford entered Peggy Jo's office the following morning carrying a travel mug of coffee and looking as if he'd just gotten out of bed. His bleary eyes focused on Jack's dark sunglasses.

"You're damn lucky you didn't get any closer to that stuff," Gifford said. "By the way, how's the girl... Gayla...Kayla? I understand she actually touched the stuff."

"The doctor told us she'll be fine," Peggy Jo said. "Her breathing has cleared up, but her eyes aren't quite back to normal. She's taking the rest of the week off, as much to recuperate emotionally as physically."

"Yeah, I can imagine." Gifford pulled a chair up to Peggy Jo's desk and slumped down into it, then rummaged around inside his overcoat pocket and pulled out a sheet of paper. "Got the lab report back."

Jack rose from where he'd been sitting on the edge of the desk. Peggy Jo had tried her best to get him to stay at her house and had even offered to cancel today's show, but Jack had adamantly refused. Damn stubborn man! His only concession to having a severe eye irritation was wearing dark glasses to shield them from light and to conceal their bloodshot appearance.

"And just what can you tell us about the substance Kayla dumped out of the envelope addressed to Peggy Jo?" Jack asked.

Gifford scanned the report. "First of all there were no identifiable fingerprints, other than Kayla's, on the envelope. The address was hand-printed in black ink. The envelope itself was the kind you can buy anywhere. We're running a DNA test, just in case there's any saliva on the flap or the stamp, but we don't expect to find anything.

"Now as to the chemical inside the envelope—that brownish powder was Malathion, which is used to wipe out bugs on lawns and plants. There were also trace amounts of—" he glanced down at the report again "—capsicum, which is a component in pepper spray."

"A nice little surprise package," Jack said, a grumbling agitation evident in his voice. "Nothing deadly, unless consumed, but poisonous enough upon breathing to cause eye irritation and minor breathing problems for anyone coming into close contact with it."

"I'm sure he was hoping I'd open the envelope myself." Peggy Jo felt guilty about what had happened, guilty that Kayla and Jack had suffered at the hands of her stalker.

"Maybe he was. Maybe he wasn't," Jack said. "But either way, he knew that if you or someone in your employ opened the envelope, he'd get his point across. He can hurt you and those near you. This was just a warning. He's getting more deadly."

"Parker's right," Gifford said. "This guy isn't going to back down. He's going to eventually move in for the kill."

"Damn, Gifford!" Jack's words roared from his scratchy throat.

"Sorry, Ms. Riley," Gifford said. "I'm a plainspoken man. You're in danger and there's no point in pretending otherwise."

"I understand." Peggy Jo couldn't ignore the truth. Someone hated her enough to torment her, to harm those around her, and probably enough to want to see her dead. "Recently you said that you didn't think my daughter or my housekeeper were in danger. What do you think now?"

"My guess is that he won't harm them unless they're in the way when he's trying to get to you," Gifford said. "But you can't be a hundred percent sure when you're dealing with a nutcase like we have here."

"Thanks for sharing this report with us." Peggy Jo held out her hand to the detective.

He shook her hand. "By the way, we found out where your ex-husband is living."

"What?"

"Where?" Jack asked.

"He's living in Sale Creek. Not that far away. He's working for a man who owns a nursery and greenhouse out there. Forbes's record is clean...except for a few domestic-violence charges. Seems Buck's got a thing for beating up women. In the past thirteen years, three former girlfriends and an ex-wife filed charges and then dropped them. His third wife recently left him and took her two children and is living in a shelter right now."

"Poor woman," Peggy Jo whispered.

Jack eased up beside her so quietly that she wasn't aware of his presence until she felt the weight of his big hand as it splayed across her back. At first she tensed when he touched her, then when she reminded herself that this was Jack—gentle, caring, understanding Jack—she relaxed.

"We appreciate the information," Jack said.

"Yeah, well, I'm just sorry that we didn't take this problem more seriously from the beginning." Gifford looked directly at Peggy Jo. "We're taking it seriously now, Ms. Riley. And so is the FBI."

"The FBI?" she glanced from Gifford to Jack.

"Yeah, I got a call from an Agent McNamara this morning. He said he was flying into Chattanooga today to head up the FBI's investigation into this case."

"Good ole Sawyer." Jack grinned.

"I take it that he's a friend of yours?" Gifford asked.

"He's an acquaintance," Jack replied.

"Let's hope he can help us." Gifford headed for the door, paused momentarily and glanced over his shoulder. "Don't let her out of your sight for a minute."

"I don't intend to." Jack maneuvered his hand across

Peggy Jo's back and around her waist, then pulled her up against him. "If this guy wants to get to her, he'll have to come through me first."

By that afternoon Jack had removed his sunglasses. His eyes felt much better. Only a slight irritation remained. Peggy Jo had rescheduled the guests from yesterday's show, and today's segment had gone off without a hitch. She had called to check on Kayla again, and they'd both been relieved to know that the young woman wanted to return to work on Thursday. For the second day in a row Ross Brewster hadn't shown up for work. He had called in sick this morning. Jack couldn't help wondering if the boy was running scared with good reason or if the police had frightened him so much that he was simply steering clear of Peggy Jo altogether.

Peggy Jo came out of her dressing room, two apples in her hands, and tossed one of the apples to Jack. "Midafternoon snack," she said. "I'd prefer a couple of doughnuts, but I'm being good and watching my girlish figure." She patted her hip and laughed.

"I happen to like your womanly figure," Jack said.

She bit into the apple, chewed and swallowed, all the while her gaze connected to his. He tossed his apple into the air and caught it, then lifted it to his mouth and took a bite. He had hoped she'd respond to his comment about her figure, but she didn't take the bait. Apparently she had decided not to let him involve her in any personal conversation about the two of them.

"I'm thinking about sending Wendy and Hetty to my cousin's farm in Spring City," she said. "I had planned to take Wendy up there for a few days after Christmas, but with the way things are here, I wonder if Wendy's safe."

"Getting them out of town might not be a bad idea. When were you thinking of sending them?"

"As soon as Christmas break begins. In two weeks."

"You might want to think about doing it sooner."

"Why? Do you know something that I don't?" she asked.

Jack shook his head. "No, not really. Just call it a gut feeling."

"About my stalker?"

"He's going to strike again. Soon. Then he'll back off and wait a few days before he makes another move. If Wendy or Hetty are in the way... Protecting you would be easier if I didn't have to worry about them."

"I can't send Wendy away before the school play this Thursday. It would break her heart if she didn't get to be an angel."

"Then let's make plans for Hetty and her to leave over the weekend." Jack considered several different ways of distracting Peggy Jo's stalker so that he wouldn't be aware of Wendy and Hetty's departure. "I'll need to call in another Dundee agent to help us get them out of Chattanooga."

Before Peggy Jo could respond, Jack sensed someone's presence, then heard a knock at the door. Peggy Jo gasped. Another knock. Jack crossed the room and opened the door.

"Sawyer." Jack grasped the FBI agent's hand. "Come on in. Detective Gifford said you'd called him this morning."

"Yeah, I did a little finagling so I could take this case myself instead of sending a flunky down here."

Sawyer McNamara had the smooth, polished look of a high-powered businessman, all Mr. *GQ* in his dark tailor-made suit, Italian loafers, tan overcoat and leather briefcase. Unless you looked right into his stern, calculating blue eyes, you'd never suspect that hidden beneath the civilized facade beat the heart of a dangerous warrior. But Jack had seen Sawyer in action. Cool under fire. Deadly in his unemotional ability to execute battle plans.

"Peggy Jo, I'd like to introduce Sawyer McNamara," Jack said.

"Ms. Riley." Sawyer held out his hand as he approached Peggy Jo. "I'm pleased to meet you, ma'am, but I'm sorry it's under these circumstances."

Peggy Jo came out from behind her desk to shake Sawyer's hand. "Thank you for coming, Mr. McNamara. Jack has told me that the FBI might be able to help us."

"We'll sure do what we can." Sawyer laid his briefcase on her desk, then snapped open the locks. "I have the FBI's profile our psycholinguistics expert put together after reading your stalker's letters and studying all the pertinent information. And while I had a stopover at the Atlanta airport earlier today, Ellen sent a Dundee agent out there to bring me the profile their man came up with."

A knot of apprehension formed in Jack's gut. "Have you had a chance to read both reports?"

"Sure have. And guess what?"

"What?" Peggy Jo asked.

"Both experts came up with similar psychological profiles on the stalker," Jack said.

"Bingo." The corners of Sawyer's mouth twitched, but he didn't smile as he removed two manila file folders. "I compared the two reports on the plane ride over from Atlanta."

"Want to share the findings with us?" Jack glanced at the folders.

"Our experts think we're dealing with a man who blames Ms. Riley personally for something bad that's happened in his life. He's the type of man who holds grudges and he's prone to violence. While he hates Ms. Riley, he's also sexually attracted to her. He's probably had a series of bad relationships. Might or might not be married, but isn't happy in whatever relationships he's had with women. High school education, but not college. At least they concluded that from studying his writing skills. Agewise, they think he's over twenty-five, but under forty.''

Glancing at Peggy Jo, Jack noted how suddenly she'd gone pale. ''Does this description remind you of anyone?''

''Yes. My ex-husband. Everything Agent McNamara said describes Buck.''

''Hmm.'' Sawyer handed the file folder to Jack. ''Can we eliminate any suspects because of the profile?''

''Yeah, our top two guys,'' Jack replied. ''Both men work here at WLOK. Ross Brewster is only twenty, he's attending college and he has no history of violence. Then there's Chet Compton, the station manager. He's the right age and doesn't exactly score with the ladies, but he's got a college degree. However, I'd say he's the type to hold a grudge.''

''We won't completely rule out either man,'' Sawyer said. ''But for now, I think we'll concentrate on the ex-husband. Do you happen to know where he is now? I'd like to pay him a little visit and introduce myself.''

''Better you than me,'' Jack said, fury rising inside him at the thought of confronting Peggy Jo's ex. He'd find it difficult not to beat the guy senseless for his past sins.

''Detective Gifford found out that Buck is living in Sale Creek, which is about a forty-minute drive from here,'' Peggy Jo said. ''But why would Buck come after me now? We've been divorced for thirteen years, and I haven't heard anything from him in all this time.''

''We can't be sure it's your ex-husband,'' Sawyer told her. ''There's a chance that your stalker is someone you don't even know. He could be some guy who's watched your TV show, gotten pissed off by something you've said and decided to come after you.''

''Thinking it's someone I don't know is just as frightening as believing it's someone I do know.'' Peggy Jo frowned, anxiety obvious in her expression.

''I'll call the police station and talk to Gifford,'' Sawyer said. ''I'd like to get the information he has on Buck Forbes so I can pay Mr. Forbes a friendly visit in the morning.''

''Where are you staying in case I need to get in touch with you?'' Jack asked.

''I've booked a room at the Choo Choo,'' Sawyer replied. ''I rented a car and came straight here from the airport, so I'll have to call you at Ms. Riley's later and give you the room number.''

''Mr. McNamara, why don't you come home with us for dinner?'' Peggy Jo offered Sawyer a gracious smile. ''I can call Hetty and tell her to expect a guest tonight.''

Jack didn't like her smiling at Sawyer that way. He might get the wrong idea and think Peggy Jo was fair game. *Damn it, Jacky-boy, what's gotten into you? That's exactly what she is—fair game. She's not wearing anybody's brand. She doesn't belong to you or to any other man.*

''Why thank you, ma'am,'' Sawyer replied. ''I'd enjoy a home-cooked meal for a change.''

''I've pretty much finished here for the day.'' Peggy Jo glanced at Jack. ''Why don't we follow Mr. McNamara over to the Choo Choo so he can register and then he can follow us home.''

''Please, call me Sawyer.''

Peggy Jo giggled. Damn her, she giggled. Jack didn't like the way this friendly association was developing.

''Only if you call me Peggy Jo.''

Jack clamped his hand down on Sawyer's shoulder, but looked right at Peggy Jo. ''Why don't you call Hetty, then finish up in here. I need to speak to Sawyer privately for a couple of minutes.''

He didn't give her a chance to reply before he ushered the FBI agent out into the hall and backed him up against the wall.

''What the hell was that all about?'' Jack asked.

Sawyer knocked Jack's hand from his shoulder and straightened his trench coat by tugging on the lapels. ''I didn't know you were personally involved with Ms. Riley.''

''I'm not!''

''Then what's the problem?''

*Yeah, Jacky-boy—what's the problem? Why do you care that Sawyer's putting the moves on Peggy Jo and she's responding favorably.*

''Okay, so I am,'' Jack said.

''You're what?'' Sawyer asked with a straight face, but a devilish glimmer appeared in his eyes.

''I am personally involved with Peggy Jo.''

''Say no more.'' Sawyer held up his hands in a don't-get-bent-out-of-shape gesture. ''Believe me, all I was doing was being friendly.''

''Yeah, sure you were.''

''Look, Jack, it's none of my business, but do you think it's smart to become personally involved with a client?''

''You're right—it's none of your business.'' Jack heaved a deep sigh. ''And, yeah, I know it's not a smart move on my part.''

Peggy Jo emerged from her office, closed the door, locked it and then walked over to Jack and Sawyer. ''Ready?''

''Yes,'' the two men replied simultaneously.

As they walked down the corridor and out of the building, Jack stayed at Peggy Jo's side, his hand resting at the base of her spine.

Rain clouds had moved in, darkening the sky to a sooty gray. A cold November wind cut right through to the bone. The threesome hurried out into the parking lot, but just as Sawyer separated from them to go to his rental car, Peggy Jo stopped dead still.

''Oh, my God, no!''

Jack had been looking right and left, but now he focused his attention straight ahead, at Peggy Jo's Sebring. Or something vaguely resembling her car. The convertible hood had been slashed repeatedly, leaving large gaping wounds in the material. The body of the silver Chrysler had been scratched, leaving ugly marks the entire length of the vehicle, and every window had been smashed.

Standing only a few feet away from the Sebring, a terrified look on his face, Ross Brewster shook his head back and forth, the motion an obvious denial.

"What the hell?" Jack grabbed Peggy Jo's arm. "Go straight over there to Sawyer."

"But, Jack—"

"Do what I say!"

When she headed toward Sawyer, he met up with her and called out to Jack. "What's going on? Is that Peggy Jo's car?"

"Yeah, I think we just might have caught the culprit red-handed," Jack said.

Ross froze to the spot, not moving a muscle as Jack zeroed in on him. Damn stupid boy. Did he think he could vandalize a car in the middle of the afternoon on a busy downtown street and not get caught?

"I didn't do it, Mr. Parker." Tears welled up in Ross's eyes. "I swear to God, I didn't do it. I just got here a couple of minutes ago and saw Peggy Jo's car. I was coming in to tell you when I saw y'all coming out of the studio."

"Why should I believe you?" Jack asked.

"Because I'm telling the truth. Honest I am."

"Fine. You can tell that to Detective Gifford when he gets here," Jack said. "But for now, you can come inside with us and tell it to Agent McNamara."

"Who's Agent McNamara?" Ross asked.

"See that guy over there with Peggy Jo? He's Sawyer McNamara, an FBI agent."

"FBI?" Ross went white as a sheet. He moaned softly and then fainted dead away.

"I'll be damned," Jack said.

## Chapter 14

Jack heard Peggy Jo when she left her bedroom and went downstairs. He hadn't slept well most of the night and had been awake for the past half hour, thinking about yesterday's events. Now he rose from the bed, picked up his discarded jeans and pulled them up over his pajamas, then reached out and jerked his sweater off the footboard. A distinct wintry chill permeated the old house early in the morning, before Hetty turned up the central heat's thermostat. After pulling the sweater over his head and sliding his feet into his leather house slippers, he made his way out into the hall and quietly descended the stairs. He halted on the landing where the staircase split in two. From his vantage point above the foyer, he could see into the living room. Peggy Jo stood in the doorway, her back to him, completely unaware that he had followed her.

Across the room, near the windows, the large, gaily decorated Christmas tree stood, the miniature white lights blinking on and off. She must have thrown the switch just inside the door that turned on the lights. She looked so alone. An overwhelming urge hit him—an urge to go to her and put his arms around her. Despite the calm, almost serene way she stood there looking at the tree, he sensed the tension inside her, the turmoil of uncertainty and tightly controlled fear. She was on the edge emotionally, but hanging on for dear life.

He supposed if anyone had a right to fall apart, Peggy Jo did. But she wasn't the type to go to pieces, to wring her hands and cry, "What am I going to do?" No, she was the type who worried about others more than herself. And she was the type who got angry and said, "I want this guy found and stopped!"

If only Ross Brewster had turned out to be her stalker, they could all rest easy. But despite what Jack had assumed was obvious evidence against the college kid, Ross not only had an eye witness who saw him arrive after Peggy Jo's car had been vandalized, but one who actually saw a man leaving the scene only moments earlier. The witness, Mrs. Murray, the wife of one of WLOK's video engineers, described the man as tall and slender, with a dark beard and mustache. And he'd been driving an older model car that fit the description of the vehicle Jack had seen speeding away from Peggy Jo's house the day a paper-covered baseball had been thrown through her window. Mrs. Murray hadn't seen the man doing anything to the Sebring, but she had seen him getting into his car and zooming out of the parking lot just seconds before Ross arrived.

If Sawyer's visit with Peggy Jo's ex-husband didn't provide them with any new information, it was highly possible that they were facing an unknown enemy, someone Peggy Jo had never met. Except in her nightmares. If that were the case, his identity would remain a mystery until he made his move directly on Peggy Jo.

Jack walked down the remaining steps and said her name softly. She tensed, then turned slowly to face him.

"Before I said your name, you knew I was there," he said.

"Yes," she replied. "I didn't hear you, but I felt your presence. Besides, I know that you never let me get very far away from you."

"Couldn't you sleep?" he asked.

She shook her head. "I couldn't shut off my mind. I kept thinking about what's going to happen next."

He took a tentative step toward her. "Peggy Jo—"

"No, please. I have enough to deal with right now. Don't..." She drew in a deep breath, obviously trying to control her emotions.

Disregarding her plea, he hurriedly closed the distance separating them and, without giving her a chance to try to rebuff him, cradled her face with his hands.

"Don't you get it? Neither of us can turn off what we're feeling just because it isn't convenient right now. But I promise you that I'm not going to do anything except protect you and comfort you. I know you're a strong woman, but, darling, even the strong sometimes need a shoulder to lean on. Can't I be that for you, if nothing more? Can't you lean on me?"

She swallowed tears that she refused to acknowledge and nodded. Jack kissed her forehead. She moaned softly.

"I'm afraid—" she said.

"Shh. I understand. And it's all right."

"No, Jack, you don't understand." She placed her hands over his and dragged them away from her face, but held on tightly as she put their hands between them. "Yes, of course, I'm afraid of my stalker. But I'm even more afraid of...of not being strong, of letting myself lean on you, rely on you. I don't dare give in to weakness. If I depend on you and you let me down, I wouldn't be able to stand it."

"Peggy Jo, I'm not going to let you down." He brought her hands to his mouth, opened her palms and placed warm, soft kisses in the center. "I'm going to be with you, right at your side, until this is all over and your stalker is behind bars. I want to protect you and keep you safe, but if you'll let me, I can give you the emotional support you need, too.''

''Why couldn't Dundee have sent me a female body-guard?'' Her lips formed a fragile smile. ''I wouldn't have tumbled into bed with a female agent.''

Jack chuckled. ''Darling, you wouldn't have tumbled into bed with any other agent, male or female. Only with me.''

''Yeah, I know. I must be susceptible to big, rugged cowboys with wicked smiles.'' She jerked her hands free and playfully swatted him on the chest.

''Only to this cowboy.'' Even though he halfway ex-pected a fight out of her, Jack pulled her into an embrace. He was pleasantly surprised when she not only willingly accepted him, but actually wrapped her arms around his waist and laid her head on his chest.

''I'm not good at this—leaning on a man.'' She avoided looking at him. ''But until this is over…I need you, Jack. Please, please don't let me down.''

He held her fiercely, longing to convey to her that she could trust him completely. More than anything he wanted Peggy Jo to believe in him. As much as he wanted to make love to her again, to possess her and find fulfillment in her sweet body, he understood that without trust between them, Peggy Jo would continue to resist him and to deny the way she felt about him. And there was no way of getting around the truth—he had as big a problem with trusting as she did.

When he heard footsteps on the stairs, Jack refused to relinquish his hold on Peggy Jo even though she tried to free herself.

''It's Hetty,'' she whispered.

''So?''

''So, she'll make a big deal out of this.''

''And you don't want it to be a big deal,'' he said, then

pivoted her slowly so that he could glance over his shoulder. "Morning, Hetty."

"Morning yourself." Hetty padded up the hall toward them. "You two are up mighty early. Or maybe y'all haven't been to bed yet."

"Hetty!" Peggy Jo's tone attempted outrage, but failed to produce the desired effect.

"I figured after the way Jack was acting all territorial around you while Mr. McNamara was here last night, he would stake a claim before morning." Hetty's facial expression didn't alter as she walked past them, went straight toward the front door and punched in the security code.

"Hetty Ballard, of all the outrageous things to say." Peggy Jo glared at Jack. "Well, aren't you going to deny it?"

Jack glanced at Hetty, who had opened the front door and gone onto the porch to pick up the morning newspaper, then he looked point-blank at Peggy Jo. "I can deny only half of it."

"What?"

When Hetty came back into the house and walked up the hall past them, Jack said, "I need to clarify something." Hetty paused. "I didn't stake my claim, as much as I would have liked to, but you're right about my being territorial where Peggy Jo is concerned."

"Humph. Thought so." Hetty disappeared down the hall.

Peggy Jo struggled to free herself, but Jack refused to release her. "Darling, you're the first woman who was so damned and determined to get away from me. And you're also the first woman I never want to let go of."

Peggy Jo's gaze crashed into his, her eyes filled with surprise and uncertainty. "Jack, please...you promised. Comfort. A shoulder to lean on. You said I could trust you."

Damn! Condemned by his own gentlemanly vow. He grasped her arms tenderly and ran his hands down to her wrists, holding on to her loosely. "And I'm a man of my word." He released her.

She took several steps away from him, an appreciative smile lighting her face. "I think I'll go get a cup of coffee and then call Betsy. If we're going to send Hetty and Wendy to the farm this weekend, I need to make arrangements."

"Good idea. While you're doing that, I'll grab a quick shower and then contact Ellen and see about getting another agent down here to drive Hetty and Wendy to your cousin's."

The morning went by in a flash. Phone calls were made. Arrangements were set. They dropped Wendy by school. And when they arrived at the studio, they found Kayla back in the office. She told them that Ross had taken the rest of the week off from work. And to make the day perfect, Chet avoided her like the plague.

Jack had ordered takeout and they shared the sweet and sour pork, fried rice and sesame chicken on paper plates at her desk. Not one dark cloud had appeared on the horizon today, but Peggy Jo couldn't relax. She kept waiting for the other shoe to drop. Was it possible that they could get through the rest of the day without incident?

Just as she was wiping her hands off on her napkin and contemplating whether or not to indulge herself by eating one of the cream-cheese stuffed wontons, Sawyer McNamara sailed into her office, an irritated expression marring his handsome features. She supposed some women would find Sawyer's polish and sense of style very appealing. And those same women might think him better looking than Jack, who was like a piece of rough-hewn lumber compared to the FBI agent. But Sawyer didn't appeal to her in the least; not the way Jack did. All the big cowboy had to do was smile at her and skyrockets exploded inside her.

Jack downed the last drops of his hot tea, then set his cup aside, wiped his mouth and hands on his napkin and stood to greet his ally. "I had expected to hear from you before now."

"I got held up," Sawyer said. "First of all, Buck Forbes wasn't at work when I arrived at the nursery this morning. His boss had sent him off on a delivery, so I had to wait."

"You saw Buck?" Peggy Jo asked. "You spoke to him?"

"Yes, eventually." Sawyer removed his overcoat and hung it on the brass hat rack in the corner. "But I found out a few interesting things about the man from his boss."

"Like what?" Jack asked.

"Like the guy drives a car that fits the description of the vehicle you saw screeching away from Peggy Jo's and the one Mrs. Murray saw yesterday."

"I'll be damned." When Jack cast his gaze in Peggy Jo's direction, he realized she'd gone pale, so pale that the freckles covering her nose and cheekbones appeared darker.

"That's not all," Sawyer continued. "Seems Mr. Forbes is sporting a beard and a mustache these days."

"Buck can't be my stalker," Peggy Jo said. "He just can't be. It doesn't make any sense. What motive could he have? We haven't seen each other in thirteen years."

"I'm not saying he's our man, but just in case he is, I gave him fair warning," Sawyer told them. "Of course he denied being Peggy Jo's stalker, but his attitude toward her was downright unfriendly. He made several rather rude remarks about Peggy Jo, her TV show and her books."

"He's watched my show? He's read my books?"

"He gave me that distinct impression."

"I hope you made it clear to him that if he is harassing Peggy Jo, he won't get away with it," Jack said. "You warned him, didn't you, that not only would he be facing a prison sentence, but he'd have to deal with me if he tries to get to Peggy Jo."

"Oh, I told him all right. I told him that the police and the FBI were involved in this case and that Peggy Jo had a highly trained bodyguard with her twenty-four/seven. And the son of a bitch laughed in my face.''

Peggy Jo stood, rounded her desk and went straight to Jack's side. She reached down and grasped his hand in hers.

He squeezed her hand, looked at her lovingly and said, ''I'm right here, darling, and I'm not leaving your side.''

Costumed children of various ages and sizes covered the stage as they took their final bow. Wendy Sue Riley stood on the front row looking every inch the angel she had portrayed in the Christmas play. Peggy Jo was so proud of her little girl, the precious child who had come into her life after tragedy had ripped Wendy's birth parents from her. Every day of her life, Peggy Jo thanked God for the chance to be a mother. On the day she brought Wendy home with her, she had made a solemn vow that she would be the kind of mother to her daughter that she had always longed for herself.

The audience of parents, grandparents and other family members broke out into thunderous applause and rose to give their little darlings a standing ovation. The children beamed with happiness, basking in the show of love and acceptance.

''Wasn't she wonderful?'' Peggy Jo said as she applauded.

''The kid's a natural. She didn't miss a word of her angel speech.'' Jack continued clapping.

''I don't think I've ever seen her so excited about something.'' Tears glistened in Hetty's brown eyes.

When the applause died down, the teachers led the students off the stage and the audience dispersed. Jack reached under his seat and pulled out a florist box, then followed Peggy Jo and Hetty down the row and out into the aisle.

''She's going to be thrilled when you give her those flowers,'' Hetty said.

''She's our little star, and stars should receive flowers

after a performance.'' Peggy Jo slipped her arm though Jack's. ''Thank you for thinking of the flowers. She'll love the rainbow colors of the miniature carnations in the nose-gay.''

Making their way through the crowd, they paused for Peggy Jo to speak to several parents she knew and others who knew her from her TV show. By the time they arrived backstage, Wendy was jumping up and down in an effort to see over the taller children's heads as she searched for her family.

''Mommy!'' She came running toward them. ''Jack! Hetty!''

Peggy Jo picked Wendy up and gave her a big hug. ''Sweetpea, you were the star of the show.''

''Ah, Mommy, I wasn't the star. I was just one of the angels.''

''But you were the best angel,'' Jack told her. ''The prettiest, brightest, best one.''

''Was I really?''

''Really.'' Jack held out the florist box. ''Mommy and Hetty and I have something for you. Flowers for m'lady, to celebrate her brilliant performance.''

Wendy's eyes widened, and her mouth opened in surprise. ''For me. Flowers?'' She grabbed the box, ripped off the lid and squealed with delight. ''I love it! My own bouquet!''

Jack discarded the empty box, then glanced around, checking out the crowd. ''You girls ready to go?''

Wendy took Peggy Jo's hand and held the small nosegay with the other. ''Mommy, did that man from WLOK come and film the play?''

''He sure did. And he's supposed to be waiting outside to give us the tape so we can watch it tonight, if you want to.''

''I want to.''

''Well, let's get moving,'' Jack said.

"Are we still stopping for milkshakes on the way home?" Wendy asked. "Remember, you promised."

"Absolutely," Jack replied. "Chocolate milkshakes for Mommy and Hetty, vanilla for me and strawberry for you."

"Yippee!"

Part of the crowd lingered inside the building, but over half had already gone outside and rushed to their cars. The weather forecaster had predicted a possibility of light sleet tonight and temperatures dropping to well below freezing before midnight. As they came closer to the outside doors, Peggy Jo felt the frigid night air invading and destroying the inside warmth.

Wendy tugged on Peggy Jo's hand. "Wasn't tonight the best?"

"You're the best, Miss Riley, the very best. I'm so proud of you."

"Ah, Mommy, you just say that because you love me."

Peggy Jo caught a glimpse of Mick Hamm, one of WLOK's camera crew, who waited just inside the front doors. When he saw her, he came forward and held out the videotape.

"I got it all," Mick said. "From beginning to end." He glanced down at Wendy. "You were great, kid. Your mother will be talking about your performance for the next month."

"Thanks, Mick," Peggy Jo said.

"Sure. No problem." He nodded to Jack. "See y'all tomorrow."

Jack stayed on Peggy Jo's right side as they walked out of the building. Hetty and Peggy Jo flanked Wendy, whose attention was completely absorbed by the colorful carnation nosegay she held.

"I'm glad we got here early this evening and found a parking place close by," Jack said. "Looks like the drizzle has started."

Cars drove by slowly. Headlights glowed in the darkness

and taillights glimmered like large, dazzling rubies. Voices carried on the night air. Parents grumbling about the weather. Children laughing. Babies crying. And a light, freezing rain chinked against the vehicles and pavement and coated the ground with sparkling moisture.

The car came out of nowhere, headlights off, traveling at an ungodly speed. Dear God, the car was headed straight for her. Peggy Jo froze to the spot. It was too late for her to move out of the way. Her body shut down. Her heart stopped. Her mind cried out for help.

Suddenly Jack spun around and shoved her backward, accidentally causing Wendy's hand to slip loose from her mother's tenacious hold. Wendy fell into Hetty, knocking the housekeeper to the ground. Having missed Peggy Jo, the car careered directly toward Wendy. Peggy Jo screamed. Jack lunged forward, reaching for Wendy just as the car sped by.

Everything seemed to have happened in slow motion and yet in the blink of an eye at the same time. Hetty moaned as she lifted herself up into a sitting position. Peggy Jo came up off the pavement. The bloody scrapes on her hands and knees stung, but she barely noticed. Despite the soreness radiating through her legs, she rushed over to where Jack lay huddled on the ground, his big body shielding an unmoving Wendy.

# *Chapter 15*

Matt O'Brien and Domingo Shea arrived at Erlanger Hospital's emergency room just as the nurse wheeled Hetty out into the waiting area. Peggy Jo's housekeeper sported a cast that covered her broken ankle, and a tired, worried expression deepened the fine wrinkles around her mouth and eyes.

"Well, they're finished with me, and I'm ready to go home," Hetty said. "Looks like I'll have to get used to using crutches for the next few weeks." She glanced down at Wendy, who lay asleep in Peggy Jo's lap. "How's our baby?"

"The doctor said she'll be fine. She just had the wind knocked out of her, and she has a few scratches and bruises." Peggy Jo gulped, swallowing the tears lodged in her throat. "But she was so scared. She cried herself to sleep."

Jack nudged Peggy Jo. "There's Matt and Dom. Y'all stay right here. After I speak with them, we'll take everybody home."

Peggy Jo nodded her head wearily. Stress etched her features with a haggard expression. She pushed back stray tendrils of disheveled red hair that had fallen onto her face. Tattered pantyhose and mud-stained clothing added to her unkempt appearance. Without conscious thought, Jack reached out and caressed her cheek. She rewarded him with a weak smile.

"I'll be back in a minute," he said, then got up and met the two Dundee agents as they approached. After shaking hands with both men, he motioned for them to follow him to a more private area. He didn't want Peggy Jo or Hetty overhearing their conversation.

"Thanks for coming, guys." When Jack had called Ellen several hours ago, he'd specifically requested that she send Matt and Dom. Dundee's CEO had obliged him since both men had recently completed their assignments and were temporarily free.

"Ellen said this was a personal matter for you." Matt glanced across the room at Peggy Jo. "Is she the reason it's personal?"

"Hey, I might have exaggerated a bit when I told Ellen this case had become highly personal to me," Jack replied. "But I knew that would be the easiest way to get her to send me the agents I wanted."

Grinning, Dom elbowed Matt's arm. "I told you Jack hadn't gone soft on some woman. You owe me fifty bucks."

"Yeah, yeah, I know what you told me, but I'm not convinced." Matt eyed Jack. "So, which is it—you lied to Ellen or is Peggy Jo Riley more than a client?"

Jack cleared his throat. "I haven't gone soft on her, not exactly, but…to be honest, she is more than a client to me."

Dom's swaggering smile broadened. He lowered his voice to a discreet whisper and said, "Which means he's screwed her."

"Damn it, it's not like that! Not with her." Jack glared at Dom, whose triumphant grin vanished instantly.

"I think *you* owe *me* fifty bucks," Matt told Dom.

"What the hell were you two doing on the drive over from Atlanta, making bets on my love life?"

"Yeah, something like that," Dom admitted.

"If either of you knuckleheads say one word to Peggy Jo about your insights into our relationship, I'll skin you alive," Jack warned them. "Now, let's get down to business."

Matt and Dom nodded, but wisely kept quiet, apparently realizing that they'd said more than enough.

"We're sending the housekeeper and the daughter to a cousin's farm in Spring City as soon as we can get their suitcases packed," Jack said. "I need y'all to take them to the farm and make sure they get there safely and without being followed. Then one of you will stay at the farm with them until Peggy Jo and I come up there in a couple of weeks so she can spend Christmas with her family."

"Dom's staying at the farm," Matt said. "Ellen's shipping me out to Los Angeles day after tomorrow."

"Fine. For now I need you two to get Hetty—the housekeeper—into your car and follow us home," Jack said. "Once we're there, we'll finalize some plans for the trip to Spring City."

When Jack turned around, Matt grabbed his arm. "Wait up a minute."

"What?"

"Sawyer contacted me right before we got to the hospital," Matt said. "He paid a late-night visit on Ms. Riley's ex-husband. Seems Buck Forbes had a car wreck last night and messed up his car pretty bad. Wrapped the old Pontiac around a tree and just left it there while he staggered out onto the highway."

"Son of a bitch!" Jack clamped his hands into tight fists. He had the overpowering urge to ram his fists into the wall, just to let off a little steam. "Quite a coincidence. He just happened to wreck his car the same night somebody tried to run us down."

"Sawyer said when they found the guy, he was in the local jail, charged with a DUI," Dom said.

"What time did his accident happen?" Jack asked.

"Around ten-thirty." Matt inclined his head in Peggy Jo's direction. "Are you going to tell her?"

"Later, not now. She's had just about all she can take for the time being. Telling her that there's more evidence pointing to her ex as the stalker can wait."

Three hours later, right before daybreak, Peggy Jo and Jack said goodbye to Hetty and Wendy. Last night's sleet had turned into a light snow, but the flakes melted on the pavement as they hit the ground. Although her heart was breaking because she had to send her child away for her own safety, Peggy Jo put up a brave front, assuring Wendy that she was going to have a wonderful time at the farm with Betsy's family.

"Remember your cousins, Shane and Molly. Y'all can play games and feed the animals and do all sorts of fun things," Peggy Jo said.

"But I'm going to miss you, Mommy."

"I'm going to miss you, too, sweetpea, but I will call you every day, and Jack and I will come to the farm for Christmas. And you'll have Hetty and Fur Ball there with you."

She hugged her child one final time, kissed her cheeks and helped her into the back seat beside Dundee agent Domingo Shea, then she picked up Fur Ball's pet carrier and handed it to Wendy.

"I'll take good care of Wendy," Hetty said.

Peggy Jo hugged Hetty, then moved out of the way so that Jack could assist Hetty into the front seat alongside Matt O'Brien.

What had happened to her sane, safe, orderly existence? Before some madman had made it his mission in life to torment her, her world had made sense to her. She'd been able to take care of herself and those she loved. But not now. She hated living like this, hated being put in a position where she couldn't protect her own child.

With Jack at her side, Peggy Jo stood on the brick walkway and waved farewell as Matt backed the midsize Buick out of the driveway. She continued waving even after the car disappeared up the street. Tiny snowflakes melted as they hit her hair and face. Jack grasped her hand, pulled it down and turned her toward the house. She didn't protest when he guided her up the steps and across the porch. Once inside he kept his arm securely around her waist as he locked the front door, punched in the security code and then led her toward the staircase.

"They'll make sure no one is following them, won't they?" she asked.

"They'll make sure. Don't worry."

"Easier said than done."

"Yeah, I know," Jack replied. "But remember that this guy isn't after Wendy or Hetty. They just happened to be in the line of fire last night because they were with you."

"Do you have any idea how that makes me feel? To know that my daughter could have been killed because some lunatic tried to run me down. And knowing that Hetty has a broken ankle—"

Jack grabbed her shoulders and shook her gently. "Stop it. Don't do this to yourself. None of it's your fault."

"Then whose fault is it? I'm the one who made this man, whoever he is, so angry that he's decided to torment me. To...kill me."

"You haven't done anything wrong. And we're going to catch this guy and put him behind bars." Jack slid his hands down her arms and grasped her wrists. "Come on upstairs. You need a hot bath, some clean clothes and a few hours of sleep.''

"I can't sleep. Not until I know that Wendy and Hetty are safe at Betsy's.''

"As soon as we get the call from Matt, I'm putting you to bed.''

She nodded agreement, then went with him upstairs. He walked her to her room and paused in the doorway.

"Bath or shower?'' he asked.

"What?''

"Do you want to take a bath or a shower? I thought if you wanted a bath, I could draw the water or I could turn on the shower and lay out some towels for you.''

"Oh, Jack.'' Tears gathered in her eyes as she touched his cheek. "You're such a sweet man.''

Sweet? Jack Parker? Women had used many an adjective to describe him, most of them flattering, but Peggy Jo was the first one who'd ever told him he was sweet. And he knew by the look in her eyes that right at this particular moment it was the highest compliment she could pay him.

"You're pretty sweet yourself, darling.''

She inhaled and exhaled slowly, then said, "I can handle the shower by myself, but thanks for offering. However, there is something you can do for me.''

"Name it.'' He longed to wrap his arms around her, keep her safe and blot out the rest of the world.

"After you take your shower, would you go down to the kitchen and fix me some hot cocoa? We missed out on those milkshakes last night, and I feel a powerful need for a dose of chocolate.''

"How about a couple of Hetty's chocolate chip cookies to go with the cocoa?'' he suggested.

"Ah, Mr. Parker you sure do know how to tempt a girl. But just cocoa. No cookies.''

"I want to tempt you, Peggy Jo. Only you.''

The words had rolled off his tongue so easily. The emotion materialized verbally before his brain had adequately processed its meaning. A sudden, deafening silence hung between them. Time stood still for one breathless moment as they stared into each other's eyes. Jack realized that he had meant exactly what he'd said. For the first time in his life there was only one woman he wanted to tempt, to impress, to please. Only one woman he cared about. No one else mattered.

Peggy Jo broke eye contact. "Go. Go. Get your shower."

"Yeah, sure." Reluctantly he left her, all the while wishing he had the guts to tell her how he really felt about her.

When she emerged from her shower, she found the mirrored wall foggy with steam. Although the room was relatively warm, her body chilled instantly after having just left the heated, watery cocoon behind the shower curtain. She dried off hurriedly, then slipped into her yellow robe. After digging out a large-toothed comb from a drawer in her vanity table, she set to work untangling her long, wet hair. She took her damp towel and rubbed a clear circle on the mirror, then sat down at the vanity table and finished combing her hair before she plugged in the blow dryer.

When her hair was almost dry, she turned off the dryer and laid it aside. She was bone tired. Despite the therapeutic effects of the hot water, her body still ached from her tumble onto the pavement, and her raw hands and knees burned. She needed to put some salve on her injuries, something to help them heal faster. When she got up and rummaged through the contents of the medicine cabinet, she heard a knock on the bathroom door. Her heart leaped into her throat.

"Hot cocoa's ready," Jack called through the closed door.

"Come on in," she told him. "I'm decent."

"How about coming out or opening the door for me. I've got my hands full."

She grabbed the tube of antibiotic ointment, then turned the doorknob and opened the door. Jack stood there in her bedroom, a mug of steaming cocoa in each hand and a wide, cheerful grin on his face. She loved his optimistic, be-happy attitude toward life. He was definitely the type who, if life handed him a bunch of lemons, would find a way to turn them into lemonade. No matter how bad the situation, she could count on Jack to put a positive spin on it. Mercy me, how she needed a man like that in her life.

He was such a welcome sight. His glistening hair appeared almost black in its damp state, not quite dry after his recent shower. And apparently he hadn't taken the time to shave because a heavy five-o'clock shadow darkened his face. A fabulously masculine face that she was beginning to love. When had it happened? she wondered. When had she started falling for Jack Parker? That very first day at the studio when he'd been so damn rude to her? Or that first night when she had watched how kind and loving he'd been with Wendy, how considerate he'd been with Hetty? Or had it been almost a week ago when they had made love? Had sex, she reminded herself. No. Made love. At least for her it had been more than sex. But had it been more for Jack?

While musing about the unthinkable—Jack as a permanent fixture in her life—she let her gaze travel from his face to his body. His big, beautiful, partially nude body. He wore his navy-blue pajama bottoms, but instead of his usual white T-shirt, he'd put on the matching pajama shirt, but left it unbuttoned, revealing his broad, hairy chest, his lean washboard stomach and his round, shallow belly button.

Jack eyed the tube of ointment in her hand. "You should have let them check out your hands and knees at the hospital."

"I'm okay. Really. It's nothing. Besides, I was too concerned about Wendy and Hetty to bother with my minor cuts and scrapes."

"Sit down." He nodded toward the vanity stool. "Let me take a look."

"Honestly, I'm fine. I can rub some of this stuff—" she held up the tube "—on my hands and knees and they'll be all right."

"Woman, sit down and stop arguing with me." He walked her backward toward the stool, then reached around her to set both mugs of cocoa on the vanity table. "Sit."

She sat, but glared at him, feigning anger. If any other man on earth had dared to order her around this way, she would have taken a couple of inches off his hide. So, why accept such treatment from Jack? Because she knew that he was trying to take care of her, and right now she needed someone to do just that.

"Stop staring daggers at me." He took the tube of ointment from her, then reached out, grasped her right hand and opened her palm to inspect her wounds. He clicked his tongue. "These look pretty rough." He opened the tube, squirted cream into her palm and tenderly massaged it into her red, raw skin. When he finished with the right hand, he doctored the left, then finished up by placing a kiss on the inside of each wrist.

Dear Lord, the man was most definitely lethal. He had a way about him. A gentle, loving kindness that impressed her as much—no, even more than—his sexy smile and to-die-for body. She had believed herself immune to any man's charm, had thought she could never trust again, never risk getting hurt again. But in less than two weeks, Jack had changed all that. She found herself trusting him and easily succumbing to his Texas charm. Suddenly, opening herself up to love and joy seemed the most natural thing in the world. *Even if he leaves you?* an inner voice demanded. *And he will leave you. No matter how kind and loving he is to you, by his own admission he's not the marrying kind.*

Before she realized what he was doing, Jack knelt down, parted her robe to reveal her thighs and placed one hand beneath her right knee. Her mouth opened on a silent gasp. The intimacy of the moment couldn't possibly escape his notice when it was so blatantly obvious to her. He soothed the cream into the raw flesh on one knee and then the other, his touch featherlight. She couldn't bring herself to look directly at him, afraid of what he might see in her eyes, what hidden longing she would reveal to him. When he finished doctoring her, he laid the tube on the vanity, then slid his hand between her legs to part her thighs. She held her breath. He lowered his head. She whimpered before his mouth ever touched the sensitive skin along her inner thigh. The moment his lips skimmed over her flesh, she keened softly, deep in her throat and grabbed his shoulder. With his head still bowed and his tongue forging a moist trail up her thigh, Jack reached up to undo the tie belt that held her robe in place. If she were going to stop him, she had to do it now. In a few minutes she wouldn't be able to stop either him or herself.

The minute her robe parted he covered one breast with his hand. As his mouth moved closer and closer to his objective, he rubbed his thumb across her nipple until it puckered and tightened. Quickly, he moved to the other breast and begin a see-saw motion, dividing his time between the two pebble-hard peaks. Using his other hand he cupped her hip and pushed her forward, to the very edge of the vanity stool, so that his mouth could press hotly against her feminine mound.

When his tongue caressed her intimately, she cried out, stunned by the intensity of the sensation that jetted through her. She ached and throbbed with need. A need that grew with each flick, each hard, heated motion of his tongue and lips. While he made love to her with brash, mindless abandon, she forked her fingers through his hair and gripped the back of his head, holding him as he lavished all his attention on the act of giving her pleasure.

Suddenly every nerve coiled tightly, every muscle tensed, preparing for the maelstrom of fulfillment her body anticipated. And with one final, precise stab of Jack's tongue, Peggy Jo fell apart, shattering, quivering uncontrollably, as spasms of release claimed her. While she was still in the throes of passion, Jack hurriedly took off his pajama bottoms, removed a condom from the pocket of his undone shirt and prepared himself to take her. The moment he lifted her off the stool and set her on the vanity table, she grabbed the edge of the table and hoisted herself up just enough to accommodate him. He thrust into her, his sex hard and heavy, filling her completely, stretching her to the limit.

They mated in a raw, unbridled frenzy, their mouths devouring, their hands roaming, their bodies pumping wildly. Jack tensed, then he grabbed her hips and shoved her back and forth in a rapid, repetitive motion that soon brought him to the brink and set her afire all over again. The moment he peaked, his big body trembled with the force of his climax, and Peggy Jo frantically sought another. When the aftershocks rippled through him, her second release hit her, even more intense than the first. She cried out his name as her body shook with pleasure.

In the distance, somewhere far away from the hazy, sated weightlessness that cushioned her, surrounded her, consumed her, Peggy Jo heard a ringing telephone. Jack nuzzled her throat and kissed the rise of each breast, then lifted her and set her down on the vanity stool.

"That's my phone," he said. "I left it on your nightstand."

"Wendy!" Peggy Jo tried to stand on wobbly legs.

Jack eased her back down on the stool. "I'll get it."

She nodded, then waited for him to retrieve his cell

phone. He returned in a flash and handed the phone to her. She put the phone to her ear.

"Mommy, we're here all safe and sound. Betsy's going to let Molly and Shane stay home from school today to play with me. And Fur Ball likes Molly's cats, Snowball and Fluffy, and he even likes Shane's dog, Boots."

"Oh, sweetpea, that's wonderful."

"I gotta go now. Betsy's fixing pancakes for breakfast. Bye, Mommy. I love you."

"I love you, too."

Peggy Jo handed the phone to Jack. When he walked back into the bedroom, she could hear him talking to someone. One of the Dundee agents, no doubt. Just hearing Wendy's voice eased a heavy weight of worry from her heart. She could rest now, knowing that her child was safe.

Hurriedly she cleaned herself, belted her robe and followed Jack. He sat on the edge of her bed, immersed in conversation and totally oblivious to his nude state. She pulled back the covers, removed her robe and slipped into bed, loving the feel of the cotton flannel sheets beneath her.

"Yeah, Matt, thanks," Jack said. "Tell Dom I'll be in touch."

He closed the small cell phone, tossed it onto the nightstand, then crawled into bed beside Peggy Jo. When she snuggled against him, he pulled her into his arms and kissed her temple. Neither said a word. They lay together in the quiet, cool semidark room and drifted off to sleep.

# Chapter 16

The days that followed were bittersweet for Peggy Jo—for so many reasons. She missed Wendy terribly, but even though they weren't together, both handled their separation as best they could. Having Hetty with her and being part of Betsy's loving family helped Wendy adjust. And having Jack at her side helped Peggy Jo. She tried to meet each new day with her usual spunk and enthusiasm, knowing that Wendy was not only having fun being with Betsy's children, but that she was safe under Domingo Shea's constant surveillance. Peggy Jo spoke to Wendy and Hetty daily, sometimes twice a day, and she continued her heavy workload at the station. And every night she lay in Jack's arms and tried to convince herself that what they shared would be enough to keep him in her life forever. The word *love* was never mentioned, although she'd come close to shouting her feelings from the rooftops more than once. Every time Jack made love to her, she wanted to tell him the depth of her feelings and longed for him to tell her that he felt the same. But she was afraid she was deluding herself, that for Jack their affair was a temporary liaison. He had made her no promises beyond the passion of the moment.

For over a week after Wendy and Hetty left, Peggy Jo's life settled into a peaceful routine during the day and a marathon of nightly lovemaking. It was as if her stalker had disappeared off the face of the earth. For a while she hoped that the stepped-up police investigation and the FBI's involvement in her case had scared off her tormenter. As day after day passed without incident, she began to relax, began to feel safe once again. But as suddenly as they had stopped, the cruel, filthy letters began again. Two, sometimes three every day. And the threats were more specific and described in graphic detail the madman's intent.

She held the latest missive in her hand, scanning once again the evil words a truly demented mind had conceived.

You think you're safe. You're not. I'm waiting. Waiting for the perfect moment. I'll come after you when you least expect it. I'll know when the time is right, when you're the most vulnerable. And when that time comes, no one can save you. Not the police. Not the FBI. And not your damn cowboy lover.

"I wish you would stop reading that thing over and over again," Jack said. "By letting it torment you, you're giving him just what he wants."

"If only we knew for sure who he was." Peggy Jo stuffed the letter back inside the envelope and tossed it onto the desktop. "Buck is the only real suspect the police have, and despite some circumstantial evidence against him, they can't be sure it's him."

"My gut instincts tell me that Buck is our man," Jack told her. "If we could just get some substantial proof against him, the police could arrest him."

"I'm willing to go along with Sawyer's idea of setting a trap for him. If you'd agree to—"

Jack grabbed her so quickly that she gasped in surprise. "I will not agree to let the FBI use you as bait. If we bide our time, this guy's going to make a mistake without our having to put you in more danger than you're already in."

"I can't go on like this much longer." She laid her hand on his shoulder. "Separated from my daughter. Living in fear. Wondering when he's going to strike next and what he's going to do."

Jack tightened his hold on her shoulders. "I won't let you do something foolish."

"Jack, you should know me well enough to realize that if I decide to cooperate with the FBI, you can't stop me."

He released her so quickly that she swayed from the force of his withdrawal. And when he slammed his closed fist down on top of her desk, she jumped.

"Don't do it." He spoke through clenched teeth.

"If after Christmas, nothing has changed, I'm going to tell Sawyer that he'll have my full cooperation."

"No, damn it, no!"

"Yes. I want my life back. And if using myself as bait to trap this lunatic is our best chance of capturing him, then that's what I'll do."

Jack turned his back on her. When she crossed the room and touched him, he jerked away from her.

"Please, let's not argue about this again," she said. "I want these next few days at Betsy's farm to be wonderful for all of us. You and me and Wendy and Hetty. All together for Christmas."

"That's what I want, too." He reached out and pulled her around to his side, his body still rigid with anger but his voice softened. "We'll shelve this discussion until we come back to Chattanooga. But don't think you've won this argument."

"And don't you think you can change my mind."

\* \* \*

Betsy and Darrel Mitchell lived on a two-hundred-acre farm outside the small town of Spring City, Tennessee. The house had been built by Darrel's great-grandfather in the late-nineteenth century and each successive generation had added on and remodeled, thus creating the huge, rambling two-story structure with wide porches and a homey inviting facade. Darrel grew some corn and soybeans, but he made his living raising beef cattle. Betsy supplemented the family income with her job as a grade-school teacher. They lived a simple, contented life together with their eleven-year-old son, Shane, and their seven-year-old daughter, Molly. And anyone seeing Betsy and Darrel together would instantly realize how deeply in love they were. Peggy Jo had long ago given up any hope of ever having what her cousin had, but since Jack had come into her life, she had allowed those long-ago, silly teenage dreams to resurface.

*You keep thinking stupid things like that and you'll wind up getting your heart broken,* an inner voice warned. But the truth of the matter was that it was already too late to save herself from heartbreak. She was head over heels in love with Jack. Although logic and common sense cautioned her not to expect a future with him, her heart dared to dream impossible dreams.

"I've figured it out," Betsy said, her hazel eyes sparkling. "Sleeping arrangements won't be a problem. Mr. Parker—Jack—you can use the day bed in my sewing room. That's where Mr. Shea slept. And Peggy Jo, you can share a room with Hetty."

"I don't mind moving into the sewing room," Hetty said.

"There's no need for that," Betsy said. "Besides, it wouldn't work. That would leave Jack no place to sleep, unless he— Oh, I see."

Peggy Jo blushed when her cousin's gaze connected with hers. Betsy had realized the reason for Hetty's suggestion.

Why hadn't Hetty just kept her mouth shut? Better yet, how did Hetty know that she'd been sleeping with Jack for the past couple of weeks?

"I'm sorry. I didn't realize that...well, I certainly don't disapprove...but..." Stammering uncontrollably, Betsy's embarrassment stained her round cheeks with a rosy hue. "I'm afraid Darrel and I are rather old-fashioned about this type of situation. If it weren't for the children asking questions and—"

"I understand." Peggy Jo glared at Hetty. "Hetty shouldn't have said anything. The sleeping arrangements you've made will be just fine. Besides, Jack and I will be here only three nights."

"Are you leaving the day after Christmas?" Betsy asked. "I do wish y'all would stay on until New Year's day."

"I'm afraid we can't." Peggy Jo didn't even glance Jack's way. The last thing she wanted was to revive their argument over whether or not she would allow the FBI to use her as bait in a trap for her stalker. If Hetty even suspected her intentions, she would side with Jack, and then she'd have the two of them to contend with for the next few days.

"I'll go get the luggage, and you can point out which rooms to put the bags in," Jack said. "If you ladies will excuse me."

The minute Jack was out of earshot, Hetty pinned Peggy Jo with her inquisitive gaze. "What's going on? And don't try to tell me nothing. I recognize that look on your face. You're in love."

"Oh, Peggy Jo, this is wonderful," Betsy said. "I wondered the minute I saw you two together. You're positively glowing and he...well, he can't keep his eyes off you."

"It's his job to keep his eyes on me. He's my bodyguard." Peggy Jo glanced out the window. "I thought Wendy would be here to meet me the minute we arrived."

"I'm sure the children will come back to the house any

minute now.'' Betsy laid her hand on Peggy Jo's shoulder. ''But a new litter of puppies being born is an event around here. Wendy was so excited about going to the barn to witness the birth. Of course, Shane and Molly have been through this before, but they get excited every time. This is the fourth litter Boots has had. And every puppy has already been claimed.''

''After watching your dog giving birth, I'm sure Wendy will have a million and one questions for me.'' Peggy Jo had hoped she could postpone any in-depth discussions about the birds and the bees until Wendy was older. ''She's never been curious about where babies come from, and I haven't rushed into explaining something she hasn't asked about.''

''One of the advantages of living on a farm is that your children learn quite young about birth and death. Shane and Molly have witnessed the births of puppies and kittens, as well as calves and colts.'' Betsy squeezed Peggy Jo's shoulder. ''Don't worry about having to explain things to Wendy. You'll do just fine. But remember to keep it simple. Don't give her more information than she needs.''

When he returned, Jack slammed the front door with his hip, shook the last dusting of snow from his hair and wiped his feet on the hooked rug in the foyer.

''Where do I put these?'' He held up his duffel bag and Peggy Jo's burgundy leather overnight case and clothes bag.

''We put Hetty in the bedroom Darrel's mother used when she lived with us,'' Betsy said. ''It's down the hall and to your right. First door. And my sewing room is the very last door on the left.''

''Want some help?'' Peggy Jo asked, needing an excuse to speak to Jack alone.

''Maybe you should come with me,'' he replied. ''I might get lost.''

Betsy giggled. Hetty rolled her eyes heavenward.

"Excuse me for a few minutes." Peggy Jo quickly escaped before either woman had a chance to comment.

When they were safely down the hall, away from the living room, Jack dropped the bags to the floor and pressed her up against the wall. His mouth hovered over hers, warm and damp.

With his nose almost touching hers, he said, "I don't like the sleeping arrangements."

She placed her hands on his chest. "Neither do I, but I don't want to have to explain to Wendy why you and I are sleeping together any more than Betsy wants to explain it to her children."

"Yeah, I know. I understand. But I still don't like it."

He kissed her. Fast and furious. Mouths devouring. Tongues thrusting. When they broke apart, Peggy Jo sucked in several deep breaths. Jack Parker had become an addictive drug to her. The more she had, the more she wanted. How would she ever survive the withdrawal symptoms once he went away?

After a huge supper of fried chicken, corn on the cob, fried potatoes, butter beans, cornbread and a blackberry cobbler, Peggy Jo helped Betsy clean up the kitchen, while Hetty retreated on her crutches to her favorite chair in the den.

"Mommy, may I go with Shane and Molly back to the barn to check on Boots's babies?" Wendy asked.

"I'll go with them," Darrel said.

Peggy Jo nodded. "Sure, sweetpea."

Dom Shea shook Darrel's hand then nodded to Betsy. "I want to thank you folks for your hospitality. I enjoyed my stay here."

"Please, come back anytime for a visit, Dom," Betsy said.

"Thank you, ma'am. I just might do that." Dom's smile curved his wide, full lips and crinkled the fine lines around his black eyes. "It would be worth the drive over from Atlanta just to eat one of your fabulous meals."

"Jack, don't you want to come with us to see Boots and her puppies?" Wendy asked.

"I sure do," Jack replied. "Let me see Dom off, then I'll meet y'all in the barn."

Darrel hustled the children into the mud room to put on their coats, while Jack and Dom got their jackets from the hall tree in the foyer before going outside to Dom's car. Jack knew his fellow Dundee agent had a long drive ahead of him if he wanted to make it to his sister's in San Antonio by the next night.

"Thanks for postponing your Christmas plans," Jack said. "You could have pulled rank and gotten another agent to fill in for you."

"No problem. Working holidays is sometimes just part of the job."

"Yeah, well, I appreciate it all the same."

Dom opened the trunk, tossed his bag inside and looked up at the dark night sky. "You know, worse things could happen to a man than getting married, settling down and having a couple of kids."

Jack laughed. "Is this Domingo Shea, the confirmed bachelor speaking?"

"Yeah, yeah, I know. But I didn't say the white picket fence thing was for me, I just said a man could do worse. Darrel Mitchell seems like a might happy man. And my brother-in-law, Rico, is happier now than he was when he was single."

"What's your point?"

Dom shrugged. "Wendy's a terrific kid."

"Yeah, she is."

"You're the kind of man who'd make a great father."

"Whoa...hold on just a minute," Jack protested. "Just because Peggy Jo and I... We've known each other only one month."

Dom patted Jack on the back. "Yeah. Sure." Dom slammed the truck lid. "I'm going to head out. I may run into some bad weather between here and Little Rock. I want to make as much time tonight as I can. I can always crash once I get to Marta and Rico's."

"Have a good Christmas."

Jack shook Dom's hand, and when his fellow agent backed out of the driveway, he turned and went toward the barn, all the while his mind processing their brief conversation. What was it with Dom? If he didn't know better, Jack would think the guy had encouraged him to get married. Hell, he wasn't going to get married! Not ole love-'em-and-leave-'em Jack Parker. He'd had a few close calls before, but had always managed to come to his senses.

Yeah, but Peggy Jo was different from any of those other women. With her it was more than just liking her and enjoying sex with her. The woman was unique. He admired her more than any woman he'd ever known. And he respected her. She was no weak clinging vine, no manipulative gold digger, and certainly not the hard-nosed, man-hating feminist he had thought she was. She was strong, brave, loving, generous. Damn, he sounded like a lovesick teenager. No wonder Dom had gotten the wrong idea. Was it that obvious to everybody how he felt about Peggy Jo?

"Jack, Jack, come here." Wendy ran out of the barn and came to meet him. She grabbed his hand and tugged. "Come on. You've got to see Boots's babies. They're eating their supper. They're so cute."

He clasped Wendy's hand securely in his and followed her to the barn. "Maybe you can talk your mama into letting you have one of the puppies for a Christmas present."

"All these puppies are sold to other boys and girls," Wendy said. "And I've already got Fur Ball. I don't think Mommy would let me have two pets." She tugged on Jack's hand again, leading him into the barn. "Besides, I've already asked for an awful lot of stuff for Christmas. But

I told that Santa Claus we saw at the mall that if I could have one very special present, I'd give up all my other gifts.''

Boots, a golden retriever, lay in the hay in one of the barn stalls, four tiny puppies sucking away on her tits. Wendy joined Shane and Molly, the three children forming a semicircle around the new mother and her babies.

"Okay, kids," Darrel said. "I think it's time we let Boots have a little privacy. Molly, you and Wendy go back to the house with Jack, while Shane and I bring the horses in from the pasture." He glanced at Jack. "They're predicting about three or four inches of snow for tonight. It'll be the first white Christmas we've seen in a while."

"Come on, girls." Jack put Wendy and Molly on either side of him and grasped their little hands securely.

On the walk back to the house, little Molly Mitchell jabbered away about Christmas and Santa Claus with the excitement most kids her age felt on the day before Christmas Eve. Suddenly she stopped, moved around in front of Jack so she could see Wendy and asked, "Did you tell him—" she glanced up at Jack "—what you wished for, what you want most this Christmas?"

"No, I didn't tell him," Wendy said. "I told you that I didn't tell anybody except that Santa Claus in the mall."

"Christmas wishes aren't like regular wishes," Molly said. "If you tell a Christmas wish, it will still come true."

"Don't you think Santa Claus will get me what I asked for? Doesn't he bring you the presents you want?" Wendy asked.

"Yeah, that's true," Molly said. "But if you tell him—" she pointed at Jack "—he can make your wish come true and that way you can still have all the presents from Santa Claus, too."

"Want to tell me?" Jack asked.

"Maybe." Wendy seemed to be deep in thought.

Molly jerked on Jack's hand. "It's cold out here."

"Yes, it is," Jack replied, then hurried them through the yard and onto the back porch.

They entered the house through the mud room and quickly removed their coats and hung them on the wall racks. When Molly rushed into the kitchen, Jack grabbed Wendy's shirttail and pulled her toward him.

"Hey, kiddo, are you going to tell me your Christmas wish?"

She shrugged her little shoulders, then peeped up at Jack. "Well, it's sort of a test for Santa Claus," she admitted. "If I get my Christmas wish, the present I want most in the world, then I'll know he's real. But if I don't get my wish, then I'll know there's no such thing as Santa Claus or magic or happily-ever-after. Just like Mommy said."

Uh-oh, this would never do. Getting Wendy to accept the possibility that Santa Claus might be real hadn't been easy, even though she'd been eager to believe. He supposed he should find out what present she had her heart set on and then make sure she got it. Even if it meant a last-minute trip into town tomorrow. He just prayed the item wasn't something that had already sold out.

"So, how about sharing your wish with me. That way, I can put in a good word with Santa."

"Oh, Jack, you're funny. You don't know Santa."

"Maybe not, but I can help you wish, can't I? Two of us wishing for the same thing should help make it happen."

"I guess…but if I tell you, you've got to promise not to tell Mommy, not until the wish comes true, of course."

Jack crossed his heart. "I promise."

"Okay." Wendy inhaled deeply, let out her breath and said in a rush, "I wish that you'd marry my mommy, so you could be my daddy."

## Chapter 17

Christmas Eve on the Mitchell farm reminded Jack of something out of an old movie. An honest-to-God real family, who were laughing and loving and enjoying being together at a season meant for family togetherness. Wasn't this what everyone really wanted? It sure as hell was what little Wendy Riley wanted. After her great revelation last night, he hadn't thought of much else. How could he and Peggy Jo explain to this child, who had just begun to believe in magic and miracles, that she wasn't going to get her Christmas wish?

"Get bundled up, kids," Betsy said. "Daddy's ready for y'all to go outside and build a snowman!"

"Yippee!" Shane shouted.

"I wanna put on his nose and eyes this year," Molly whined.

"I'm sure Daddy will let everyone take part in putting the snowman together," Betsy said. "And if you're good and don't argue, I'll make some snow cream."

"What's snow cream?" Wendy asked.

"It's like ice cream, silly," Molly said. "Only it's made out of snow."

Jack glanced at Peggy Jo, who stood at the sink. She looked rather domestic in one of Betsy's aprons. If he told her so, she'd probably slap him. He wondered if she had missed him as much last night as he had missed her. He'd grown accustomed to their nightly lovemaking sessions and to waking up with her beside him.

"Why don't you go with them, Betsy?" Hetty suggested. "I can take care of things in here in the kitchen until you get back. You can bring some snow in with you and make the snow cream later."

"Thanks. That's a wonderful idea." Betsy removed her apron and hung it on the back of a nearby chair. "Peggy Jo, do you and Jack want to come with us?"

Peggy Jo opened her mouth to reply, but before she could speak, Jack said, "We'll catch up with y'all in a few minutes."

Betsy smiled, then hurried the children into the mud room to bundle up for their afternoon adventure. The minute the back door slammed shut, Jack nodded, motioning for Peggy Jo to come with him.

"Hetty, I'll be right back," Peggy Jo said.

"Uh-huh."

Hetty gave Jack a suspicious look, and he responded with a sly grin. Peggy Jo followed him out of the kitchen and into the hall. As soon as they were halfway down the hall, he eased her up against the wall outside the powder room and kissed her. She draped her arms around his neck.

"Miss me last night?" He nuzzled her neck.

"I never dreamed sex could be so addictive," she admitted.

"Then you did miss me."

She rubbed against him seductively, and his sex hardened instantly. "How about a quickie in the bathroom?" she asked.

Jack backed her several feet down the wall and through the open door, straight into the powder room. Keeping one hand on her hip, he reached behind him to close and lock the door. She fumbled with his belt buckle, finally loosening it, then unzipped his jeans. The moment she reached inside his briefs and touched him, he thought the top of his head would blow off. He'd nearly climaxed just from the feel of her fingers on his sex.

"Do you have a condom?" she asked, as she hurriedly removed her apron, then her jeans and panties.

"Do bees make honey?"

He whipped a foil packet from his back pocket and prepared himself, then closed the commode lid, sat down and pulled her to him. She straddled his hips and sat on his lap, easing herself down and onto his erection. With a hot, thrusting kiss, he captured the moan of pleasure as it escaped from her lips. He gripped her hips and began a slow, steady rhythm. They kissed and touched. She unbuttoned his shirt and ran her hands over his chest. He groaned. She whimpered. He growled. She moaned. Within minutes the pace quickened to a frantic undulating dance as they mated with animalistic fury. His release came first, then hers followed seconds later. She dropped her head to his shoulder and he hugged her fiercely to him.

When her breathing slowed enough for her to speak, Peggy Jo said, "We'd better get out of here before someone catches us."

He laughed. "You think Hetty's going to come looking for you?"

"Not Hetty, but one of the children might come back in or—"

"Then we'd better clean up, put our clothes on and get out of here." He released her so she could stand. When she turned her back to him, he swatted her playfully on her behind. She glanced over her shoulder at him. "Anybody ever tell you that you've got a mighty fine ass, Miss Peggy Jo?''

"If I wasn't so flattered by that comment, I'd accuse you of being a male chauvinist, which of course you know you are.''

They took turns at the sink, dressed quickly and sneaked out of the bathroom. The instant they came through the door, Jack grabbed her and kissed her again. No matter how many times he made love to her, he still wanted her. He wanted to hold her, kiss her, keep her close to him all the time.

"Look, Wendy, they're kissing,'' Molly Mitchell cried out as the two little girls approached.

Jack and Peggy Jo broke apart and faced their audience.

"What are y'all doing back inside the house so soon?'' he asked.

"We came to get a hat and a scarf for our snowman,'' Molly said, then turned to her cousin. "I guess this means you're going to get your Christmas wish.''

Wendy's exuberant smile created a tight fist of pain in Jack's stomach. How the hell was he going to get out of this one? What could he say to Peggy Jo's daughter that would explain why he'd been kissing her mommy? To a child her age, kissing probably meant love and love meant marriage.

"What Christmas wish is that?'' Peggy Jo asked.

"The one I told to that Santa Claus in the mall when you and Jack and me went shopping,'' Wendy said. "I told him that if I got my wish, I'd believe in Santa Claus forever. Oh, Mommy—'' Wendy ran toward Peggy Jo and Jack ''—I believe now. I really do believe.'' She grabbed Peggy Jo around the waist and hugged her, then turned to Jack and hugged him. "And I got my present a day early.''

Jack lifted Wendy onto his hip. "Darling, I think there's something I need to explain to you.''

"I wish someone would explain to me what's going on," Peggy Jo said.

Wendy wrapped her little arms around Jack's neck and kissed him on the cheek. "I love you, Jack." She looked at Peggy Jo. "Can I call him Daddy now?"

"What?" Peggy Jo gasped.

"Now that y'all are going to get married, Jack will be my daddy, won't he? That's what I wished for, for Christmas."

"Oh, God!" Peggy Jo moaned.

"Molly, why don't you go get the things you'll need for the snowman," Jack said. "Peggy Jo and I need to talk to Wendy."

"About when you're going to get married?" Molly's big hazel eyes widened into sparkling circles.

"About Wendy's Christmas wish," Peggy Jo said.

"Okay." Molly winked at Wendy, then scurried down the hall.

Jack nuzzled Wendy's nose. "Let's go in the living room."

Jack carried Wendy. Peggy Jo followed. The three of them sat on the sofa, Wendy in the middle. What should he say? How did he even begin to explain to Wendy that his kissing Peggy Jo didn't mean what she thought it meant?

"Wendy, you know I love you more than anything." Peggy Jo removed Wendy's hat and mittens and laid them in her lap. "I've tried to give you everything you needed and most of what you want. But I can't give you a daddy."

"That's okay, Mommy, you didn't have to do anything. Santa did it." She looked up at Jack. "And you helped him, didn't you?"

"Wendy, darling..." Jack was suddenly at a loss for words.

"Jack and I are not getting married," Peggy Jo said.

Wendy's smile turned into a frown. "But I saw you kissing Jack, and Molly said that mommies and daddies hug and kiss.''

Peggy Jo groaned. ''Look, sweetpea, sometimes grown-ups hug and kiss just because they like each other, not because they plan to get married.''

''But I wished it!'' Wendy jumped off the sofa and glared at the two adults. ''I wished with all my might. And I promised that if I got this one special present, I would give up all my other presents.''

''Sweetie, just wishing for something doesn't make it happen.'' Peggy Jo reached out for her daughter, but she slapped Peggy Jo's hands away.

''I hate you! I hate both of you!'' Wendy stomped her feet. ''You weren't supposed to be kissing if you aren't getting married.''

Wendy turned and ran out of the room, tears streaming down her face. When Peggy Jo jumped up, Jack rose to his feet, grasped her wrist and said, ''Leave her alone for a few minutes. She'll calm down after she's had herself a good cry.''

''How could I have let this happen?'' Peggy Jo wrung her hands together.

''It's as much my fault as it is yours. I knew about the wish. I should have told you. And I should have been more careful.''

''How did you know?''

''She told me,'' Jack said. ''Last night.''

''I'm going to just peep in on her.'' Peggy Jo jerked her wrist free and ran out of the living room.

Jack blew out an exasperated huff, then headed for the mud room. He needed some fresh, cold air to clear his head.

Even though Peggy Jo made her come to the table, Wendy refused to eat supper. She sat through the meal, pouting and glaring daggers at her mother. When Molly mentioned their catching Peggy Jo and Jack kissing, she was shushed immediately. Later, when Peggy Jo put Wendy to bed, Wendy turned her head when Peggy Jo tried to kiss her good-night.

"Wendy, I'm sorry that I disappointed you, but I can't marry Jack just because you want him to be your daddy."

"Why not?" Wendy crossed her arms over her chest and stuck out her bottom lip. "Don't you love him?"

Great, just great. How could she respond to that question without lying? She'd never lied to Wendy and she wasn't going to start now, but she'd have to be very careful how she responded.

"I care about Jack and he cares about me, but Jack doesn't want to get married."

"Do you, Mommy? Do you want to marry Jack?"

"I...I, er, I wouldn't want to marry anyone who doesn't want to marry me. Jack and I are very good friends, but one of these days...soon...Jack is going to leave."

"He doesn't love us." Wendy shook her head sadly. "He calls us darling, but he doesn't mean it. You're not his darling and I'm not, either." Wendy wrapped her arms around Peggy Jo's waist and buried her face against her breasts.

"Oh, sweetpea." She eased Wendy down into the bed, kissed her forehead and pulled the covers up to her neck. "In the morning you'll have lots of presents under the tree and maybe some surprises from Santa Claus."

Wendy turned her back to Peggy Jo. "There is no Santa Claus."

With a feeling of hopelessness weighing heavily on her heart, Peggy Jo left the door halfway open when she walked out of the bedroom. She almost ran into Jack, who apparently had been waiting for her.

"How's she doing?" he asked.

Peggy Jo shook her head, tears choking her and making speech impossible. How could she not have anticipated something like this? Why hadn't she made sure Wendy understood that her relationship with Jack wasn't permanent?

"I'm sorry." He wrapped his arms around her. "I'll talk to her and try to explain, if you think it would help."

Peggy Jo shook her head again, then buried her face against his chest. He lifted his hand to stroke her hair. When she shivered, he held her all the tighter and for one fleeting moment she understood the hurt and disappointment Wendy was feeling. That romantic part of her soul that had somehow survived her father's abandonment and Buck's brutality wanted Jack to stay with her forever.

Swallowing her tears, she lifted her head and looked into his beautiful, golden-brown eyes. "There's nothing you can say right now to make things better for her. Maybe tomorrow, after she opens all her presents and she's not so upset with us, you can talk to her."

Jack slipped his arm around Peggy Jo's waist. "Do you want to take a walk in the moonlight?"

She offered him a weak smile. "Not tonight. I'll need to help Betsy and Darrel put the presents under the tree pretty soon. Even though Shane is eleven, he goes along with the Santa thing for Molly."

"I almost had Wendy believing," Jack said. "Damn! I hate that she wished for something we couldn't give her."

"Yeah. Me, too." But Peggy Jo's heart whispered, *We could make her wish come true, if you loved me the way I love you.*

Wendy pretended to be asleep when her mommy came in to check on her again. She kept her eyes tightly shut and her back to the half-open door. She could hear them whispering, Mommy and Hetty, but she couldn't make out what they were saying. She looked over at the other twin bed and said her cousin's name softly, but Molly didn't answer. She must be asleep, Wendy thought. Good. She wouldn't have to tell her anything about what she was doing.

As soon as Hetty and her mommy walked back down the hall, Wendy slipped out of bed and hurriedly took off her pajamas and put on her clothes. She wasn't going to stay here in the house and watch Shane and Molly opening all their Christmas presents in the morning. It wasn't fair that they had a mommy and a daddy and they got to believe in Santa Claus, too. And they lived on this wonderful farm, with animals all around them. She was lucky that her mommy had let her keep Fur Ball. She bet if she asked her for a puppy, her mommy would say no. But if Jack was her daddy, he'd talk her mommy into letting her have a puppy. And if Jack was her daddy, she could get a baby brother or sister, too. Molly had said so.

Wendy lifted Fur Ball up off his pillow on the floor and crept out of the bedroom and down the hall. The kitchen was dark, but moonlight came through the windows, just enough so she could see where she was going. Standing on tiptoe, she yanked her coat off the rack in the mud room, eased Fur Ball inside her coat and opened the back door, being careful not to make any noise. The cold night air hit her full force the moment she walked outside. Snowflakes melted against her skin and stuck in her hair.

For just a minute she wondered if maybe she should go back in the house where it was warm, but when she thought about how mad she was at Mommy and Jack, she kept trudging through the snow, heading for the barn. She and Fur Ball could sleep with Boots and her puppies tonight, and in the morning after everyone had finished opening their presents, she'd tell Mommy that she wanted to go home, back to Chattanooga. If she couldn't have a daddy, then she didn't want to stay here and be around Molly and her daddy.

She could see the barn now. It wasn't very far. She wished she'd gotten her mittens and cap. Her hands were cold and her hair was wet. Hetty would probably fuss at her, but she didn't care. Let 'em fuss at her. She wasn't going to open presents and laugh and have fun. Mommy said she couldn't get her what she wanted most, but she knew that wasn't true. Her friend at school, Martha Jane, had told her that she'd overheard her mother telling her father that Peggy Jo Riley didn't like men and thought women were better off without husbands. She'd told Martha Jane that was a lie, but now she wondered if it was true. Maybe that was the reason Jack wouldn't marry Mommy.

Wendy grasped the handle to the single door that opened up into the barn from the side. She pulled and pulled, but it wouldn't budge. Wind whipped around her, and the snowfall grew thicker. Suddenly she felt scared. She was cold and it was dark. If she couldn't get the door open, she'd have to go back to the house.

A big hand reached out and grabbed her. She opened her mouth to scream, but another big hand covered her mouth. She wiggled and squirmed, but the big hands held her tight.

"Well, well, what have we here?" a man's voice asked. He turned her around and lifted her, then laughed in her face. "How lucky can I get? Peggy Jo's little girl walked right into my arms."

# Chapter 18

When Jack's cell phone rang, his heart stopped for a split second, gut instincts warning him that something was wrong. Bad wrong. But how was that possible, with Peggy Jo and Wendy safe in their beds? Rising from the half bed in the corner of Betsy's sewing room, he fumbled around in his pants pocket, pulled out the small phone and flipped it open.

"Parker here."

"Jack, it's Sawyer McNamara. Just tell me that Peggy Jo and Wendy are safe."

Suddenly his heart, which had only minutes before paused for a millisecond, began beating at breakneck speed. "They're safe."

"Okay, listen up. Buck Forbes is our guy, and if he remembers where Peggy Jo's cousin lives, there's a good chance he's headed your way. Somebody broke into Peggy Jo's house late last night and we figure it was Forbes, who'd gone there searching for her. We were on our way to her house when Detective Gifford got the call that the security alarm had gone off.''

Jack pressed the phone between his ear and his shoulder, holding it in place so he could speak with Sawyer and put on his jeans at the same time. ''Why were y'all going to Peggy Jo's? You knew we were—''

''You need to get Peggy Jo and Wendy up and be ready to leave the farm as soon as we get there. I've already alerted the Rhea county sheriff about the situation, and Gifford and I are on our way there now to meet y'all.''

''What the hell's going on?'' Jack put on his socks and yanked on his boots, then reached for his shirt.

''Forbes has been visiting his ex-wives,'' Sawyer said. ''He stopped by wife number two's trailer in Maryville, up around Knoxville, early yesterday evening. When she came to the door, he shot and killed her. Her current husband was there. He identified Forbes as her murderer.''

Jack felt as if a building had fallen in on him. His chest ached and he could barely breathe. ''And wife number three? She and her kids are safe in a women's shelter somewhere, aren't they?''

''They were,'' Sawyer replied. ''Seems she moved in with her sister in Sweetwater several days ago and one of the kids called Buck and he got the kid to tell him where they were.''

Jack knew before Sawyer told him that wife number three was dead. ''Son of a bitch!''

''Got that right. The bastard killed her right there in front of their two kids and shot her sister, too. The sister's in surgery, but they think she'll pull through.''

''Where's Sweetwater? How many miles from here?'' Jack pulled on his shirt and buttoned it.

''Not far. It's a pretty straight shot up Highway 68, then right onto 27. Damn it, the guy could already be there. And Jack…''

''Yeah?''

"He's armed to the teeth. A rifle and a couple of hand-guns, or that's what our eyewitnesses told the authorities."

"I'll get Darrel Mitchell up and apprize him of the situation, then I'll tell Peggy Jo and she can get Wendy up and ready." Jack ran his fingers through his hair. He checked his Glock, then strapped on his hip holster. "If he shows up, I'm going to shoot first and ask questions later."

"You do what you have to do," Sawyer told him.

Two minutes later Jack knocked on the closed bedroom door down the hall, and within a couple of seconds a bleary-eyed Darrel Mitchell eased open the door. "Yeah, what's up?"

"Buck Forbes killed his second wife in Maryville and his third wife in Sweetwater last night." Jack kept his voice low. "The FBI believe there's a good chance he's headed here, that he might already be in Spring City."

"Honey, what's wrong?" Betsy called.

Darrel looked at Jack, his gaze questioning. "Go back in there and tell her," Jack said. "I have to wake Peggy Jo and have her and Wendy ready to leave when the FBI and the sheriff get here."

"I've got several rifles." Darrel glanced at the hip holster Jack wore. "In the locked gun case in the den. I'll get the key."

"Thanks. And try not to alarm Betsy and the kids any more than necessary."

Darrel nodded and closed the door. Jack went up the hall, eased open the partially closed door and walked over to Peggy Jo's side of the big bed. When he shook her gently, she jumped and gasped. Jack covered her mouth with his hand.

"It's me," he told her, then removed his hand.

"What's wrong?"

"Get up and come with me."

"I'm awake," Hetty said, then reached over and turned on the bedside lamp.

"You need to wake Wendy and get her dressed," Jack said. "Sawyer and Detective Gifford are on their way here now, and the local sheriff will probably get here soon."

Peggy Jo sat up, slid her legs to the side of the bed and grabbed Jack's arm. "What's happened?"

"Buck Forbes killed his second wife and his third wife. Last night."

Peggy Jo's mouth opened on a silent gasp. Jack lifted her to her feet. She closed her eyes and swayed against him.

"Come on, darling. I need you to be strong. Show me how tough you are. Do you hear me, Peggy Jo?"

"What makes them think he's coming here?" Hetty asked as she slid out of bed and reached for her crutches.

Jack grabbed Peggy Jo's shoulders. "Does Buck know where Betsy lives?"

"Yes. He knows. He was still my husband when Betsy and Darrel got married here in this house fourteen years ago. We came to the wedding together. But how can he know I'm here?"

"Process of elimination." Jack cursed a blue streak under his breath. "Go wake up Wendy and tell her that we're leaving. Make up something, tell her anything you need to tell her so she won't be scared."

"I understand." Peggy Jo groaned. "What about Betsy and Darrel and the children?"

"The local sheriff will take care of their protection, if it's necessary." He squeezed her shoulders and then released her. "I'll be in the den with Darrel. Y'all get dressed as quickly as you can. We need to be ready to leave as soon as Sawyer gets here."

Jack and Darrel met outside the den and went in together. Darrel handed Jack the key to his locked gun cabinet. Just as Jack inserted the key in the lock, a loud, hysterical cry echoed through the house.

Peggy Jo ran screaming down the hall. Molly came running after her. Betsy emerged from her bedroom and grabbed Molly's arm. Shane opened his door and asked what was going on.

"Wendy's missing," Peggy Jo yelled, as she raced into the den and straight toward Jack. "She's not in her bed and her pajamas were lying in the floor. Fur Ball's gone, too."

"She probably ran away." Molly stood at Betsy's side in the doorway. "She was awfully mad at you and Jack."

"Oh, God, where is she? It's freezing cold and snowing and—" Peggy Jo gasped for breath.

"She can't have gone far," Jack said. "We'll find her."

"Shane, you and Molly search the house," Darrel said. "Jack, I'll go with you outside to take a look around."

"I'm going, too," Peggy Jo said.

Jack started to tell her to stay put, but thought better of it. "Get on some clothes first." He glanced at her yellow robe.

Betsy and the children searched the house while Jack and Darrel armed themselves with hunting rifles, then they and Peggy Jo bundled up and went outside. After checking inside all the vehicles, they circled the house, searching for any sign of Wendy.

"Look, isn't that footprints?" Darrel pointed his flashlight to the ground. "The snow hasn't completely covered them. They're small enough to be Wendy's and they're headed toward the barn."

Using his flashlight, Jack inspected the trail in the snow and followed it several feet from the back door, then stopped dead still. "There's another set of prints starting right here. A large pair of prints."

Peggy Jo ran toward the barn. Jack caught up with her and whirled her around to face him. "Don't panic."

"Don't tell me not to panic," she said. "Buck may have Wendy and if he does... Oh, God, Jack, if he hurts her..."

"Will you, please, go back to the house and let me—"

"No! He doesn't want Wendy. He wants me."

"Damn it, will you, for once in your life, let somebody else take care of you?"

She jerked free, and before Jack could catch her, she screamed at the top of her lungs, "Buck Forbes, if you want me, here I am!"

"Damn it to hell!" Jack wanted to strangle her.

The barn door burst open and a millisecond before the gunfire erupted, Jack grabbed Peggy Jo and pulled her behind the top of the old storm shelter that rose several feet out of the earth. Darrel Mitchell hit the ground and rolled until he found shelter behind the toolshed on the opposite side of the yard.

"Peggy Jo, honey, I want you, all right," Buck shouted from where he stood in the open door. A dim light from inside the barn cast shadows and silhouetted Wendy, whom he held in his arms, a handgun pointed directly at her head.

"Let her go, Buck," Peggy Jo pleaded.

"Sure thing," Buck replied. "Just as soon as you come here to me, I'll put her down. Then you and me will take us a little drive."

"She's not going anywhere with you, Forbes," Jack said.

"You gonna let your cowboy lover tell you what to do?" Buck laughed. "I thought you were the boss of yourself, Miss High-and-Mighty-Self-Made-Woman. It wasn't enough that you ran out on me, but you had to tell the whole damn world what a sorry bastard your ex-husband was. You talked about me on your TV show and wrote about me in your damn books."

"Keep him talking," Jack whispered. "But whatever you do, stay right here."

"I didn't use your name," Peggy Jo told Buck. "Not ever."

"My second wife left me. Walked out on me. And you know what she said when I tried to get her to come back to me? She said she was taking Peggy Jo Riley's advice. She watched your show and believed every rotten thing you said about me.''

"How did she know you'd been married to me?"

Jack eased out from behind the storm shelter and, crawling on his belly, made his way across the frozen ground to the opposite end of the barn. All the while he thanked God for the cloudy night that obscured the moonlight. If he could get up the small rise overlooking the barn without Forbes noticing him, he'd be able to get into position. And if he was fast enough, he could take Buck down before Peggy Jo's ex-husband could pull the trigger on his pistol.

"I told her we'd been married.'' Buck laughed. ''I thought it would impress Tammy that my ex was a local celebrity, but that was before I knew what kind of garbage you were preaching."

"Did you beat her the way you used to beat me?''

"I knocked her around when she deserved it.''

"What about your third wife?'' Peggy Jo asked.

That's it, darling, keep him talking until I can make my way to a point where I can get off a clean shot.

Damn, what he'd give to have David Wolfe here right now. The former Dundee agent had been a crack shot. But he was a pretty good shot himself. And this was one time he couldn't afford to miss his target.

"My third wife?'' Buck sneered. Wendy squirmed in Buck's arms and whimpered. "Damn it, kid, be still.''

Jack wanted to rush the man and beat the hell out of him. Poor little Wendy had to be frightened senseless. *Just hang in there, baby, I'm coming to get you. Daddy's going to save you.*

*Daddy?* Jack questioned his choice of words. Wendy's daddy? Odd how at this precise moment he felt such an intense connection to Peggy Jo's child, the little girl who wanted him to be her daddy.

"Yes, Buck, what about your third wife?'' Peggy Jo hollered. ''Did you knock her around, too? Did she watch my TV show and read my books and tell you to get lost?''

''You got that right, honey. Lindsay was good and scared of me and that kept her in line, but after she heard you preaching women's rights, she took my kids and run off. You're all alike. All you women. You don't know what's good for you. When all a man does is try to take care of you, you walk out on him.''

In the distance a siren screamed, its singsong wail traveling on the crisp night wind. Jack prayed the distraction didn't send Buck over the edge.

''Do you hear that, Buck? They're coming after you,'' Peggy Jo told him. ''The sheriff knows you're here. You can't get away, so why don't you let Wendy go?''

''I'll let her go. You come here and I'll put her down.'' Buck rubbed the gun up and down the side of Wendy's face.

''Mommy!''

''I'm coming, sweetpea. Mommy's coming.''

Don't! Jack wanted to scream. Not yet, darling. Another couple of minutes and he'd be able to get a clean shot. But not right now. In his peripheral vision he saw Peggy Jo's shadow as she came out from behind the storm shelter and walked toward the barn. Preparing himself to take a quick shot from where he was, he continued maneuvering into position. Almost there. A few more feet.

Peggy Jo walked right up to Buck. ''I'm here. Put her down.''

Jack held his breath and ran the last few feet, then crouched down and aimed his rifle. Buck eased Wendy to her feet, and she ran toward Peggy Jo. But Buck grabbed Peggy Jo, hauled her up against him and placed his pistol under her chin.

''Run, Wendy,'' Peggy Jo cried. ''Run into the house.''

''Mommy? Fur Ball's in the barn.''

''We'll get Fur Ball later. Now, go! Run!''

Wendy ran, but before she got more than a few feet away, Buck pulled another pistol from where he'd stuck it under his belt and aimed the 9mm at Wendy's back. Peggy Jo screamed.

Darrel Mitchell called out from his hiding place behind the tool shed, "You sorry son of a bitch," then revealed himself, brandishing his rifle.

Thank you, God. Thank you, Darrel. Whether or not the man realized what he was doing, Jack didn't know. It didn't matter. Darrel had distracted Buck long enough so that he had lowered the gun at Peggy Jo's throat. A split second. That's all the time Jack had.

Jack took aim and fired. His every thought was a prayer. A deadly prayer that the bullet would hit its mark. Buck Forbes gasped. Blood squirted out of the wound in his head, spit out all over Peggy Jo and sprayed the white snow at their feet. Buck's eyes rounded in shock. He crumpled to his knees and fell over, knocking Peggy Jo to the ground as he dropped on top of her.

Darrel ran forward and scooped Wendy up in his arms. Jack raced down from the small hill east of the barn and rushed to Peggy Jo. He rolled Buck's body over and lifted Peggy Jo off the ground.

"Wendy?" Peggy Jo asked, as Jack hugged her fiercely.

"She's fine. Darrel's got her."

He felt Peggy Jo trembling, tiny tremors at first, then unmistakable shaking. When she lifted her face to look up at him, tears streamed down her cheeks. He covered her damp face with kisses, all the while holding her fiercely, every fiber of his being grateful that she was alive. Nothing else mattered except that Peggy Jo and Wendy were all right.

The next few hours were a flurry of activity as the sheriff arrived with several deputies. Sawyer and Detective Gifford drove into the driveway five minutes after the shooting.

Jack had taken Peggy Jo inside the mud room, wet a towel and washed the blood from her face. Once she saw for herself that Wendy was all right, she told Jack she needed a shower. He hadn't wanted to leave her alone, but she'd insisted she would be all right. By the time she emerged from the bathroom, wearing her gray sweat suit, an ambulance had arrived to take away Buck's body.

What had happened didn't seem real somehow, Peggy Jo thought. But it had been real, all too real. Buck Forbes was dead. Jack had killed him, and by doing so had saved her life and Wendy's.

The house was oddly quiet as she searched for the others. She found Jack sitting in the sewing room on the half bed, Wendy in his lap. Hetty held Fur Ball, stroking the kitten as she clucked over Wendy and Jack like the mother hen she was.

"Where is everybody?" Peggy Jo asked.

"Betsy and Darrel and the kids are in the kitchen," Hetty said. "The sheriff's gone, but Agent McNamara and Detective Gifford are still here. They've been hanging around to see what you want to do."

"I don't understand," Peggy Jo said, her mind still in a daze.

"Do you want to go home?" Jack asked. "Or do you want to stay here?"

"Oh." Peggy Jo sat down on the bed beside Jack and reached out to caress her daughter's cheek. "Hi, there, sweetpea."

"Mommy, the police took that bad man away, and Jack said he'll never bother us ever again."

"That's right. He'll never bother us again." Her gaze met Jack's as they looked at each other over Wendy's head. "Wendy, do you want to go home or do you want to stay here?"

"All my presents are here, aren't they? I guess we should stay here for Christmas, shouldn't we?" Wendy crawled over onto Peggy Jo's lap and put her arms around Peggy Jo's neck. "Mommy, I'm sorry I left the house and made you worry and… Jack made me promise that no matter how angry I get at you or at him, I'll never run away again. He said y'all wouldn't punish me this time, but if I ever scared y'all again, he'd have to ground me for life."

"Of course we…I won't punish you. But, Wendy, what are you talking about? Since Buck—the bad man—is gone for good, we don't need Jack to look after us anymore. He'll be leaving soon. Maybe tomorrow."

"No, Mommy, Jack's not going anywhere. He's staying with us forever and ever."

"Wendy, wherever did you get such a crazy idea? I thought I explained to you—"

"Why don't you listen to your daughter?" Hetty said. "While you were taking a shower, Jack and Wendy made a few decisions about the future."

Peggy Jo stared directly at Jack, her heart beating wildly. "Just what decisions about the future did y'all make?"

"Wendy and I decided that I'm going to be her daddy," Jack said.

"What?" A hot flush warmed Peggy Jo's body. "Jack, I don't know what kind of game you're playing, but—"

He covered her lips with his index finger. "Let's just say that what happened tonight made me realize that you and Wendy are the most important things in my life. I love you, Peggy Jo, and I want us to get married." He ruffled Wendy's black curls. "And I love you, my little darling."

"You love me?" Peggy Jo stared at him, unable to believe what she'd just heard.

"Tell him you love him, Mommy. Tell him, so we can get married."

"Yeah, Mommy, if you don't tell me you love me, too, we can't make our little girl's Christmas wish come true."

"I love you, Jack. I love you."

Jack wrapped his arms around his two best girls.

Hetty smiled triumphantly. "About damn time."

# *Epilogue*

Wendy helped Peggy Jo and Jack carry the presents from the hiding place in their basement up to the living room. While Jack busied himself putting training wheels on Jed's shiny red bike and Peggy Jo assembled the child-size kitchen set for Margie, Wendy stacked the wrapped items under the tree. Once everything was set, Jack flipped the switch that turned on the twinkling white lights, illuminating the nine-foot spruce tree towering toward the ten-foot ceiling in the living room of the old ranch house. The smell of evergreen permeated the area, mingling with milder spice scents lingering in the air from Hetty's Christmas cooking. The grandfather clock in the foyer struck eleven. Christmas day was only an hour away.

"Dad, you'd better eat the cookies and drink the milk." Wendy pointed to the tray of edible delights Jed and Margie had placed on a table near the tree. "I'll run outside and pick up Rudolph's carrots off the porch."

"Thanks, darling." Jack winked at his eldest child as he picked up a couple of small sugar cookies and popped one and then the other into his mouth. "By the way, I saw you shaking a couple of your presents."

"Just checking to see if I could guess what surprises Santa brought me this year." Wendy winked back at her dad, then left to retrieve the carrots her younger brother and sister had left for Santa's lead reindeer.

Jack gulped down the glass of milk, wiped his mouth with the back of his hand and made a face at Peggy Jo. "Yuck. I don't see how the kids drink this stuff."

"You're a very bad influence on our children. As a good father, you should set a better example. Hating milk, refusing to eat spinach and letting them eat sweets before their meals. What am I going to do with you?"

Peggy Jo slipped her arm around Jack's waist and sighed contentedly. Jack hugged her, kissed her temple and then laid his hand over her protruding belly.

"You're going to keep having babies with me, Mrs. Parker. That's what you're going to do."

"Absolutely not. This is the last one." She laid her hand over Jack's where it rested on her stomach. "When this little boy makes his appearance around Valentine's Day, we'll have our two boys and two girls. That's enough family for me."

Jack pivoted her around to face him, then pulled her into his arms. "I'm a mighty lucky man. I have the most wonderful wife in the world, great kids, my father's ranch and more love than any man has a right to expect in one lifetime."

"I'm the lucky one," Peggy Jo told him. "I'm your wife."

"My wife, my best friend and the love of my life."

Standing in the open doorway, thirteen-year-old Wendy cleared her throat. "Excuse me, but if we're going to get any sleep tonight, we'd better go to bed. Jed and Margie will be up before daylight hollering for us to come see what Santa brought them."

"She's right," Jack said. "Our little hellions will be up at the crack of dawn. Let's hit the sack, woman." He swatted her playfully on the behind.

As they walked past Wendy, Jack reached out and pulled her toward them, then he and Peggy Jo kissed her goodnight.

On their way down the hall, Jack and Peggy Jo paused by each open door. First they checked on six-year-old Jed, who slept in a room filled with cowboy paraphernalia. Their redheaded, freckle-faced son loved the time they spent on the ranch, and even his room in their Atlanta house reflected his Texas heritage. Next they tiptoed into Margie's room, a fairy-tale-princess suite of pastel yellow gingham. A *sunshine* room. She looked like a little brown-haired angel snuggled up with her stuffed bear in her arms.

When they entered their own room, Fur Ball curled around Jack's leg and purred. Not to be outdone, Wishbone, one of Boots's offspring from her fifth litter, bounded up to Peggy Jo, demanding equal attention. She knelt, hugged the big dog and stroked his silky coat.

Her life was as close to perfect as it could be. A dream come true. A wish fulfilled. She was married to the absolutely best man in the world, whom she found out only days before their wedding was a multimillionaire, having inherited his late stepfather's sizable fortune upon Libbie Reid's death. And she was the mother of three—she rubbed her tummy—four great kids, as well as a spoiled cat and equally spoiled dog. And her highly successful career had made her a national celebrity. Fortunately, she had Hetty at her side, overseeing the care of the children and the running of two households—one in Atlanta, where *Self-Made Woman* was televised for national syndication, and the second here in Texas, on Jack's family ranch that he had been able to buy back from the people Libbie had sold it to years ago.

"Go to bed, darling," Jack said. "I'll join you in a minute."

He picked up Fur Ball and grabbed Wishbone by the collar. He dropped the cat off in Wendy's room, then settled the dog down on the rug by Jed's bed. When Jack returned to his bedroom, he closed the door, undressed and joined his wife. She waited for him in bed, smiling and naked, her arms waiting to hold him.

And in the quiet, peaceful moments before their eighth Christmas morning together, Jack made slow, sweet love to his wife.

\* \* \* \* \*

*Look for more books in*

*THE PROTECTORS*

*series, coming in 2002!*

*Only from Beverly Barton*
*and Silhouette Intimate Moments.*

**Silhouette**

# INTIMATE MOMENTS™

## presents a riveting new continuity series:

# FIRSTBORN SONS

Bound by the legacy of their fathers, these Firstborn Sons are about to discover the stuff true heroes—and true love—are made of!

### The adventure concludes in December 2001 with:

**BORN ROYAL** by Alexandra Sellers

In a moment of weakness, sheltered princess Julia Sebastiani surrendered to her forbidden desire for Firstborn Son Rashid Kamal. Now she's pregnant with the boldly sexy sheik's heir—and their rival royal families are up in arms! Can these tempestuous lovers set aside their passionate discord and find a way to unite their feuding kingdoms?

July: **BORN A HERO**
by **Paula Detmer Riggs** (IM #1088)
August: **BORN OF PASSION**
by **Carla Cassidy** (IM #1094)
September: **BORN TO PROTECT**
by **Virginia Kantra** (IM #1100)
October: **BORN BRAVE**
by **Ruth Wind** (IM #1106)
November: **BORN IN SECRET**
by **Kylie Brant** (IM #1112)
December: **BORN ROYAL**
by **Alexandra Sellers** (IM #1118)

*Available only from*
*Silhouette Intimate Moments*
*at your favorite retail outlet.*

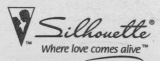

**Silhouette®**

*Where love comes alive™*

Visit Silhouette at www.eHarlequin.com

SIMFIRST6

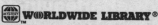

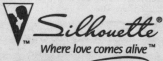
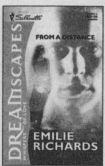

**Take a walk on the dark side of love
with three tales by**

MAGGIE SHAYNE

WINGS IN THE NIGHT

For centuries, loneliness has haunted them from
dusk till dawn. Yet now, from out of the darkness,
shines the light of eternal life…eternal love.

Discover the stories at the heart of the series…

**TWILIGHT PHANTASIES
TWILIGHT MEMORIES
TWILIGHT ILLUSIONS**

*Available December 2001 at your favorite retail outlet.*

*Silhouette®*

*Where love comes alive™*

Visit Silhouette at www.eHarlequin.com          PSWITN